To L

We met in the summer o – – – ,
and you quickly became the
first true love of my life.
Ever since you have been in my
heart with loving feelings.

Your loving friend,

Terrence (Terry) Kero

WALKING *the* WORLD

WALKING *the* WORLD

A NOVEL

Book One of the Migration Trilogy

TERRENCE KERO

outskirtspress
DENVER, COLORADO

Walking the World
Book One of the Migration Trilogy

v3.0

Novel edited by Joy Johannessen, Arlene Robinson, and Kaila Kero

Outskirts Press, Inc.
http://www.outskirtspress.com

Paperback ISBN: 978-1-4787-6319-2
Hardback ISBN: 978-1-4787-6344-4

PRINTED IN THE UNITED STATES OF AMERICA

Table of Contents

1
Ancestors

San Francisco, October 1999

Andy Koskinen studied the package that sat on the coffee table in front of him. About the size of a loaf of bread, it was from Finland, and it was addressed to Lisa Koskinen. Andy reached out to pet his black-and-white Havanese lap-dog, Sukie, wondering what was in the package and why his daughter's name was on it. He didn't recognize the sender's name or address. Yes, his parents' families had emigrated to the USA from Finland, but that was more than a century ago, and except for one visit there eighteen years ago, before Lisa was born, he'd had little contact with his Finnish relatives.

Sukie suddenly stood up on Andy's lap, barked, and jumped to the carpeted floor, sprinting across the family room toward the hallway that led to the garage. Andy chuckled, knowing it was Lisa coming home from after-school soccer practice. He always marveled at how Sukie could hear the hallway door open when he couldn't.

"Lisa," he called, "come here, I've got something for you."

With Sukie yapping at her heels, Lisa appeared in the

family-room archway to see her father holding out a brown package. She walked over and peered at it.

"Finland? Really?" she said, giving Andy a kiss and taking the package.

"Yep. Haven't heard from that part of our family since I visited there when you were just a twinkle in my eye. And your mother's, of course."

Lisa grinned. "So what is it?" She tore away the wrapping paper and found a white envelope taped to a pine box. She freed the tape, handed Andy the box, and opened the envelope. "It's a letter," she said, her brown eyes scanning it. "It's in English."

Andy settled into his recliner across from her. "Good, then I don't have to translate. What's it say?"

Lisa plopped onto the couch, took a deep breath, and read aloud, "'Dear Lisa Koskinen, I'm Tapio Hakeminen, a distant cousin.'"

She looked up at Andy with a question in her eyes, but he shook his head. "Must be really distant. I never heard of him. Whoever Tapio Hakeminen is, he wasn't at the big family reunion eighteen years ago."

Lisa went on. "'Before my Aunt Tulli died last month at age ninety-six, she asked me to send you this necklace. Her mother Outti gave it to her years ago, saying it was a family tradition to pass it to the oldest daughter.'"

She paused again and glanced up. Andy waved for her to continue.

"'Aunt Tulli was Outti's only girl, and she had no daughters or granddaughters,'" Lisa read. "'She learned your father's mother was the granddaughter of Outti's sister Sari, who moved to the USA in 1888. Aunt Tulli wondered if your father had any children, and I looked him up on the family tree he helped put together years ago when he was in Finland, and there you were. He must have updated the tree after you were born. I hope you enjoy the necklace, and will pass it on to your own daughter to keep the family tradition going.'"

Lisa folded the letter and returned it to its envelope. "A necklace?"

"Apparently so," Andy said. "You know, the women's names ring a bell, Tulli and Outti, but I don't know this Tapio or anything about a family necklace. When I visited, there was no mention of it." He handed her the pine box. "Here, open it."

Lisa hesitated for a moment, then released the two simple latches on the box, lifted its hinged top, and pulled out a leather pouch about the size of a wine bota. They both stared at it as if it might contain some magical object. Was Lisa's hand trembling? Andy didn't have time to pursue the question, because Sukie started barking again, and he looked up to see Eva standing there, her curly black hair done up in a red scarf. Their twins, Henry and Hanna, stood next to her, bouncing with ten-year-olds' energy.

"How was work, honey?" he asked.

Eva reached up and massaged her temples. "Same old biotech firm, same old issues. I was almost late to pick these two up." With a playful swat, she sent the twins to the kitchen for snacks.

"Mom, look." Lisa held up the pouch. "I just got this from Finland. There's supposed to be an old family necklace inside. Can you believe Dad doesn't know anything about it?"

Eva stepped closer, a smile lighting her smooth mocha face. "What? The Koskinen family historian doesn't know about it? Then it's definitely a mystery. Gosh, maybe it's a gold necklace. Or diamonds!"

Andy chuckled. "In my family? More likely, agate stones from some river up there."

"My guess is pearls," Lisa said, opening the pouch and turning it upside down. "*Ewww!*" she shrieked as the necklace dropped into her lap. She recoiled and brushed it off as if it were a spider.

Andy frowned at what lay on the carpet. It was a necklace, all right, a large one, but Lisa's reaction didn't surprise him. He didn't think any average person would have expected to see a necklace made out of big teeth strung on a knotted leather strip two feet long.

He reached down and picked it up, gingerly examining it. "You know, if it wasn't so interesting, I might be saying *ewww* myself, honey. But it's fascinating, isn't it? See? Each tooth's about two inches long. And look. Each one's got parallel scratches. Wonder what those are about." He counted the teeth. "Fourteen. And they all look like canine teeth from some large animal, like a lion or bear."

When he got no response, he looked up to see Lisa scowling and Eva's lovely forehead wrinkled, perhaps in thought or perhaps in aversion too.

"Is Cousin Tapio playing some kind of joke on me?" Lisa said, her voice tight. "Why would he send me something so gross? I don't even know the guy! And it's not just ugly, it's . . . scary-looking. Are tooth necklaces some kind of weird tradition in Finland, Dad?"

He fingered the teeth. "God, no. I've never heard of anything like this from Finland."

She winced. "Could you stop *fondling* it, Dad? That's creeping me out."

Eva gave Lisa's knee a reassuring pat. "Actually, it looks like something from Africa, or maybe from a Native American tribe. More like something *my* ancestors would have worn. I've seen pictures of jewelry like it. Check out that mailing label again, will you?"

Andy stood and held out the necklace, nearly touching Lisa's bare arm. The ivory teeth looked good against her golden skin, a blend of his pale white coloration and Eva's African American hue. "Put it on. Let's see how it looks—"

"No!" Lisa jerked away.

Her shouted refusal brought Hanna and Henry running from the kitchen to see what was going on. With Eva's help, Andy explained how the necklace came to be in their family room. He admitted it was a bit ratty-looking, but there was artfulness to its design. The parallel markings on the teeth were straight and carefully made. Each tooth was snugly tied with exactly the same style of knot, and the knots between the teeth were equally precise. He pointed these things out to Lisa and said, "Look, I don't know Tapio, but I don't think any of my Finnish family would prank you, honey. One of them wanted you—you alone—to have this necklace. That means they think you're special in some way. Or maybe they think our family"—he let his eyes rest on Eva and the twins—"maybe they think we deserve the honor of owning something that's been in their family for who knows how long." He extended the necklace to her again.

"You don't have to if you really don't want to, but . . . this is yours."

Lisa flinched when her hands touched the necklace, but with the same determination she displayed in her toughest soccer games, she slipped it over her head, allowing it to hang down over her red soccer shirt. She grimaced and shrugged her shoulders. "It feels strange. Kind of eerie."

Henry stepped closer and grasped a tooth. "Cool," he said. "Why are you acting like you're scared of it?"

"I'm not scared, it's just spooky, that's all."

"I like it," Hanna said. "I wish I had one."

"Well, I hate it," Lisa said, blinking. "It's ugly. It's just so gross! I never want to touch it or see it again. I'm sorry, Dad, I know it's a special gift from your family—"

"No, it's okay, honey." He reached out for the necklace, which Lisa hurriedly removed. "We'll put it back in the box and write a thank-you note to your cousin, and then I'll put it away and that will be that."

Late that night, Andy and Eva woke up to screams from Lisa's bedroom. They rushed in to see her sitting up in bed with her hands over her face.

"Mom, Dad, I just had a dream that a bear was attacking me."

"It was only a dream, honey," Eva said. "Don't worry, we're right here, go back to sleep."

"I'll try, Mom."

For the next three nights there were more screams after more nightmares. On the fourth night, Eva returned from Lisa's bedroom to find Andy in the family room.

"How is she?" he asked.

Eva gazed at him with worried eyes. He was sitting in his leather recliner, the tooth necklace out on the coffee table before him.

"She had another nightmare," Eva replied. "She's calmer now, but she says she's not going to sleep tonight."

"She has to sleep, honey. She has to."

On soundless feet, Eva went to the sofa and sat down. She crossed her legs—legs that had once competed in races at the national level, had once run toward and then away from a chance at Olympic gold—and joined Andy in staring at the strange gift from Finland.

"This is crazy," she said. "Lisa told me she wishes it never came."

Andy sighed. After the first couple of nightmares, he blamed himself—maybe his casual mention that the teeth might have belonged to a lion or bear had upset Lisa—but she was a level-headed kid, always had been. Something was wrong. Seriously wrong.

"Honey, I think it's time to call your mom," Eva said, breaking into his thoughts. "We have to do something. Lisa's exhausted from not sleeping, from the stress—maybe your mom knows something she's never told you."

Andy liked to deal with his own problems. To him, self-reliance was a point of pride that he attributed to his Finnish genes. Asking for help, even asking family for help, was something he abhorred. He rose from the recliner. "What could Mom possibly know about that old necklace? If I tell her about Lisa's dreams, it'll only upset her."

He saw the resolve in Eva's face and sighed again. "If Lisa can't sleep tonight, I'll call Mom tomorrow. I promise."

Andy put down the cordless phone and leaned back in his chair at the dining room table. For now, things seemed nearly normal. In spite of sleeping so little, Lisa insisted on going to school each day, and she'd just gone up to her room to do her homework. Eva was clearing the dishes. He watched her pick up the meat platter, then realized she was staring at him.

He leaned forward and folded his arms on the table. "Mom had no clue. She said she didn't know a Tapio Hakeminen or anything about a family tooth necklace."

Eva pursed her lips as she turned toward the kitchen. "Why don't you go online and take a closer look at that genealogy site of yours. Or you could—"

"I did."

She wheeled on him. "What? Why didn't you say anything?"

"I wasn't sure what I'd turn up," he said, instantly regretting his sharp tone. Softening it, he continued. "I found a listing for a Tapio Hakeminen in a village near Oulu. That's in central Finland, on the coast of the Baltic Sea, so at least I'm sure he's real now. I got out all the family photos from the reunion and looked them over. Nothing. No one was wearing anything like the necklace. I thought about going to see Tapio and the rest of my relatives, but I'm swamped at the university, full teaching load this quarter. And the cost of the trip to Finland? Even if I go by myself . . ."

Eva put the platter down. "Yes. And I just don't think it would be good for you to go so far away. Not until things settle down for her."

Nodding, Andy stood and prepared to head upstairs. An idea was forming in his head, but it was one he didn't want to think about. His pride in his independence kept getting in the way.

Andy looked out at San Francisco Bay through the sliding glass doors of the dining room as his family ate their breakfast of bacon, eggs, and grits. The grits were a gift from Eva's Mississippi background—once she introduced them, everyone loved them. The fog season was just about over, and the sun threw sharp shadows from neighboring homes on the hillside. Thankfully, last night had brought no screams from Lisa's room, so Andy wouldn't be sleep-fogged today while teaching his microbiology class at San Francisco State University. He stood to leave the table.

"Dad?" Lisa said, sopping up egg with her bread. A blessing, she was eating today.

"Yes, honey?"

"I had a weird dream last night."

Andy and Eva exchanged a look. "Was it the bear one again?" Eva asked. "You should've woken us—"

"No, no bears this time, and no drownings either, like that last one. This time I was flying."

"Okay, kids," Eva said a little too cheerily, forcing a smile at the twins. "Hanna, Henry, your bus will be here any second. Get your backpacks, okay?"

The twins were sitting raptly, waiting for their big sister's next words. With moans of disappointment, they left to comply. Andy could see what had Eva so rattled. Their bright and athletic oldest daughter's face held a vacancy he hadn't seen since she was feverish with a bad strep throat when she was eight. Better than terror, he supposed, but he cursed himself for not noticing that empty expression sooner.

He sat back down. "You were flying?"

"Not like in a plane." Lisa bit off a piece of egg-soaked bread, chewed and swallowed, wiped her mouth. "I was floating, in the sky. With my arms stretched out, gliding like a bird over this long, winding river. I could change directions by turning my arms. And I could go higher by stretching out and catching the wind, or go lower by bringing my arms in."

He needed to ask. "Were you scared?"

"Not even a little. I followed the river until I saw a herd of animals. I couldn't tell what they were, so I swooped down to look at them. They were deer, nothing scary about deer. Then . . . I woke up."

Andy sipped the remains of his coffee and set the cup on its saucer. Was it too much to hope that the dreams would no longer terrify her? "So it was really different? And nothing bad happened this time?"

"Well, just before I woke up, I remember thinking I shouldn't follow the river anymore, just the deer. That maybe something bad would happen if I stayed near the river. But I didn't want to lose sight of it." She fixed his eyes with her own, eyes that now held trepidation. "What if I dream about the river again tonight, Dad? If I keep following the river, if something bad happens to me—"

Squealing brakes outside announced the arrival of the school bus. Andy had an eight o'clock class. The idea that had come to him last night returned. "Honey, can I take the necklace to work today? Have the Anthropology Department look at it?"

Lisa shifted her eyes to her plate. "Sure. If I'm lucky, maybe some grad assistant will lose it."

Inside the main building Andy turned left, his shoes squeaking on the marble floor, and stopped at a door emblazoned with Professor Paul Rutherford's name and title, informing whoever was about to enter that the man inside headed the department.

At Andy's quick tap, Rutherford looked up and said, "Come in." He shuffled the papers he'd been reading, laid them on his laden credenza, and smoothed his unruly white hair, joking to Andy that it probably made him look a little too much like Einstein.

After a few more pleasantries, Andy pulled the pouch from his briefcase, retrieved the necklace, and handed it over. "A cousin from Finland sent it to my daughter," he told Rutherford. "His note said it was an old family necklace that was to be handed down from daughter to daughter, and . . . well, Lisa was next." On the way here, Andy had decided not to tell Rutherford about the dreams. Lisa's emotional turmoil needed to stay within the family.

Rutherford brought the necklace close to his round wire-rimmed glasses, rolling it in his fingers and squinting at its details. "Hmm, looks like something the old Viking warriors might have worn. That would put it back to the Viking days, so I'd guess it's about a thousand years old. Excellent condition, but considering its age, it should be in a controlled climate, and—"

"Wow! That old?" Andy looked at the necklace with fresh interest. "But how could it be Vikings? This thing came from Finland."

Rutherford smiled. "Why, Dr. Koskinen, aren't you up on

your history? Sweden invaded Finland around AD twelve hundred and controlled it for the next six centuries. That's why many towns and cities in western Finland have two names, one Finnish, one Swedish. This necklace could easily have come with the Swedish Vikings. Only one way to find out."

Without waiting for Andy's reply, Rutherford stood, turned to the credenza, opened a cardboard box, and lifted out a clay pot in a plastic bag. "There've been some remarkable archeological discoveries up there in Finland in the past few decades," he said, brushing plastic peanuts from the bag. "I daresay nothing like your necklace, however. I'm taking this pot to the Lawrence Livermore Lab tomorrow. I believe it's from a Chumash Indian tribe. The lab agreed to age-date it for me. If you like, I'll take your necklace along."

Andy's instinct was to say no, but as he opened his mouth, Lisa's face popped up in his mind, the way she looked when she said, "I never want to touch it or see it again."

"Thanks, I'd appreciate that," he said, and watched Rutherford return the necklace to the pouch, wrap the pouch in tissue paper, and carefully place it and the clay pot in the cardboard box.

"I'll let you know what I find out," Rutherford said. "But remember, Livermore is a very busy research lab, so it might take a while."

A while. For the sake of his daughter, Andy had to confide in someone.

"Dr. Rutherford? There's something else. What do you know about dreams?"

2
Junk DNA

At breakfast the next morning, Lisa nibbled on her toast and set it down. "I had another dream last night. This time I was walking along a river in a forest, and a big bear just . . . it just appeared. It opened its mouth wide and roared. I could see its teeth. They were huge."

She stared down at her hands. Her words were careful, spoken in the tone of someone who feels obligated to report a terrible event but doesn't want to convey alarm or fright.

When Lisa didn't continue her account of the dream, Eva and Andy exchanged glances. In a private conversation the night before, Eva had suggested that Lisa see a psychologist.

"No," he'd said vehemently. "Yes, I agree this is upsetting. *I'm* upset about it. But it's only nightmares. Dreams. Just dreams." He'd reached out and taken her in his arms. "Before you know it, Lisa will be right back to kicking butt at soccer and talking about which college she wants to go to."

He'd been so sure when he said that last night. Now he glanced from Lisa to Eva, inwardly cringing at the I-told-you-so in Eva's eyes.

Finally, Lisa looked up. "At first I was scared. I just knew the bear was coming after me and I wouldn't be able to run away in time. But then a woman appeared next to me. She said something in a strange language, and I couldn't understand a word. Then I know—I *know* that bear saw me. But it walked past us, like we weren't there."

She was still holding back, but at least the robotic tone had softened. If this was some sort of breakthrough, Andy was all for it. "It walked right past you?" he said. "Wow. Did you fly again?"

She shook her head, and tears formed in her eyes. "I wish. I wish I had flown away from those awful teeth. Those *horrible* teeth. Dad, if it hadn't been for that woman . . ."

Andy's heart twisted. He'd told her that Professor Rutherford was taking the necklace to Livermore for dating, but Lisa shared his independent-minded streak, so he'd thought it best not to mention that he'd talked to Rutherford about dreams and nightmares. Still, he had to say something now, something to reassure her, to distract her from this dream that had clearly terrified her.

"Honey, I . . . did some research," he said. "It's not uncommon to dream about flying. And I read that there's some evidence suggesting that our DNA can inherit memories from ancestors, just like we inherit things like our skin, hair, and eye color. About ninety-seven percent of our DNA hasn't been coded yet—it used to be called junk DNA. Now some scientists think there's useful information in the junk DNA. That the junk DNA could be where some of that ancestor-memory kind of DNA exists."

Understanding his intent, Eva leaned back in her chair. "So we inherit a brain's memory? That's fascinating, isn't it,

Lisa? And what a great research topic for your science paper. You said you were still deciding what to—"

"Dad, could that be true?" It was as though Lisa hadn't heard her mother; her eyes were boring into Andy's. "Do you really think my dreams about flying, and about the rivers and deer and bears, could be inherited from the past?"

With a casualness he didn't feel, Andy shrugged. "It's an interesting theory, but so far it's been hard to prove, especially for really old memories. It's real enough for shorter-term memory, though. There was a study of monarch butterflies, which migrate from Canada to Mexico every year. Their migration's so long it requires five or six generations of butterflies, and yet they manage to end up in the exact same location in Mexico year after year."

Lisa didn't reply, and that dreadful empty stare was back. She drew in a ragged breath. "Dad, Mom, if I keep having these nightmares . . . I can't concentrate on anything else, just these stupid dreams. I keep screwing up at soccer practice, I don't know why I even bother to go anymore. I can't concentrate on classes, and I'm afraid to go to sleep." Tears were threatening flood her eyes and roll down her cheeks. "Why are these crazy dreams *happening* to me?"

Andy thought again about what he'd learned about dreams. "Listen, honey," he said gently, "I also read that if you think about the same subject every night before you go to sleep, it significantly increases the chance that you'll have dreams about that subject, so try to think about something pleasant and positive tonight, all right?"

That evening, Lisa appeared in the family room, notepad and pencil in hand, eyes animated. Before Andy could open his mouth to greet her, she held out the notepad.

"I have a big hole here," she said.

Alarmed, Andy lowered his recliner's footrest to sit upright. "I don't understand. A hole in what?"

"The tooth necklace came from your mom's family, but except for the letter from that guy Tapio, I don't know anything about them. And I thought maybe it would help with . . . you know . . . if I could find out more. More about Finland and Finns too."

He smiled and leaned back to engage the footrest. "Oh, that kind of hole. I never thought you were interested, so I was waiting for you to ask."

"I'm ready now. I want to know more," Lisa said with determination.

"Well, okay, I'll give it a whirl. For one thing, you know you're pretty good at track. That's because long-distance running's in your blood from both sides of the family. The world's first famous distance runner was Hannes Kolehmainen. He won three gold medals at the 1912 Stockholm Olympics. And there was Paavo Nurmi, who won three golds at the 1920 Antwerp games, five in Paris in 1924, and one in Amersterdam in 1928. He became known worldwide as the Flying Finn."

"A flying Finn?" Lisa stopped taking notes. "Did he fly like I did in my dreams?"

Andy laughed. "No, honey. But he did fly past everybody in all the races. The nickname 'Flying Finn' has a nice ring to it, doesn't it? There are other famous Finnish runners too, like Lasse Viren, another gold medalist in the seventies. Long-distance running is in the Finnish genes, as it is for the Kenyans. And your mom was a great runner in college, so you probably inherited her sprinter speed and my Finnish endurance."

"Thanks, Dad." She rolled her eyes. "I always thought my endurance came from my long hours of training. So, is running the only thing Finland's famous for?"

"Oh no, there's more. Like the sauna. The Finns developed it because the winters were long and cold, but they use it year-round now. All the farms have saunas. Most of the homes in villages and cities too."

"Huh, I never thought of a farmhouse having a sauna before. That's cool. Or maybe hot." She giggled. "What else?"

"Well, you probably know that Minnesota is famous for having so many pine trees and more than ten thousand lakes. Hence its nickname, the Land of Lakes. But Finland has over a hundred and eighty thousand lakes and millions of pines. Timber and wood pulp is a big industry in Finland. Shipbuilding too. Finland's also known for its outstanding architects."

Andy leaned over and picked his cell phone up from the coffee table. "And this was made in Finland."

"Really? I thought Nokia phones were Japanese."

Andy laughed again. "A lot of people think that because Nokia sounds like a Japanese word and the Japanese are known for electronics, but Nokia is a Finnish city. The Nokia company started there a long time before developing their cell phones."

"Cool," she said as he set the phone down.

"Another unique thing. Finnish names are easy to recognize. They use a lot of *k*'s and double *k*'s and double *t*'s in their names. Jaakko, Matti, Antti, Heikki. They don't use the letter *c* at all. The Finns also use the suffix *nen* on many of their last names."

"Like our name," Lisa said. "Koskinen."

"Right. And others, like Pollarinen, Jokinen, and Makinen. If you see a name ending in *nen*, you can bet it's Finnish."

"Does *nen* mean anything?"

"I don't think so. Many other Finnish names end in *la*—Varila, Matala, Paavala, Mikkola—but the *la* has no special meaning either. I guess somewhere along the line those endings just sounded good to somebody."

She nodded, but the smile he expected wasn't there. "Those things are interesting, Dad, but they're more like . . . trivia. Tell me about your family in Finland."

"Glad you asked. Finally." He chuckled. "Now I won't have wasted all the research I did when I went to the family reunion. I'll tell you what I remember."

"Ooh, with your memory? I'd better get comfortable and get out my special pen." Lisa curled up on the sofa, tucked her pencil into the notepad's pocket, and pulled out the pen the twins had stuffed into her stocking last Christmas, bright blue, with crystals inset at the tip. And large, because Lisa was known to the family as a voracious note taker.

Andy paused for a moment, thinking. "Can't remember exactly when, but a long time ago a girl named Sari left her parents' farm to marry Johan Jarvinen. The Jarvinens lived in central Finland, near a village called Olhava. They had five kids and shared another farm with Sari's sister Outti and her husband, who had nine kids, eight boys and a girl named Tulli."

Lisa looked up from the notepad. "What? You mean Tulli and Outti and Sari from Tapio's letter? The Outti whose daughter gave me the tooth necklace?"

"Yes, it's all been coming back to me since I started trying to figure out where Tapio fits into the family tree."

Lisa was silent as she took this new information in. Finally she said, "What else do you remember? Tell me more about Tulli. She had eight brothers? I love Henry, but if you ask me, one is plenty. And nine kids on one farm?"

"That wasn't unusual back in those days. Dairy farmers needed big families to help with the crops and milk the cows twice a day, three sixty-five a year. Remember, there weren't any tractors back then, or milking equipment."

Lisa smiled. "And to think I give Mom a hard time about doing the dishes."

Andy returned her smile, grateful to see it. "But all those children did make things crowded. Sari and Johan read about free homestead land in America and decided to move there to start a new farm. Outti didn't want her sister to leave, but Sari had made up her mind. She and Johan traveled through Sweden and Denmark to Germany, and from there took a steamship to New York. They went to Brainerd, Minnesota, and found work at a hotel, and in their spare time they looked for land to homestead. Then . . ."

"What's wrong, Dad? Is that famous memory of yours failing?" Lisa asked as his voice trailed off.

Andy had to force a smile because he was struggling inwardly. He recalled the rest of the story, but was it too much for Lisa to hear, given the dreams that were tormenting her? One look at her expectant face told him he had to go on. If he made some excuse for not telling her everything he knew about her ancestors, she might clam up again, and that would be terrible.

With a sigh he tried to suppress, he said, "After Sari and Johan got to Brainerd, . . . well, a terrible thing happened . . ."

* * *

Minnesota, Summer 1888

Sari Jarvinen leans against the oak tree overhanging the picnic spot, watching the children play by the Mississippi River. A dutiful wife should care little for fashion, but this is a special outing—a grand annual event put on by Sally, who owns the hotel where Sari and her husband are working—so she's wearing her best hat and nicest skirt. She is glad her fair skin is well covered; some guests at the hotel have been saying that the summer of 1888 is surely the hottest of the decade. She closes her eyes, remembering the cool breezes of her childhood. Homesickness overwhelms her until she reminds herself that someday she and Johan will have saved enough money to homestead and establish a dairy farm of their own.

She glances over at her husband dozing next to her, then back at the children. Some are wading close to shore between clumps of cattails in the calm knee-high water. Sally's son, Erick, is climbing onto a rickety little raft made of old boards found along the shore.

Sari doesn't recognize the sound at first. Her mind is occupied by the thought that it is very nice of Sally to invite her employees to the picnic. Then she knows what she's heard. She bolts upright and sees the children yelling and pointing to the river.

"Johan!" she shouts. "Erick is drowning!" She runs to the water, hears her husband behind her. The small raft is bobbing a hundred feet from shore. Beside it, Erick waves and screams.

Johan runs past her, dives into the river, and swims toward Erick. As she watches in horror, the current sucks them both downstream toward a bend. When Johan finally reaches Erick, the boy disappears, and Sari's heart stands still. At last they pop up, Johan swimming toward shore with one arm, his other wrapped around the boy. Erick grabs wildly at him, almost pulling him under. Johan treads water furiously, calling out, "I can't hold him, I need help!" His voice is tight with fear. Another man dives into the river, swims to him, grabs Erick's arm, and sidestrokes to the shore. Others wade out and bring Erick in, crying and kicking.

Johan is still out in the river. Sari hears him yell something she can barely hear. What is it? Cramp? As her mind tries to sort out what he's saying, as her heart prays to God, he sinks under the water. "Johan! Johan!" she screams, running into the river as far as she can before her sodden skirts stop her. Several men swim out to where he went under and frantically look for him.

For naught. A few minutes later, the men drag Johan's limp body to shore. Sari's pleas to God have gone unanswered.

The day after the funeral, Sally finds Sari and asks her to sit with her. "I'm so terribly sorry," she says, "I know what plans you had, I know how much you and Johan looked forward to homesteading."

Sari nods, saying nothing, until she hears clinking from the kitchen as the staff prepares for lunch. "I must get back to work, I must—"

"Wait," Sally says, putting her hand over Sari's. "Before James and I bought this hotel, we owned a smaller one west of here, in New York Mills. We have it up for sale, and we want to sell it to you."

"What?" Sari says. "I can't afford to buy a hotel."

"Yes, you can." Sally hands her an official-looking piece of paper. Sari stares at it, then reads it over quickly. Her eyes widen.

"Is this right? Only one dollar?"

"Yes. Johan saved our son. His life is worth more than we can ever repay you."

"But . . . but you shouldn't—"

Sally holds up a hand. "You can go next week, if you wish. I already wrote to the manager about helping you get started. I will send the local store money to take care of food and supplies until you're settled. There's absolutely no reason you can't do this, Sari."

***

Lisa sat frozen, tears streaming down her cheeks, and Andy was certain he'd made a mistake in telling her about the drowning. "Honey, I'm sorry, I—"

She scribbled on her notepad, then looked up at him. "How awful that Sari's husband died before they could get their farm. What happened then, Dad? Did she make a success of it? The hotel? Way back then, did women even own things?"

Andy felt a surge of relief. "You're like a sponge, aren't you? Women did own things, and yep, she sure did run the hotel successfully. They built more railroads in rural Minnesota, to bring in more farmers, and all the hotels filled up with railroad workers. Later, Sari's oldest daughter, Amelia, married one of them." He searched his memory. "A Finn named Ole Niemi. Amelia and Ole raised four children in New York Mills. Amelia's oldest daughter, Lisa, married Erik Jokinen, another Finn. Erik and Lisa moved north to Hibbing and started a general store, and then—"

"Lisa?" Her eyes were animated again. "Is that the Lisa I was named after?"

"Yep. Lisa Jokinen is your great-grandmother. Our family has often taken the names of our relatives. Lisa is a popular name in our family."

She began scribbling again. "Dad, I can't believe you never told me that!"

"Sorry, honey, Mom and I always meant to tell you, but we were waiting for the right time. Guess that's now." Andy leaned back, thinking. "You know, for most of our history, Finnish people didn't even use last names. I recall reading that last names started around the thirteenth century, because with cities growing and getting crowded, single names alone couldn't identify individuals. Because Finland was an agrarian culture—"

"Agrarian? That's when there are a lot of farms?"

"Right. In western Finland where our people came from, a surname was given according to the farm where each family lived. Several families on the same farm used the same last name. If they started a new farm, they chose whatever last name they wanted."

More scribbling. "I can't believe people could just pick any last name they wanted."

"Remember, we're talking hundreds of years ago. Some chose last names based on places, like Joki or Jokinen, which means 'river,' or Koski or Koskinen, which means 'rapids,' or Jarvi or Jarvinen, which means 'lake.'"

Lisa was no longer writing, and her eyes had that faraway look again. After a moment's panic, Andy realized she wasn't upset, just thoughtful.

"So our name—Koskinen—it means 'rapids'?" she asked.

He nodded, fearful again, but Lisa just shrugged. "I guess . . . when I came in here, I guess I was trying to find out something about our family, something that might help explain why I keep dreaming about rivers, about drowning. But"—she shook her head—"I don't see how our name could have anything to do with that. I mean, I've had the same last name all my life."

"Yes, honey, just a coincidence. Would you like to hear more about our history?" Andy asked, eager to take her mind off the dreams. "I don't want you accusing me of holding out on you."

Lisa laughed, her pen poised over her notepad.

"Well, my mother's family was always very proud of living in Hibbing. It produced two-thirds of the world's iron ore for years. Many Finns, like Lisa's Erik, worked in the mines, and he saved money to start his own store. By 1915, Hibbing's population topped twenty thousand. The place got so crowded and busy that two men started a bus line there to help people get around, and it became the famous Greyhound Lines."

Lisa gave him an exaggerated yawn, clearly not as interested in these facts as in her namesake, but Andy, charged up by the memories and relieved that she seemed calmer now, told her about a large iron ore deposit that had been discovered directly below Hibbing. "The mining company paid to move the entire city two miles away. They built a big redbrick high school with two indoor swimming pools, one for boys and one for girls. The school still exists today."

"Two swimming pools? I'd settle for one."

Andy laughed and looked at his watch. "Yes, that would be nice, but I'm afraid our school district doesn't have the bucks. Your mom should be home with the twins any minute now, so I guess I'd better hurry if I want to finish the story."

Lisa rolled her eyes. "Yeah, the minute Hanna and Henry get here, you won't get a word in edgewise."

"Right. So Lisa and Erik Jokinen's store did really well. Well enough that they were able to send all three of their children to college. They were the first children in either of their families to attend college."

Being college-minded, Lisa was interested in this. "Was Grammy Amanda one of them?"

He nodded. "Yep. My mother became an elementary teacher in the small village of Makinen, near the city of Eveleth, in a two-room schoolhouse. She taught the first three grades. See the picture on the mantel? That's her, in her classroom with the kids."

Lisa jumped up and went to the fireplace. She brought the picture back to the couch and studied it. "Grammy sure was pretty. What happened to her?"

"She loved teaching, but during the war she got lonely, and there were no young men around. She said she always dreamed of meeting a handsome Finn. There's a lot more to *that* story, of course."

"Oh, a love story? Grammy's love story? That's my genes too. Tell me everything."

Just then, they heard the sound of the front door being flung open, followed by Hanna's frantic cry: "Dad! Come quick! It's Mom!"

Andy and Lisa sat quietly in a waiting room at UC San Francisco Medical Center, where they'd been sitting for two hours, trying to make small talk but unable to. Hanna and Henry were with a neighbor. Andy and Lisa were the only people present.

A doctor in green scrubs came into the room and looked around, his eyes settling on Andy. "I'm Dr. Coleman. Are you a friend of Eva Koskinen's?"

"I'm her husband, Andy Koskinen. How's my wife?" Andy thought the doctor had probably been looking for a black man.

Dr. Coleman's next words upended Andy's world and caused Lisa to fall into his arms. *"Severe kidney failure . . . dialysis . . . possible transplant."*

3
Koskinen History

San Francisco, November 1999

Lisa's dreams seemed to abate in the worry over her mother's health, but she still dreamed often of flying near a river. Though they didn't speak of it much, Andy was worried, terribly worried, about Eva. Dialysis was working well enough, but there was no telling for how long. Eva was able to return to work, and except for her dialysis appointments, which she jokingly called her "day spa visits," the family functioned normally. But dialysis alone would not cure the kidney disease no one had known about until her collapse. Eva was on a transplant list.

Late one afternoon after school, Lisa answered the ringing phone and yelled, "Dad! It's Professor Rutherford."

Andy took the phone. "Hello, Professor, any news?"

"There certainly is news, Andy. I was wrong about the necklace being from the Vikings about one thousand years ago. The tooth the lab tested is six thousand years old, and it came from a bear."

"Yikes! Six thousand years old? That's about when I

thought the Finns first came to Finland."

Lisa looked over at him, eyebrows raised in surprise.

"This necklace is a historical relic, Andy. Livermore Labs wants to test a second and third tooth to verify its age. Is that all right?"

Andy turned to Lisa. "The lab wants to test two more teeth. Is that okay with you?"

"Sure. I can't believe the first tooth is really six thousand years old. That's incredible!"

After Professor Rutherford's call, Lisa began to seem more curious about the necklace than bothered by it. She was almost her old self, bouncing into the house after soccer practice to tell about a great play she'd made or a class that had gone particularly well. Andy was grateful for that, and grateful too for her continuing interest in their shared family history. It helped keep him from dwelling on Eva's medical problems.

That evening, Andy was reading a journal article in his recliner when Lisa appeared with her notebook. He'd already told her all he could recall about his mother's Finnish background, and now she wanted to know about his father's side of the family.

"Well, there were four Koskinen brothers and one sister, and . . ."

* * *

Finland, 1890

Matti Koskinen knows he's in trouble. How can he break the news?

He and his brothers have just finished the milking and are doing their other chores when their father, Tuomas, comes into the barn and says he wants to see Matti in the kitchen. Just Matti. As he trudges toward the house, Matti knows that something he has been dreading for months is about to happen.

"I want you to take over the farm next summer, son," Tuomas says. "Mother and I will help you as much as we can."

Matti's throat clenches. He swallows. Here it is. "Father, I don't want to be a farmer anymore."

Tuomas stares at him in disbelief. "Why? The farm has everything you and your future family will need."

Matti swallows again. "Because I don't want to milk cows twice a day all my life. It's 1890, and there are plenty of opportunities to do other things. I know this is a valuable farm and most men would love to have it, but . . . not me."

Tuomas rises from the table and begins to pace. "What will you do? These are hard times. There are no jobs around here."

"I've heard there are good-paying jobs . . . in the copper mines in America."

Tuomas drops heavily into his chair. "You will leave Finland? If you go to America, we will never see you again."

Matti looks at the floor, thoughts flashing in his mind. His family had lived in the Kemi area in the north for hundreds of years, moving to Kokkola just twenty years ago to start this new dairy farm. His father took the surname Koskinen because a river with rapids flows through the farm. His father is right, times are difficult, and have been the whole time Matti and his brothers and their sister, Hilda, have been growing up. But the dairy farm has done well, and they grow their own potatoes and vegetables, and they want for nothing. Now his father is ready to retire, and by tradition his oldest son will take over the farm, but Matti has other ideas.

Neither speaks until Matti, unable to bear the silence any longer, looks up to see tears in his father's eyes. He has never seen his father cry.

Tuomas swipes his hand over his eyes and says in a hard voice, "All right, then the farm will go to your brother Tuomas, and Antti and Johan will help him. Hilda will stay on the farm until she marries."

Matti takes a deep breath. "Father, Antti and Tuomas are going to America with me."

Matti Koskinen and his two brothers leave for America the next spring, going first to Germany and then taking a steamship from Bremerhaven to New York. After Ellis Island and travel by train to Michigan's Upper Peninsula, they find jobs in the copper mines.

The work is hard and dangerous, and Matti asks the mining company for more safety precautions and better pay. The company ignores him. Matti tries to organize a union. The company threatens to fire him and tells him to stop having meetings, but he keeps holding them in secret.

One warm summer Saturday evening after work, Matti, Tuomas, and Antti are walking along a dirt street known for its bars. Matti stops. "I'm going to the Red Bar for a few beers. I'll see you later at Sally's Saloon."

The Red Bar is already crowded with drunken miners. Matti yells to a man across the room, "Over here, George. I'll buy you a beer." He talks to George about the union. Several more miners join in the discussion.

A tall stranger walks by and bumps George hard, knocking his beer bottle to the floor. "You clumsy donkey," George bellows. "You owe me a beer!"

"Nobody calls me a donkey." The stranger grabs George's shirt, pulls him off his bar stool, and pumps his fist at George's face.

Matti jumps up. "Stop it! Let him go!"

A burly stranger approaches Matti. "You're the union guy, ain't you?"

"Yeah," Matti replies. "You interested in joining?"

The stranger reaches out as if to shake hands, and Matti feels something sharp slice into his belly.

"No damn unions here!" the stranger yells as Matti falls to the floor, bleeding to death. The stranger disappears into the night.

One month later, still grieving, Tuomas and Antti decide their father was right: farming offers a safer and better life. They travel to Minnesota, where they share a homestead claim in the new Finnish farming community of Makinen. Their neighbors help them clear the land and build their houses and barns, and they become dairy farmers as they'd been in Finland. The Finns living nearby make their early years easier because of the shared language, but English quickly becomes a necessity. Eight years of school is now mandatory for all the farm children, who learn English in their classrooms and then teach it to their parents.

* * *

"I was named after my grandfather Antti," Andy said, "and remember what I told you about big farm families? Antti had five sons and three daughters. The three oldest sons left the farm during the Great Depression and found work in Duluth and Minneapolis. The youngest sons, Matti and your grandpa Thomas, joined the army at the start of World War II, but they came back to the farm when the war ended."

He smiled as a memory popped into his head. "Remember what we were talking about the day Mom got sick?"

Lisa stopped writing, her forehead furrowed in thought. "About Grammy. About her being lonely, wanting to meet a nice Finn boy, but all the boys went to the war." She gave Andy an eager grin. "So are you finally getting around to that love story, Dad?"

"Seems like as good a time as any."

* * *

When the bombs hit Pearl Harbor, things moved quickly. But dismantling a massive military force stationed all over the world and getting it back to America takes longer. It is 1946 by the time Thomas and his brother Matti come home from the war.

Eager to resume their former lives, they spend their first few days on the farm working from sunup to sundown. Thomas feels new muscles developing, but every day those muscles get a little sorer. The war was rough, he thinks as he unhooks the horses from the manure spreader, but not as hard as farm work.

His father approaches and calls him and Matti over.

Thomas stands with the team's traces in his hand, wondering what's up.

"The school's starting again pretty soon," Antti says, "and they need a bus driver to pick up the farm kids. I want one of you to take the job."

The boys look at each other. "Matti can do it," Thomas says.

Matti snorts. "Yeah, right. In your dreams."

Antti pulls a coin from his overalls. "Call it, Thomas."

"Heads."

"Come on, tails!" Matti yells as the coin spins in the air. When it lands, they all lean down to see it. Matti grins. "Tails! You lose, Thomas. You have to drive the bus."

The first day, in fact the first morning, Thomas is ready to quit by the time he picks up the last screaming kid, drives up to Makinen's two-room schoolhouse, and helps each of his whiny charges off the bus.

The last one, a little girl, trips on the steps, but Thomas catches her and carries her to the school's front door. He stops. He's been to war, he's seen a lot of women, but standing on the steps of that little schoolhouse is the most beautiful woman in the world.

Amanda Jokinen smiles at the handsome blond man standing there, peering at her with bright blue eyes.

"Hello, ma'am. I'm . . . well, here's one of your children."

"Hi. I'm Amanda." She glances at the little girl in his arms. "Are you a parent?"

He sets the girl down and crosses his arms. "No, ma'am. I'm Thomas Koskinen, the bus driver this year."

Amanda tells herself to stop breathing so hard, it isn't ladylike. Two children are tugging at her, but she hardly notices. "Are you from this area?" she asks. "I didn't see you around last year."

"My family farms near here. I just got home from the army. Where are you from?"

"Hibbing. I came here last year after college."

Thomas hesitates for a moment. "What time should I pick up the kids?"

She manages to say, "Class is over at three," and he turns to leave. She wants to say more but thinks better of it, knowing nothing about him except that he is handsome. But he seems to like her, because he turns around, smiles, and waves goodbye.

Amanda thinks about Thomas all day. When he returns to pick up the children, he doesn't wait at the bus as last year's driver did. He waits outside the classroom door.

They exchange polite greetings, but the conversation ends there, as though they'd both agreed to simply stand there smiling, staring into each other's eyes. By the time Amanda pulls her eyes away from him, she sees that most of the children have run to the bus, obviously eager to go home and tell Mom and Dad about their first school day.

Thomas finally brings himself to walk to the bus. He turns to look back and stumbles. Fighting a giggle, Amanda waves at him, and he waves back as he drives off.

The warmth that enveloped her at first sight of him stays with her. At the boardinghouse where she lives, she tells a fellow teacher about him, and for some reason she no longer feels lonely.

That night she has a weird dream about flying like a bird, floating happily along a winding river. It's the first time she's ever had such a dream, and what an odd dream it is. When she wakes, she thinks about Thomas and lingers in bed for several more minutes than usual.

At dinner that night, Thomas sees his father wink at his mother. Ulla winks back, and Antti turns to his son. "Thomas, I've been thinking about how much you hate to drive that bus. Maybe Matti should drive it half the time."

Matti opens his mouth to reply, but Thomas speaks first. "Oh no, that's not necessary. I actually enjoy the kids."

Ulla laughs. "I'll bet you met Amanda Jokinen." Seeing her son's face flush, she says, "Last year, we heard the new teacher was a real beauty. She also turned out to be a great teacher. All the parents love her."

"Especially the fathers," Antti adds.

Matti frowns, and Thomas laughs. "Too bad I won—I mean, *lost* the flip."

For the rest of the week, Thomas and Amanda only have time for brief hellos because they both have their hands full with the children. On Friday morning, Thomas slips her a note before he leaves. Puzzled, she opens it as she walks into her classroom. The note asks if she will be attending the dance at the Makinen community center on Saturday night.

"Oh yes!" she blurts out.

The children look at her. "Why did you say that?" one little girl asks.

"I . . . just feel happy."

She begins class, but all day she thinks about how she will reply.

In the afternoon, when Thomas comes to the door, she is

waiting with a big smile. "I wasn't planning on going," she says, "but I'd love to go with you."

On Saturday night, as they're walking into the dance hall, he leans close and whispers, "I need to tell you something. I don't know how to dance."

She smiles and squeezes his hand. "I'll teach you. Look, this is a slow dance," she says, pulling him onto the dance floor and showing him how to put his arms around her. "All you need to do is hold me close." Which he seems quite happy to do.

Amanda is in heaven for the next three weeks. When Thomas asks her to come home with him for dinner, she tells her teacher friend in the boardinghouse that she has never felt so alive.

When they arrive at the farmhouse, Antti and Ulla are standing on the porch, grinning. They greet Amanda warmly.

"Miss Jokinen, you do know we have something special in common, don't you?" Antti asks.

She looks puzzled. "Do you mean being Finnish?"

"Yes, but not only that. Rivers, Miss Jokinen, rivers and rapids. Joki and koski!"

Thomas nudges Amanda "What a joki. I mean joke."

During the Thanksgiving break, Amanda takes Thomas to Hibbing to meet her family. After dinner, her father pulls her to the side.

"I like your young man," Erik says. "He's a confident and straightforward fellow. Great sense of humor. He'd be good in sales. Might work out at our store."

When Thomas and Amanda announce their engagement at Christmas break and their intent to be married the following summer, nobody is surprised. It is a good match.

After the wedding, Erik sits down with them. "I have a friend who's looking for people to start new Ben Franklin variety stores in Minnesota," he says. "If you're interested, I'll finance one for you in Moose Lake."

While they're deciding, Thomas and Amanda visit and fall in love with Moose Lake, a quaint town of fifteen hundred located on the north side of a river-fed lake, with rapids flowing down into another river on the south side. Though small, it was one of the best-known towns in Minnesota because of the state mental hospital on the south side. Moose Lakers are often asked in jest which side of the lake they live on.

* * *

Lisa sighed dreamily. "Their courtship was so romantic! Thanks for telling me Grammy Amanda's love story, Dad."

"My pleasure," Andy said. "She and Thomas were actually pretty romantic even after they got married, though they ended up having a smaller family than their parents did. Just Annie, Henry, and me."

"So Grammy and Grandpa met at a school, and you ended up working at a school too. Life really does go in a circle, doesn't—" She paused, a light dawning. "So the Ben Franklin, that's how they ended up in Moose Lake?"

Andy nodded. "Yep, old Moose Lake carries a lot of significance for the whole family. Actually, Moose Lake is an appropriate place for Finns. Moose are part of the deer family, and Mom and Dad probably didn't know this, but lakes were stopping places for our ancestors when they journeyed along the rivers, hunting deer to survive, just as the Finns did when they first migrated to Finland."

"Deer," she said, her eyes thoughtful. "And Grammy told you she dreamed about a river?"

"That's right. Who knows? Maybe you picked up one of her memories, like that theory about memory DNA claims."

"Yeah, maybe. I guess there really might be something to it. But what happened to the brother who stayed in Finland, Dad? What happened to Johan? Did he come to America later?"

"No. Johan stayed, and that's why the same dairy farm is still in the Koskinen family today. One of his grandsons still lives on the farm. Actually, I was doing some research about Johan and his sister, Hilda, and I wondered what happened to her after the three brothers left for America. I couldn't find anything about her." He rubbed his chin. "There was so much information about the brothers, but not about her. I find that pretty odd."

Lisa looked up from her notepad. "Uh-oh, looks like we have another family mystery to solve."

4
Sprinter

San Francisco, November 1999

Eva sipped her after-dinner coffee while Andy read in his recliner. Lisa was curled up on the sofa, poring over her chemistry book, studying for a test with Eva's help.

"Have you heard anything from Professor Rutherford, Andy?" Eva asked.

He looked up from his book. "Nothing about the necklace, the lab's still testing it, but there's a young professor in his department who was very interested in it when Rutherford mentioned it to him. His name's John Anderson, and he did his PhD thesis on the migration of *homo sapiens* out of Africa to Europe. He specializes in prehistory, the span of time before people began writing things down about five thousand years ago, and he seems to have some ideas about the necklace. You can ask him all about it when he and Rutherford come to dinner."

"What?" Eva set her coffee cup down with a clatter. "Dinner? When?"

"Saturday, just like I told you."

Eva glared at him. "May I point out that Saturday is tomorrow?"

"You mean I didn't tell you? I could have sworn I did," Andy said sheepishly. "I'm sorry, honey, I meant to, guess it slipped my mind."

"Such as it is," Eva said tartly.

"I'll tell them we have to cancel, I'll—"

"You know what?" Eva said. "It'll be nice to cook up a big dinner with all the fixings now that I'm feeling better. Haven't done that for a while, just tell me next time if it's not too much of a strain on your brain." She allowed a hint of a smile to cross her face. "And if this Professor John has something to say about the necklace, I'm all ears."

"Me too," Lisa said. Andy and Eva had almost forgotten she was there.

Eva regarded her daughter thoughtfully. "I know how you feel about it, Lisa, but that necklace represents your Finnish roots. Sometimes I wish I knew more about my own roots, especially about Africa. I guess I started thinking more about that after I got sick. I want you kids to know about it too. I've been doing some research about African Americans, slavery, and when modern man left Africa for the first time."

"I'm pretty much okay about the necklace now, Mom, and I've been hearing tons about Dad's family, but I hardly know anything about yours. I know you grew up in Mound Bayou, Mississippi, but that's about it. Where did your family live before that?"

Eva searched her memory, glad for her daughter's interest but reluctant to delve into the past. "Remember, honey, it was slave times, but I heard a little from my parents and grandparents. My mother's great-great-grandmother was a Virginia plantation slave, and then the plantation owner moved to near Jackson, Mississippi, to start another cotton plantation. Far as I can tell, my family worked there during the Civil War and moved to Mound Bayou about 1887."

"And then?" Lisa asked, her expression expectant.

Eva sat back, not wanting to go on but needing to. "When I was about your age, I tried to find out more, but millions of slaves were brought to America between about 1600 and the early 1800s. If any records were kept, they just listed ages and first names, and usually not even the names the slaves had been born with. The slave traders and owners gave most of them American or European names, so you see how impossible it is to find out anything about anyone except from stories handed down."

Eva hadn't meant to let her longing show, but it was too late. Lisa put her chemistry book down on the coffee table with a thump and said, "Mom, could your DNA maybe tell you where in Africa your ancestors came from?"

Surprise lightened Eva's somber mood. "You know, I was reading something the other day about how advanced the science is getting on that, something about a project doing DNA testing of tribes in West Africa so they can compare the results with African Americans."

Andy leaned forward. "Do you have any idea what country or tribe your family's from?"

Eva shook her head. "I just know that most slaves came from Africa's west coast. That's a big, big coastline. Tell you what, I'll get a DNA test kit at work tomorrow and send it off, and I'll try to find out more about that project I read about.

Who knows, maybe someone in *my* family line ended up in Finland at some point. It's a big world, you know."

"Wouldn't that be something?" Andy said.

"Mom, what was it like, growing up in Mississippi? You never talk about it."

"Mississippi is way in the past, honey, and—"

"Tell her about Mound Bayou and Cleveland, at least," Andy said. "You know, about the racism and what happened when you ran track in high school. I think that's important for the kids to know."

"Yeah, Mom," Lisa said. "Look, we've studied racism in school, and it's not like I never dealt with it. Kind of difficult not to with a white dad and a black mom, don't you think? I can handle it."

Eva took a deep breath. Where to start? She didn't know, but she knew she had to. If the worst happened and no suitable kidney was found, she'd never have the chance to tell Lisa about her growing-up years, and if she didn't tell Lisa, who would tell Henry and Hanna? Andy knew some of her story, but not all of it. She allowed her mind to travel back to Mound Bayou in the Mississippi Delta, where she grew up before and during the civil rights movement. Memories came to her, of her parents' decades-long fight against the divided public school system, and especially of the day the Mississippi schools finally integrated in the 1970s.

"All right," Eva said, "I'll tell you as much as I can. My dad was hired to teach biology in an integrated school in Cleveland, a larger town about ten miles south of Mound Bayou. I was a senior in high school then, living on our cotton farm, but Daddy decided I should transfer to Cleveland because they had more college prep classes. It was almost all white, even after integration."

"Were you scared?" Lisa asked.

"Sure. Only five percent of the students were black, and the whites were always coming at us with something awful, nigger this and nigger that."

"Tell her how you got started running track," Andy said.

Eva's mind went back to 1973 as if she were actually there. "Well, one day after class my phys ed teacher told me, 'You run like a deer,' and the next day, as I was running a hundred-yard sprint, I saw him and the school's track coach on the sideline, timing me with stopwatches. I crossed the finish line and turned to see Coach Richy staring at his stopwatch, mouth open. 'Jeez. Wow! She just beat the state high school record,' he said to my teacher. I became the track team's only black girl, and the white girls seemed to resent the time Coach Richy spent with me. They were especially upset when he made me the fourth runner on the relay team. Coach pulled the white runners aside and said, 'I don't care what the fuck you think. Eva's going to run the relay. If you don't like it, you can quit now.'"

Lisa gasped. "Mom, I don't think I've ever heard you say that word. But what happened?"

Eva gave her a small smile. "Well, none of the girls quit, but my dad thought running track was a waste of time. When I told Coach that, he said, 'Eva, you're the fastest high school girl I've ever seen anyplace. You're going to break the state hundred-yard-dash record.' And then, when I told my father what Coach said about college scholarship offers, he changed his mind about track being a waste of time."

With more prodding from Andy and Lisa, Eva went on with her story. She told them how nervous she was when she stepped out of the dressing rooms at the Northern Mississippi Spring Invitational. It was the first track meet of the year, the first time in Mississippi's history that black and white girls would run together. She glanced up at the stands, filled with white people, except for a small black group at the end. Coach had said several college scouts would be here, but which ones were they? She knew none of them had ever heard of Eva Jefferson.

She easily won her heats in the hundred and the two hundred. After the last sprinter heat, Coach took her to a big tent and handed her a bottle of water. "You're doing great," he said. "And no pressure, but I bet my friend you'd beat the state record in the hundred-yard final."

When the starting gun went off, Eva was last out of the blocks. She reached into her soul, and running like a scared deer, she soon passed the other girls. At the track's edge, Coach Richy raised his fist, yelling "Go, baby, go!" as she sped past him.

The blacks in the stadium stood up as she reached the finish line several yards ahead of last year's state champion. When her name and time were posted on the scoreboard, the announcer bellowed, "Eva Jefferson has broken the Mississippi state record!"

The day's last race was the 4 x 100 yard relay. After the third leg, Eva nervously started her run in the baton hand-off lane, looking for the pass from Amy, one of the white girls who'd said she didn't want to run with her. Amy drew nearer and nearer, and Eva reached out for the baton and completed a perfect hand-off. Behind her, Amy yelled, "Run, Eva, run!"

Eva advanced on the two leading runners. With thirty yards to go, she accelerated, and the black fans went wild. "Eva! Eva! Eva!" She shot by the other schools' runners and sprinted to the finish line five yards ahead of them. A roar went up, and Cleveland set a new state record.

The three other Cleveland runners rushed to hug Eva. Coach Richy came over to them, clapping enthusiastically. "You all did it," he said. "You're the best in the state."

Eva sighed, remembering how good it felt to hear those words from Coach. "When I looked up into the stands, I saw my dad. He was waving. I saw him remove his glasses and wipe his eyes. I never heard the other girls say a bad word about me again. We all went on to be state champions in the relay race."

There was silence when Eva stopped speaking, and then Lisa said, "Wow, Mom, awesome! But you went through so much."

Eva pulled her daughter to her and brushed a strand of hair from her face. "Well, it's all over now. And I have you and your dad."

"But Mom, that was . . . that was beautiful. You were just like a butterfly leaving a cocoon. What happened next?"

"Well, I got that track scholarship. To Northern Mississippi State University."

"Your mom did a little more than that," Andy said. "She broke all the school's track records, and was invited to try out for the USA Olympic track team. And she did more than run fast. She was fast both on and off the track."

Eva shot him a look. "Now, what on earth does *that* mean?"

He grinned. "*Meaning*, you also excelled in science. A grad school fellowship at the University of Minnesota, and a PhD in microbiology there."

Eva smiled. "Yes, I guess that was something special too. My parents worried about me going to a mostly white university so far from home. Not to mention those long, freezing winters."

"Hey, I thought you enjoyed that first winter with me," Andy said.

She patted his arm. "Yes, honey, I did. But I sure didn't like the ten-below weather. Without you, the winters would've been miserable."

On Saturday morning, Eva stood at the kitchen sink watching the twins play outside. Lisa was still sitting at the breakfast table. "I had two dreams last night, Mom," she said. "One was about running."

Eva's motherly instincts compelled her to check her daughter's expression, but Lisa didn't look upset. "Well, that makes sense. I talked your ear off about running last night. Did you win?"

"I don't know. It was a long race, and I woke up before it was finished."

"What about the other dream?" Eva asked.

"Well, there was this tribe, and they were looking for deer herds, and the chief's name was Antti—and Mom, his wife's name was Eva."

"Really? That's wild," Eva said, pouring herself a cup of coffee she probably shouldn't have. She took a seat at the table and gave Lisa a playful swat on the arm. "Maybe you can tell Professor John all about it at dinner tonight."

5
Professor John

Sukie barked when the doorbell rang a little after six o'clock. Andy answered it to find John Anderson standing there alone. "Come on in," he said as Anderson explained that Professor Rutherford had a bad case of flu and couldn't make it.

"That's too bad," Andy said. "Down, Sukie!" The dog seemed to have taken an instant liking to the new guest.

John Anderson was young, handsome, and sure of himself. He wore his jet black hair in a ponytail and was mostly clad in denim. Andy ushered him into the living room to meet Eva and Lisa.

"Have a seat," Andy said after the introductions were made. "Can I offer you a drink?"

"Scotch, neat, if you have it," Anderson said as Sukie plopped herself at his feet.

Andy didn't. "Will white wine do?"

Anderson suppressed a frown. "Sure."

Eva passed him a plate of hors d'oeuvres and excused herself to check on the twins, who had eaten early and were upstairs playing. Fifteen minutes later she came down and summoned everyone to the dinner table, seating Lisa across from Anderson.

"So I hear the tooth from that necklace of yours is six thousand years old," he said to Lisa as he tucked into Eva's dinner of fried chicken, mashed potatoes, and collard greens.

"Yes, that's what the lab tests showed, Professor Anderson, and ever since—"

"Call me John," he said, chewing a mouthful of chicken appreciatively.

Lisa blushed. "Well, ever since I put the necklace on, I've been having these dreams, and sometimes they're incredibly vivid and detailed."

John put his fork down. "Such as?"

"Well, last night there was this tribe of people camped by a river, and they looked totally ancient. They were all wearing fur—"

"Mink?" John asked. "Just kidding," he added when he saw Lisa's look of confusion. "Don't mind me, please go on."

"It was rough fur," Lisa said, "like from wild animals, and the tribe—"

"Clan," John said, picking up his fork and spearing his last bite of chicken. "It would have been a clan."

Lisa eyed him, a little annoyed. "All right, the clan was camped by this river, and they were looking for deer herds, and then there was a bear, and then—"

"A bear? You didn't tell me about any bear," Eva said as John glanced regretfully at his empty plate. "Seconds?" she asked him.

"Yes please, it's all delicious."

"The bear was dead, Mom, no big deal."

Andy gave his daughter a worried glance and changed the subject. He knew she was doing much better about the dreams and the necklace, but still, a bear, even a dead one? He hadn't told her that the first tooth the lab tested came from a bear.

"When do you think people first migrated to Finland?" he asked John.

"About six thousand years ago, about the time of your tooth necklace. Hang on a minute." John rose from the table, went to the foyer, and returned with his briefcase, pulling out a rumpled map and spreading it on the table.

"Here's how things might have gone all those thousands of years ago. Clans that lived mainly on deer meat followed the herds from Russia into Finland. They learned to adapt to the brutally cold winters, and Finland's population slowly grew. Its inhabitants shared and expanded a unique language, Finno-Ugric, unique partly because of the country's isolation and stability. The clans slowly journeyed northward within Finland, along lakes and rivers formed when the glaciers melted. They learned how to grow crops for a more balanced diet of plants and meat, they continued to hunt deer, but gradually they became farmers, especially near the slightly warmer Gulf of Bothnia on the Baltic Sea. They cleared the land for dairy farming, which was becoming common in Europe."

John paused and took a forkful of collard greens. "Sorry," he said, "I get carried away."

Lisa was looking at him intently. "But how did those clans in Russia get there in the first place? Were they there all along?"

MAP, MIGRATION ALONG VOLGA RIVER AND TO FINLAND

"No, they came from Africa, like everyone else."

"What?" Eva said.

"Yes, that's your specialty, isn't it," Andy said, "Prehistoric migration routes out of Africa?"

"Right," John said, cutting into a chicken breast. "Did you know that recent research suggests that everyone alive today is ultimately descended from forty women in Africa?"

"Forty women in Africa?" Eva said, incredulous.

"Mom, you thought the necklace looked like something from Africa the first time you saw it." Lisa pulled the map closer and studied it. "But how on earth could people get from Africa to Finland?"

"It's a long story," John said.

* * *

North Russia and Finland, 6,000 Years Before Present

"Help! Help!"

Chief Antti of the An-Eva clan hears screams coming from outside the tent he shares with his wife, Shaman Eva, and their three sons, Heikki, Tapio, and Matti. He jumps up and unties the deer fur that covers the entrance, swearing as he sees three collapsed tents crushed by layers of snow. "Boys! Come quickly. Tents down," he yells.

Antti and his sons run to lift the fallen tents. Others join in to help. Cold wind and falling snow make it difficult to rescue all the people trapped inside, but they do. Antti yells, "Everybody! Remove as much snow from your tents as you can."

This is not the first time a snowstorm has collapsed some of the clan's tall, triangular, fur-covered tents. The long winters have become their worst enemy.

But even the longest winters pass and yield to spring, and then summer. One warm day, after the clan moves to a new campsite, Chief Antti's sons come to their father. Heikki says, "We have an idea for making stronger tents. We should use big wood logs and tree branches in a different shape."

Antti is sitting near a small smoky fire that helps keep the mosquitos away. He has been brooding about whether there is any way to prevent more tents from collapsing during the coming winter. Now Heikki is proposing a possible solution. Antti is dubious, but he decides to hear his son out. "Tell me more."

"Here, let us show you."

Heikki brings out five thick wood sticks, each about two feet long. He puts two together in an inverted V and ties them together with animal-hide strips. He does the same with two more big sticks. Tapio holds one pair upside down against the ground, and Matti does the same with the other pair, next to the first. Heikki lays the fifth stick across the top of the stick pairs and ties both ends with leather strips, forming a structure in the shape of an inverted V. Tapio and Matti lean several more sticks against each side, slanted at the same angle as the big inverted-V sticks, to create a solid wall of wood.

Heikki smiles, pleased with himself. "We'll cut trees down with our stone axes and turn them into big logs, and we'll arrange the logs just like these sticks so the tent won't collapse from heavy snow or strong winds. Then we'll tie some deer fur over the wood sides to keep it dry and warm inside."

Antti is nodding. "And we can hang deer fur on both ends too. One end can be the entrance." His former despair only a memory now, he stands. "Boys, this is a good idea. Let's get to work."

The clan members watch warily as the men build the first big log tent. Their skepticism ends when they see that the finished tent is strong, and large enough for eight to ten adults and their children. Everybody wants one. The men and women team up and build new log homes for everyone. When winter comes, none of the new-style tents collapse, no matter how deep the snow or strong the winds.

In the security generated by living in safer homes, the clan continues old rituals and traditions. They sing a special hum song to their children, and Chief Antti and Shaman Eva add a cut mark to each of two teeth they have extracted from a dead bear they found. They restring the old leather thong on the sacred family necklace and add the two new bear teeth. They will perform the blood-bonding ceremony and give the necklace to Heikki when he gets married at next full moon.

Two years pass uneventfully. In the third year, there are no deer to be found. Chief Antti directs his scouts to find a new campsite closer to where several large deer herds had been spotted earlier. The An-Eva clan establishes a camp along a river where expansive plains and gently rolling hills provide deer herds a vast grazing area. Deer meat continues to be the clan's main source of food. An-Eva scouts develop traits crucial to the clan's deer-hunting success, like being able to run long distances for many hours without stopping.

The scouts find a deer herd grazing in a valley half a day north of the river campsite, and Chief Antti quickly assembles a large band of hunters. They arrive mid-afternoon and stand on a hilltop overlooking the valley, but they see no deer. Chief Antti rests his chin on hands folded atop his bow. Deer can easily travel a long distance in one day, and have most likely left the valley. Now he has to find out which way they went.

Chief Antti doesn't speak for a time. In the silence, he considers their situation. In anticipation of a big kill, they have brought with them sledges, platforms mounted on thick wood runners and secured with strips of animal hide and vines from the strongest plants. The sledges make it easier and faster to carry deer meat and hides to the main camp, but he doesn't want to tire his best hunters by having them pull the sledges somewhere else until there is a good chance they will be needed.

He turns to Heikki. "Send one of your scouts west and another east, son. You go north. We'll camp here until you return."

The scouts to the east and west return in the evening. They have found nothing. But where is Heikki? Chief Antti keeps vigil, his eyes searching the valley. In the approaching dusk, he sees someone running toward his encampment. He stares anxiously at the figure until it gets close enough to identify. Yes, it is Heikki. He breathes a sigh of relief.

Heikki sprints into camp with a big grin. He stops to catch his breath. "There's a huge herd far on the other side," he says, waving across the valley. "I saw them drinking from a stream there."

Chief Antti springs into action. "Let's go, men. We must run tonight, before the deer drink their fill and move on again."

It is midsummer, and the sky stays pale blue all night, providing adequate light as the hunters cross the valley and strike camp in the northern hills. Just as Heikki said, they see the large herd in the distance. Early the next morning, Chief Antti sends his hunters to surround the deer and prepare for the kill. When they are all in position, he signals by throwing his spear high in the air, and the hunters advance toward the herd. They release sharp stone-tipped arrows from powerful bows, wounding twelve deer, which they track down for the final kill. They butcher the deer and load the meat and furs on the sledges for the long trek back to their main campsite.

The clan repeats this same kind of hunt for many years as they journey along the big river to its source in the hills. The hunting is good even in winter, and their wooden sledges prove invaluable, easily sliding their meat over the snowy landscape. With each kill, the clan celebrates with a feast and ceremonial honors to the hunters, and to the gods.

The An-Eva clan prospers as glaciers and permafrost melt, forming freshwater lakes and small rivers. The soil becomes fertile, and tall green trees cover much of the land. The mild summer days are sunlit until late at night, the short winter days are dark and bitter, but the land is ideal for deer and for any clans that can adapt to the frigid, snowy winters.

Few clans migrate so far north. Those that do form the heart of the resilient people who hunt deer and slowly populate the area. When metal is found, the An-Eva clan forges sharp axes that make it easier to cut big logs for larger log cabins. With axes capable of more precise cuts, they also learn to make tables, chairs, beds, and wooden snow skis.

The An-Eva clan cluster stays together as they continue to follow the deer herds. The land and weather are ideal for deer to flourish, and there are few clans hunting them, so the herds don't need to move as often as in past times. The clans also learn how to grow edible plants, ensuring a steadier supply of them than from random foraging. Soon it is less necessary for the clan to move around and easier to stay in one place.

6
An-Eva Clan

With Lisa's curiosity about the necklace and her interest in John Anderson's migration theories growing by the day, Andy bought a bottle of expensive scotch and invited him to come to dinner again the following Saturday. Sukie greeted him with the same enthusiasm, and Eva greeted him with a dinner of fried catfish and all the fixings. She was interested in his theories too, and when Andy fretted about her doing so much cooking, she told him that food for information was a good trade.

Over the meal, Lisa asked about the necklace.

"You're not going to believe this," John said. "Professor Rutherford's still under the weather, but he phoned me this afternoon to tell me that the lab had finished testing the second tooth. It's ten thousand years old, and it's from a bear too."

"Good grief!" Andy exclaimed.

"A bear?" Lisa said. "I didn't know the first one was from a bear."

Andy glanced at her, but all he saw in her face was excitement. He frowned in concentration as his mind scrambled to process the news. "That means the second tooth can't be from

Finland, because people didn't migrate there until about six thousand years ago."

"And why make a necklace out of bear teeth?" Lisa asked.

"Well, bears may have had some special meaning to your ancient ancestors," John said. "Maybe they worshiped bears. The bear is Finland's national animal, you know. Or maybe they just found a lot of dead bears lying around and didn't know what to do with the teeth." He winked at Lisa. "Anyway, it's amazing they kept it in the family for such a long time."

"Truly amazing," Eva murmured, getting up to clear the plates. She returned with a pecan pie and served everyone a slice with a dollop of whipped cream.

"So where did the second tooth come from in the first place?" Lisa wanted to know.

John remembered that she had asked a similar question at the last dinner. "It'll take us a while to get back to 'the first place,' Lisa, but I can tell you a little more about the early Finns if you're interested."

"We all are," Eva said. "Let me know when you'd like more pie."

John flashed her a grin. "After I finish my lecture. Sure you're ready for it?" He brought out the same map he had shown them before.

"Ready!" Lisa said.

"All right, here goes. Some eighteen thousand years ago, during the peak of the Last Glacial Maximum—that's the last ice age to you—*homo sapiens*, aka modern man, moved south from northern and central Europe because of the bitter cold and permafrost. When things warmed up a bit, they began moving back north up the Volga, the longest river in Europe. About ten thousand years ago, some clans got to central Russia, and few thousand years later, some of those clans migrated to the Valdai Hills in northern Russia, near the source of the Volga, and eventually into southern Finland, always following the deer herds. Major rivers were a common migration path for hunter-gatherers because they provided fresh water, fish, vegetation, and game that came to the river to drink."

Lisa was poring over the map, tracing the routes John had described. "I still can't get over the second tooth being ten thousand years old. Where do you think the people who strung it on the necklace came from—"

"In the first place, I'd like another piece of pie," John said.

* * *

Russia, 10,000 Years Before Present

One warm summer, Chief Yuri's small clan treks west down a wide shallow river to get away from the brown bears in the foothills of the mountains. Yuri and six hunters, traveling south of their camp, stop near a river bend to fish. In a quiet moment, the chief hears loud footsteps and turns to see four brown bears racing toward them. At that instant, he realizes his group has encroached on the bears' fishing spot.

Shouting for his men to run, Yuri points at a cluster of tall boulders across the shallow river. They never make it. The bears come crashing through the water behind them and slash four hunters with their sharp claws. The men scream in pain, and their screams become howls when the bears tear into their flesh with powerful jaws, turning the river red. Chief Yuri and two of his hunters manage to reach the shore. They look back. There is no way they can help their clansmen. With heavy hearts, they escape to their camp.

Yuri's clan has struggled before, but the loss of four hunters leaves him with only three to find food for his clan. Many of the remaining members are women and children who have recently lost their husbands and fathers. Yuri knows that staying where they are, with all the bad memories, will only make the clan more despondent, so he announces that they're moving. The clan walks west along a big river, and a week later camps near a small river that flows into it. There have been no bears in sight for days.

Five of Yuri's clan—one older woman, two girls, and two boys—go downhill to bathe in the small river and retrieve water to take back to the campsite. They shed their deerskin clothes and prepare to dip into the cool, clean water.

Chief Antti and a group of An-Eva hunters sit on two large boulders separated by a narrow clearing that leads to a small river where clan scouts have seen deer coming to drink. They are waiting for the deer to arrive, eager to see how well their new bows will send sharp-tipped arrows into their prey. They spot five strangers approaching the river from the other side and preparing to bathe.

Two of them are girls who look to be about twelve years old. They have long, light-brown hair, pretty faces, smooth white skin, and firm breasts. Chief Antti glances over at his son Heikki and his nephew Tapio. As he expects, they are also watching the girls, trading smiles and playful punches.

Then Heikki frowns, and Chief Antti turns his head to see why. His gut clenches. Two brown bears are bolting toward the unaware bathers from the forest across the river.

Heikki jumps up and shouts as loudly as he can, "Bears! Bears!"

The bathers don't respond. Chief Antti stands and bellows, "Come across. Quickly!"

At last the bathers turn and see the bears heading toward them. The chief waves at them to come to him. Frantically they all start across the shallow river. As four reach the shore, Antti, Heikki, and Tapio leap down and run to help them get to the safety of the tallest boulder. In the rush, one young boy slips in the river and hits his head on a rock. Stunned, he sits up and starts to cry.

Heikki sprints into the river, grabs the boy, and carries him to the boulder. He quickly hands him up to Antti, who is trying to calm the other four. Heikki turns to see the two bears scrambling after him, enraged by the intrusion on their fishing spot. Antti and Tapio reach down and jerk Heikki up the boulder as one bear swings at him, barely missing. The bear huffs and grunts as the six hunters on the other boulder loose their arrows. One hits its eye, three pierce its outstretched neck, and two enter its open mouth. The bear falls backward and roars, blood dripping from its face.

The second bear roars, and the hunters unleash their arrows again. Three land harmlessly on the beast's chest, protected by its thick fur. The other three strike his head, stunning him.

Chief Antti points at the bear below him, which has recovered enough to stand on its hind legs and attempt to crawl up the boulder. "Get him!"

The hunters land several more arrows in the bear's head and neck. Roaring in pain, the bear staggers toward the river and falls to his knees. As they watch him bleed to death, the second bear retreats to the forest.

Chief Antti and his hunters help the strangers retrieve their clothing and accompany them back to their hilltop camp, where the older woman tells her clan chief about the bear attack and the rescue. He nods to her and turns to speak to Antti and his men. Some of his words sound familiar to Antti, but most do not.

"I can understand him," says Igor, one of Antti's hunters. "Before I came to your clan, I belonged to a mountain clan that spoke this language."

Igor addresses the chief, who nods and speaks in reply.

Igor translates. "He says, 'Welcome. I am Chief Yuri. Your brave men saved five of our clan.' I told him you are Antti, chief of the An-Eva clan."

Now that there is a means of communication, Yuri introduces his wife, Yena.

The older woman from the river points at Heikki and the rescued boy and says something rapidly. Chief Yuri picks the boy up, steps toward Heikki, bows his head, and speaks.

Igor listens carefully. "He says the boy you saved is his son Kuri."

Heikki beams, as does Chief Antti, who says to Igor, "Tell him Heikki is *my* son and I'm proud he was so brave."

Yuri introduces the older woman and the others Antti's men saved. The two pretty girls, Kasi and Kari, grin at handsome young Heikki, and Yena smiles warmly at him.

Through Igor, Yuri says that Kasi and Kari and the other young boy recently lost their fathers to marauding bears. "Four of my best and bravest hunters died that day, all in a brutal bear attack." He thanks Chief Antti again for his clan's bravery and asks them to stay for some roasted fish.

"Perhaps another time," Antti says, guessing that if they have few hunters now, food is probably scarce for them. "We must return to our camp. Come, let us cut up the bear and share in the meat and fur."

Yuri gladly accepts the offer, and they return to the river. While his men dress the bear, Antti cuts out its two large front teeth for his clan's sacred necklace, explaining the tradition to Yuri as he does so. He says the necklace is always passed on to the oldest daughter of the chief of the An-Eva clan and the chief's wife, the clan shaman.

On the way back to their camp, Antti hears Heikki and Tapio talking about the two pretty girls. He hides a grin as he says, "You boys are always looking for the prettiest girls, but those girls aren't pretty at all. Surely you don't want to see *them* again."

"Yes I *do*," Heikki says earnestly, missing his father's joke.

Tapio chuckles. "I'm hesitant to disagree with my chief, but those girls are two of the prettiest I've seen. I believe I'd like to see them again too."

Laughing, Antti hefts his load of bear meat higher on his shoulder, and they continue their trek home.

Several days later, Chief Antti returns to Yuri's clan with Heikki, Tapio, Igor, and Shaman Eva. When she sees Kasi and Kari, she whispers to Antti, "You're a sly one, husband."

After greetings, Antti looks around and asks Yuri, "How

big is your clan?"

Yuri opens and closes his fingers to show that they number sixteen. Antti knows this is a clan in peril. With so few hunters, it will be nearly impossible for them to support their clan of mostly women and children.

"Why don't you hunt with us for the rest of the summer," he suggests to Yuri, thinking that the arrangement will benefit both clans and give Heikki and Tapio many more chances to see the two girls. "There are several smaller clans that follow mine and live close by, and we often hunt together."

A few weeks later, Chief Yuri's clan joins the An-Eva clan cluster. Kasi and Kari quickly learn the An-Eva language, and Eva takes them on frequent trips to find plants for food and medicine. Chief Antti lets the girls come along on the larger hunts to help butcher the deer and carry the meat and fur back to camp. Antti and Eva agree that Kasi is a great match for Heikki, and Kari for Tapio. At summer's end, the two couples marry.

Although it is the clan's tradition to give the sacred tooth necklace to the oldest daughter of the chief and shaman during her marriage ceremony, Eva has borne only boys, so she and Antti decide to give the necklace to Heikki. So begins a new clan tradition of passing the family necklace down to the oldest son instead of the oldest daughter. Other traditions will change too. In past years, the chief and shaman would select the clan's best hunter to marry their oldest daughter, and the couple would become the new chief and shaman in due time. In later years, the oldest son will always become the new clan chief, and his wife the new shaman, but they will continue the tradition of taking the names of their predecessors and will be called Chief Antti and Shaman Eva.

Bear attacks continue to be a problem and eventually threaten even a clan as large as the An-Eva clan has become. After encountering too many brown bears while scouting east up the big river, the clan cluster migrates back downriver, to the other big river that flows from the north. Finding a sizable deer herd moving north, they follow it.

The next summer, Kasi and Heikki's first child is ready to be born. Early one morning Kasi's water breaks, and Eva helps Kasi's mother with the delivery. They clean and swaddle the baby girl, and then Kasi's mother holds her, staring. "What's wrong with her eyes and her hair?" she cries.

"Nothing," Eva says. "Kasi has given us a beautiful baby girl with sky blue eyes and golden hair."

When he first sees his daughter, Heikki is perplexed. "Well, I guess she's pretty enough, but are you sure there's nothing wrong with her?" he asks his mother.

"I'm sure. Many years ago, when I was very young, I saw such children in another clan, and I wished for my own children to be born with blue eyes and golden hair." Eva smiles. "And now, through my grandchild, I have my wish."

Word spreads about the new baby girl, and everyone in the clan comes to see this marvel. Word spreads even faster and farther when Kasi bears her first son, who also has blue eyes and blond hair. When her second son is born with brown hair and brown eyes, like his father and the rest of the clan, Heikki is delighted, and so is Eva. "He's every bit as beautiful as his brother and sister," she says.

7
Livermore Lab

San Francisco, December 1999

Professor Rutherford knocked on Andy's open office door and stuck his head in. "How is your dear daughter?" he asked. "And how is Eva?"

Andy stood, touched by the elderly professor's concern. "Come on in, have a seat. Thanks for asking about the family," he said as he perched himself on the edge of his desk. "Lisa's fine. She still has dreams now and then, but she isn't bothered by them, and she's doing great in school. No word yet as to whether Eva will need a transplant, but she's soldiering through. Guess it's me who's been doing most of the worrying lately."

"Well, maybe I can distract you," Rutherford said. "Livermore just called with the results on the third tooth. They tested it several times—"

"And?"

"The first tooth was six thousand years old, Andy, and the second ten thousand. This one is eight thousand years old."

"What?" Andy leaned back suddenly and had to grab

Eva's picture before it tumbled off the desk. "Eight thousand? That's crazy! Why are they all different ages? What the heck's going on with this necklace?"

"We have a mystery, that's for certain. We should to go to Livermore. They absolutely want to talk to you. With an object that old, there are considerations as to the next steps. Are you free now, by any chance?"

"Well, I just finished my last class. If you don't mind swinging by my house, we can take Lisa with us. It's a school holiday, so she's home, and she's an excellent science student. I'm sure she'll jump at the chance to visit the famed Livermore Lab."

"Fine, love to meet your daughter," Rutherford said. "Imagine her reaction when we give her the latest news."

As Andy had anticipated, Lisa was more than game for a trip to Livermore, and more than intrigued when Professor Rutherford told her that the third tooth was eight thousand years old.

"Is it a bear tooth too?" she asked.

"Yes, Lisa, and I've been thinking about that. Is anyone in your family from Lapland, Andy?"

"No, both my parents' families are from central Finland, well south of Lapland. Why?"

"Well, there's no proof, of course, but given the age of the tooth and its physical characteristics, I have a hunch that it may have come from a brown bear in Lapland and ended up on Lisa's necklace as part of a Saami tradition."

"Saami? What's that?"

Rutherford shifted into professor gear. "About ten thousand years ago, Lisa, a tribe called the Saami followed the deer herds up the western coast of Norway to northern Norway, Sweden, and Finland, and their descendants still live in these countries today. They're often called Lapps, a name many Saami consider pejorative." He turned to Andy. "Have you had your DNA tested?"

"Nope. Eva's having hers done because she knows so little about her ancestors, but both my grandparents were from Finland, and theirs before them, and theirs on back, so why should I bother?"

"To humor an old man, if nothing more, but in light of Livermore's findings, you simply must. We'll test for both your maternal mitochondrial DNA and your paternal Y-chromosome DNA, and the results should be back within six weeks."

"What can we tell from that?" Lisa was hanging on the professor's every word.

"The lab can compare your father's DNA with that of diverse world populations, even those that existed long ago, such as the Vikings and indigenous tribes like the Saami. If Saami DNA from northern Finland matches your father's DNA, the tooth necklace could have come from them, thousands upon thousands of years ago."

"That's so cool, Dad, you should do it. But how do they really know what age something is, Professor Rutherford? Especially when it's so incredibly . . . well, old."

"I'd be pleased to tell you," the professor said as Andy pulled into the Livermore parking lot, "but here we are, and I have a colleague who can do a better job of explaining it than I can."

Dr. Cheng met them at the visitor center. A tall man in an

immaculate white lab coat, he seemed all business to Andy as he got them passes and drove them to a two-story brick building five blocks away. At the double glass doors, he flashed his badge at a uniformed guard, and a gush of cold air hit them as they entered.

"This is the Center for Accelerator Mass Spectrometry," he said. "We do age testing here." He glanced Lisa's way with a hint of a smile. "Like a quick tour of the lab?"

"That would be great, Dr. Cheng."

"Then let's go." He led them down a long hallway, occasionally nodding at a co-worker. "We age-test in different ways," he explained to Lisa. "We use radiocarbon dating for objects less than fifty thousand years old, like your teeth, for instance."

They took a turn down another hallway, this one lined with industrial pictures.

"Every living thing has radioactive Carbon-14," Dr. Cheng went on. "After something dies, it takes about fifty-seven hundred years for half the Carbon-14 to decay and disappear. By measuring the amount of C-14 left in a sample, we can determine its percentage and the sample's age."

"Sounds like a clue to solving a mystery to me," Andy said with a private smile at Lisa.

Lisa barely heard him. "How does measuring how much Carbon-14 is left tell you the percentage that disappeared?"

Dr Cheng gave her an approving look. "Excellent question. When a living thing dies, it contains the same quantity of both Carbon-14 and Carbon-12. The ratio is fifty-fifty. Carbon-12 does not disappear over time. It remains stable in the dead object. We measure the amount of Carbon-14 left and compare it to the amount of Carbon-12 present. That gives us the new ratio, or percentage. And from that, we can compute the age of the sample."

Lisa nodded. "Thanks. Now I understand."

"That was a very insightful question, young lady," Professor Rutherford said. "Most people just accept the general statement that because we know the half-life of Carbon-14, that's all we need to know. They rarely ask how we can determine the actual percentage remaining."

Andy grinned. "Smart cookie."

When the tour ended, Dr. Cheng said, "As you can imagine, we plan to do further tests on the necklace, with your permission, Lisa."

"Of course," she said.

"Good, I'll call you when we have those results."

After Dr. Cheng dropped them back at visitor parking, Andy, Lisa, and Professor Rutherford climbed into Andy's car, and he drove the mandated fifteen miles per hour toward the main gate.

"You realize this is a big deal," the professor said. "Cheng gave you the royal treatment. Of course, this tooth issue is important to science. Why, just finding a necklace so old is very rare thing. I think the entire scientific world will be interested in the results."

"What happens to the necklace when they finish testing it?" Andy asked.

Lisa leaned forward from the backseat. "You know, when the dreams were really bad, I'd have told them to keep it, but when they're done, I'm going to bring my necklace home."

8
Revelations

Late the next Saturday afternoon, with the winter sun setting over the Pacific, Andy drove Lisa home from her soccer game. She wiped sweat from her forehead as they went inside and were greeted by an exuberant Sukie. Lisa picked the dog up to stop her from barking and was rewarded with a sloppy lick on the face.

"We won, Mom," she said as Eva greeted them in the hallway with a big smile, holding one hand behind her back.

"That's wonderful, sweetie," Eva said.

Andy raised an eyebrow at her. "What are you hiding?"

"Give me a kiss and I'll show you."

"Sounds like a good deal to me." He kissed her, and she handed him an envelope. He scanned the address and looked up at her.

"Your DNA results?"

Lisa put Sukie down. "Cool, Mom! What do they say?"

"My mitochondrial DNA shows that my maternal ancestors were from the Yoruba tribe in Nigeria." Unexpected tears came to Eva's eyes.

Andy took her in his arms. "That's got to be great to finally know, honey. Especially after hearing so much about my side of the family," he said, coaxing a laugh from her.

"I guess that's one mystery solved," Lisa said.

Eva shrugged out of Andy's embrace and wiped her tears away. "It's only the beginning, sweetie. I've got some serious research to do."

***

Igbo Ora, Nigeria, 1750

Life is good. Nina and her twin sister, Oni, are sitting in front of Oni's hut, an hour away from Nina's village. They are waiting for their men to return from hunting. Oni has recently married a Yoruba tribal chief's son, Lekan, in a big wedding. Nina's fiancé, Kayode, is a chief's son too, and soon Nina will have a big wedding of her own. At the thought of Kayode, Nina smiles and touches Oni's knee.

She hears leaves rustling in the forest and is sure she recognizes her fiancé's gait. "They're back, Oni!" she says. As she stands to greet Kayode, he and Lekan come running from the forest with a horde of strange warriors—at least thirty, she guesses—closing in on them. With bone-chilling cries, the intruders strike the two men down with clubs.

"No! No!" Nina screams as she runs toward them, stumbling on tree roots, with Oni right behind her. Other villagers run from their huts, mouths agape, trying to understand what's happening. Almost in slow motion, it seems, the warriors surround five villagers and club them to the ground too.

"Run, Nina!" Kayode yells. He is sprawled on the ground,

blood gushing from his head. "Run!"

His entreaty comes too late. A warrior's arms wrap around Nina as she turns to flee, and another warrior tackles Oni. Hideous yells and grunts sound all around them as the warriors club more of their tribesmen and pull others from their huts and tie them with ropes and chains.

Nina has heard of such a thing but has always thought it was a myth. It isn't. These warriors are capturing young men and women to sell to slave traders. They will take them to nearby Lagos, on the ocean, and ship them off to a terrible place called America.

Nina, her hands now tied behind her, turns back to Kayode and Lekan. The warriors are forcing the bloodied men to their feet and chaining their hands.

"Let them go! Keep us, but let them go!" Kayode shouts, and a warrior beats him to his knees. He looks up at the warrior, pleading, "I'll give you anything you want. Take me, but leave the women here!"

Nina and Oni are shoved toward a group of thirty or so villagers, all with their hands bound. Nina sees that five of their captors are dressed in white men's clothes. They must be the slave traders. The shortest of them, a black man, grins at Kayode. "You are jesting, of course," he says in a language Nina doesn't understand. "We take what we want. And we can get plenty of money, guns, and liquor for those two."

He turns to the other traders, and they speak in the strange language, but Nina makes out that they are calling him Bekoe. "As for these two," he says to the warriors in Yoruba, "take them to Lagos immediately. I want them in the next auction."

The warriors jerk Kayode and Lekan to their feet and push

them toward the forest. Kayode stares back at his beloved, fear on his face.

The reality of her dilemma sinks into Nina. The small village is helpless. The warriors herd all the old men and women, and the youngest children, into a circle and order them to kneel. They check the huts again, drag out several more healthy young women, and line them up with the other women for the slave traders to examine.

Bekoe carefully inspects them all, looking into their mouths and feeling their breasts. He pauses in front of Oni and Nina. "Beautiful twins," he murmurs. "Just beautiful." He motions them to step forward.

"What are your names?" he demands.

"I'm Oni. She is Nina."

He frowns, staring up and down the line, then back at them. "You. Oni. I have a proposition for you. Come here." He takes her arm and pulls her aside.

"I will oversee new slaves at a plantation in Brazil. I will take you as my mistress. You'll not have to work in the fields."

He pauses, staring at her. Tears obscure her vision. Around them, the villagers cry and moan while their captors laugh and joke.

"Well?"

"I . . . I want to go with my husband."

"Dammit, woman! It's a great offer. If you don't take it, you'll die in the fields. And you will not be with your husband. You'll never see him again, whatever your decision."

"Can my sister come with me?" Oni asks through a sob.

Bekoe glances back at Nina. He shrugs. "All right. We leave now."

Accompanied by ten warriors, Bekoe takes Oni, Nina, and several other young women on the two-day trip to Lagos. The women are chained together so none can run away. Three of them are raped at the overnight camp. In the morning, one tries to escape but is caught and raped in front of the other women. They don't kill her because she will be valuable at auction, Nina hears Bekoe say.

At the port, they go directly to the auction site. Bekoe unchains Oni and Nina and leads them to the rear, away from the others. During the auction, a English trader spots them and introduces himself to Bekoe.

"Nice," he says. "Very nice. Strong and healthy." He steps close and inspects their teeth. "How much?"

"My regrets, sir, they're not for sale."

"Not for sale, eh?" The trader looks Nina up and down. "Everything's for sale. I like this one. I'll give you . . ." He frowns, inspecting her again. "I'll give you twice the top price for this one."

"Done!" Bekoe says. "By God, sir, you certainly drive a hard bargain."

Oni doesn't understand his words, but she understands what just happened. She looks at Bekoe in desperation. "But . . . but you said—"

"I know what I said." He turns to the trader. "You'd best take her now. The ship bound for America leaves at noon."

The sisters cry and cling to each other until the trader drags Nina away."Come along," he says. "I got four more bought, and we got to get you settled."

"Wait!" Oni cries out. It is a word the trader understands because he has heard it so often from the men and women he buys and sells.

"No time, girl. We got to go—"

"Bekoe, I beg you, tell him to let me give my sister something first." Oni removes the necklace her mother gave her when she married.

Bekoe stares at it. "What would anyone want with two big ugly teeth? They look like lion's teeth."

"Yes, they are sacred to our family. I want to give Nina one."

"All right, hurry it up," the trader says when Bekoe explains what Oni is asking.

Oni hastily unties one tooth from the leather thong and presses it into Nina's hand. Nina tries to hug her, but the trader grabs her arm and drags her off toward the harbor.

"Please let us stay together," Oni implores.

"No!" Bekoe yells. "You're coming with me. Now!"

Bekoe takes Oni to the new plantation in Brazil. One morning she manages to escape and joins the Tupi tribe.

After Nina's slave ship arrives in America, a plantation owner in Virginia buys her at auction.

* * *

A week later, when Andy came home from a late meeting, Eva was standing in the hallway holding something behind her back.

"What, again?" he said. "Well, I know the drill." He kissed her, and she handed him an envelope.

"Hey, *my* DNA results! That was fast."

"Wasn't it, though," Eva said with a tinge of annoyance.

"Mine took almost two months. I guess being a biology professor gets you to the front of the line."

Andy laughed and took her hand and led her to the family room, where Lisa was studying on the couch. "What's up?" she asked as Eva sat down beside her.

Andy headed for his recliner, waving the envelope. "We're not the only ones who'll be glad this came," he said. "Rutherford's been bugging me about my DNA results every day for the past week." He opened the envelope and scanned several pages of text and graphics.

For an average person, reading the results would have been difficult, but Andy was a microbiologist and knew right away what they meant. Surprise bloomed on his face, not because of his paternal Y-chromosome DNA tests, which confirmed that he was of regular Finnish ancestry, but because of what his maternal mitochondrial DNA showed.

He looked up at Eva and grinned. "My God, it's true! Rutherford was right. My mother's ancestors were Saami."

Lisa jumped up from the couch to peer over his shoulder while he studied the results again.

"Yep, according to this, my mom's ancestors came from the Saami tribe in northern Finland's Lapland area. That means the ten-thousand-year-old bear tooth and the eight-thousand-year-old one probably both came from them. Wow."

"That's something, all right," Eva said.

"You know what it means? That I'm a double Finn, regular *and* Saami, from an ancient tribe that still exists. Rutherford's going to be over the moon."

Andy was right. The next day at work, Professor Rutherford was thrilled to hear that his theory about "the

Saami connection" was correct. Better yet, after weeks with no word, Dr. Cheng called Andy that afternoon about the test results on the additional teeth.

"Can I come right out?" Andy asked.

"As long as you bring Lisa," Dr. Cheng said.

"I'll do that."

When Andy and Lisa got to Livermore, they checked in at the visitor center and made their way through the maze of hallways to Dr. Cheng's office.

"Good to see you again. Sit down," Dr. Cheng said, pointing to the chairs that flanked his large desk.

"Thanks," Andy said, "and before you tell us your news, I've got some of my own. "I got my DNA test results." He described them in detail.

When he finished, Dr. Cheng leaned forward and folded his arms on his desk. "That's great news, Andy, but I think mine's going to top it. We tested three more teeth. One of them was two thousand years old, and one was eight thousand years old, the same as the second tooth we tested, remember? No surprise there. They're probably a canine pair."

"That makes sense. What about the other tooth?"

Dr. Cheng looked from Andy to Lisa. "That one is fourteen thousand years old. Fourteen thousand years old," he repeated, emphasizing each word.

"Really?" Lisa exclaimed. "That's almost twice as old as the canine pair. That's like . . . that's totally completely ancient!"

"Wow, this is really getting crazy," Andy said. "The Saami didn't get to Finland until the end of the ice age, ten thousand years ago."

Lisa frowned. "Darn. That means the necklace isn't from

Finland, right?"

"Yep," Andy said. "It means that last tooth was put on the necklace four thousand years *before* the Saami came to Finland."

Lisa shook her head. "So we have to start all over again, I guess. Or go farther back, maybe. Where did the Saami come from?"

"I don't know. Do you, Dr. Cheng?"

"I have no idea."

"Well, I'd sure like to find out," Andy said, thinking that it might be time for another dinner with John Anderson. "Bet you would too, and every researcher who studies prehistoric people."

Dr. Cheng stood up and went to his window, staring outside reflectively. He turned around. "Your tooth necklace is a treasure, Lisa, not just for your family, but for archaeologists and historians as well."

"Can we see it again?" she asked.

"Certainly. I have it right here." Dr. Cheng took an acrylic artifact box from a wood cabinet behind him. He opened the box to reveal the leather pouch covered with a layer of plastic and nestled in what appeared to be a velvet lining. Clearly, the lab was taking precautions.

Andy declined the offer of protective gloves—it was *his* family's necklace, after all—and opened the pouch. He removed the necklace almost reverently and examined it carefully. "The teeth all have the same scratch patterns," he said, as if to himself. "Ten groups of five cut marks, for a total of fifty on each tooth."

"Yes, we've been studying those too," Dr. Cheng said. "The teeth we already tested have the same marks even though they're different ages. We'd like to test the other eight teeth, if that's okay with you. Based on the pattern so far, I'll bet some are six thousand, ten thousand, and twelve thousand years old. That would work out to seven matched pairs for every two thousand years."

"But why every two thousand years?" Lisa asked. "It's all so mysterious. Please test those teeth as soon as you can, Dr. Cheng. It's the only way to know everything there is to know about my crazy necklace."

Andy wondered if Lisa was thinking about her dreams and what he'd told her about memories becoming part of each generation's DNA. It was just a theory, but what if the family necklace could play some small part in the research into that theory? Lisa could claim a contribution to science, a subject she loved.

"I agree," Andy said, "let's go for it. In the meantime, we may know someone who can enlighten us about what we might call the pre-Saami period." He winked at Lisa.

"Oh?" Dr. Cheng looked a bit puzzled.

"He's talking about John—Professor Anderson, I mean," Lisa said, her face coloring. "Professor Anderson is a specialist in . . . in . . ."

Andy came to the rescue. "In prehistoric migration. He knows an awful lot about it. And I'm going to contact the Finnish Historical Society too. You'll call me when you find out something about the other teeth, right?"

Dr. Cheng nodded. "Absolutely."

Back home, Andy and Lisa could barely contain themselves as they told Eva the latest news.

"Amazing!" she said, and then her face stilled in thought.

"What if . . . I haven't made too much progress with my research, but what if the Saamis' ancestors lived in Africa fourteen thousand years ago and started the tooth necklace before they migrated? I've always thought the necklace looked like something from Africa."

"Mom, how could that be?" Lisa said. "African people are dark-skinned, and Finnish people are light. Just look at Dad!"

"Yes, honey, but remember what John told us. We're all originally from Africa, and the sun affects skin color in several ways. People living in Africa near the equator acquire melanin, which protects the skin from the sun's ultraviolet rays. When clans from Africa migrated north, there was less sun, which meant fewer UV rays. In a colder climate, they also began wearing more clothing, which reduced their skin exposure even more. Lighter skin absorbs more vitamin D than darker pigments, and all these things led to the overall lightening of skin color as *homo sapiens* went north."

"Gosh, Mom, I thought you said you hadn't gotten too far with your research. How many years does it take for skin to change color?"

"All the way from dark to light, I read somewhere that it took some two hundred generations, about five thousand years. That's why African Americans still have dark skin. They've been out of Africa for only a relatively short time."

"So in this hot California sun? We'll see what changes in about five thousand years." Lisa held out her golden arms and laughed. "How about other physical characteristics?" she asked.

Eva considered. "We know that running fast is genetically inherited. Some African American and West African runners have a gene they call the fast-twitch gene that enables them to sprint exceptionally fast. I think I've got that gene, and you too. Think about it, you're much faster than all the other soccer players on your team."

Lisa furrowed her brow. "What about brain power, our ability to read and write and think? Is that passed on?"

Eva leaned back against the sofa. "That's a tough one. There's so much we don't understand about the extent to which our family genes can be passed on, especially when it comes to brain characteristics and mental capabilities."

"Well, what about dreams? Dad said there was some theory about inheriting memories or dreaming about things that happened in the past, like when I dreamed about flying like a bird over rivers and seeing bears."

"That might have some meaning," Eva said thoughtfully. "I'll see if I can find out more about that theory, but likely the research there is still really early."

"Yes, it is," Andy said, "or at least it was when I looked into it a few months ago."

Lisa sighed. "I just wonder if something in my head's trying to connect me to the past, or maybe something in a leather pouch. That necklace has plenty of secrets. Wouldn't it be great if I was the one to find them?"

9
Two Paths

Andy and Lisa stood in Dr. Cheng's lab staring down at fourteen teeth, each encased in a tiny plastic bag and arranged on a table in a straight line.

"What did you find out?" Lisa asked eagerly.

Dr. Cheng pointed to the last tooth on the left. "This one's fourteen thousand years old, the same age as the one next to it. A matched canine pair. All seven pairs are about two thousand years apart, going down from fourteen thousand to two thousand years old."

"You were right, Dr. Cheng. You were dead-on." Andy said.

Lisa picked up a tooth from the middle of the row. "But why that age sequence, and of paired teeth?"

"I'm not sure, but I have an idea," Andy said. "Look at these tiny cut marks. I'm betting each mark represents one generation, which is about twenty years. Fifty cut marks times twenty years gives you a thousand years for each tooth." He paused with a look of wonder on his face. "If you add all the marks up, these fourteen teeth represent fourteen thousand years of our family's life. Wow. And wow."

"You're probably right," Dr. Cheng said. "I second your wow."

"But that still leaves the question of where my ancestors lived before reaching Finland ten thousand years ago."

"And it's a good question, but as I told you, that's not my area of expertise. Did you call your friend John?" Dr. Cheng smiled at Lisa.

"He's been out of town for a conference, but I'll call him when he gets back," Andy said. "Meanwhile, I've got another call to make to a relative in Finland."

"Cousin Tapio?" Lisa asked.

"Yep, honey, let's go before it gets too late in Finland."

To his frustration, Andy's conversation with his distant cousin yielded little. After thanking Tapio for the gift of the necklace, he explained about the ages of the teeth and his DNA results and asked, "Do you know of any Saami in our family?"

"No, I'm afraid I don't. I'm amazed that the necklace is so old and that your mother's ancestors were Saami. Nobody in our family is from Lapland, or even knows any Saami people."

Andy let out a slow breath. Had he hit a brick wall so soon? "Are you sure, Tapio? Can you check to see if other family members know of a Saami connection?"

Tapio called back the next day. "The Koskinen and Hakeminen relatives had a hard time believing the necklace's history," he said. "And none of them know anything about a connection with the Saami people. Sorry."

"I guess the linkup occurred a long time ago, hundreds or thousands of years back. But at least we're certain that the necklace originated outside Finland, before the last ice age. I'll keep working on it, though as you can imagine, that'll be hard. There's little written Finnish history that talks about *anything* over a thousand years ago."

No sooner had Andy hung up with Tapio than Dr. Cheng called.

"You know, I've been thinking about those oldest teeth from fourteen thousand years ago," he said. "They're larger than the rest, and they look a lot like some brown bear teeth found in Spain, from the Cantabrian and Pyrenees Mountains during the last ice age."

"Spain? I thought the Finns emigrated from Russia. I mean, the brown bear is Russia's national animal as well as Finland's."

"Well, couldn't your ancestors have come from more than one place?"

Andy considered this new possibility. "I suppose so. Our family could've had two migrations: the Saami one from Spain to Lapland about ten thousand years ago, and the one the regular Finns made a few thousand years later from Russia to southern Finland. They probably intermarried, which would explain why my maternal DNA comes from the Saami and my paternal DNA from the Finns."

"And the Saami family started the necklace in Spain, with bears' teeth," Dr. Cheng said. "That makes sense. Tell Lisa it looks like that part of the mystery might be solved."

Over dinner, Andy recounted the details of his calls with Tapio and Dr. Cheng. Lisa listened intently, and the twins tried to follow along, but Eva found herself hiding a yawn now and then.

When he finished, she said, "It's all just fascinating, isn't it, kids? You're learning a lot about your Finnish family. That necklace isn't just a necklace, is it? It's really an amazing record of your dad's history, and yours too."

Andy pointed to a bronze sculpture of a brown bear on the sideboard. "Maybe the Finnish national animal has a different connection to our family tooth necklace than the one I was thinking about. Maybe brown bears followed the Saami from Spain to Finland after the last ice age and—honey?"

"Sorry, I just had a really busy day at work," Eva said.

The twins had devoured her meatloaf and mashed potatoes and vanished upstairs. Andy and Lisa had cleaned their plates, but Eva's was almost untouched.

"You've hardly eaten any of your dinner, honey."

"I'm just not hungry." Eva forced a smile. "I've felt a little lazy the last couple days."

"Your eyes look a little puffy to me. Maybe you should see the doctor again."

Lisa gave a confirming nod.

Eva waved a hand dismissively. "No need, I'm fine." She stood and started to clear the table.

"Leave that, Mom. Dad and I will clean up tonight. Go watch *Jeopardy*."

10
Ice Age

"What's for dinner, Eva?" John said, taking an appreciative sip of his scotch.

"Ask Andy. He's our chef tonight."

"Oh, just lihapullat and karjalanpiirakka." Andy shrugged modestly.

"Come again?"

"Meatballs with rice in a rye pastry, of course," Lisa said. "I helped with the meatballs."

"Well, I guess you're really serious about figuring out where the Saami came from in the first place." John produced two new maps from his briefcase and spread them out on the coffee table. "All right, class, let's begin by reviewing the last ice age, the good old Last Glacial Maximum. It occurred between twenty-four thousand and ten thousand years ago, and was the last major period in which severe cold weather and ice expanded over many parts of the world. Huge ice sheets slowly covered much of northern Europe, and ice caps concealed the higher mountains in southern Europe, including the Alps and the Pyrenees. Over time permafrost, bitter cold, and a dry climate made northern and central Europe uninhabitable for *homo sapiens* and animals. Humans who would not or could not migrate to southern Europe did not survive." He ran his index finger down one of the maps.

He traced likely migration paths southward along major rivers.

"Clans living in Germany migrated to Spain, journeying along the Doubs, Saone, and Rhone Rivers to the southern coast of France and down to the northeastern coast of Spain. The Saami clan was one of them, and then they migrated west along the Ebro River to northwest Spain, near the Vitoria Mountains and the Cantabrians, where those fourteen-thousand-year-old brown bear teeth in your necklace are from."

"I knew you'd know about the Saami!" Lisa said breathlessly.

"I know a thing or two about the Basques too. There were Basques living around Vitoria when the Saami arrived, and both the Saami and the Basques were resilient survivors. They may have learned each other's language enough to hunt deer together."

"Lisa and I could have used a Saami hunter to bring us some deer meat for the lihapullat," Andy said, "but we had to make do with ground beef and pork. Come on, let's eat."

* * *

Southern Germany, 22,000 Years Before Present

After a long journey, the Hei-Lee clan sets up camp on a small hill overlooking a deep blue river. On their first night, they fall asleep to the howling of wolves.

MAP, HABITABLE LAND, LAST ICE AGE, 18,000 YEARS BP

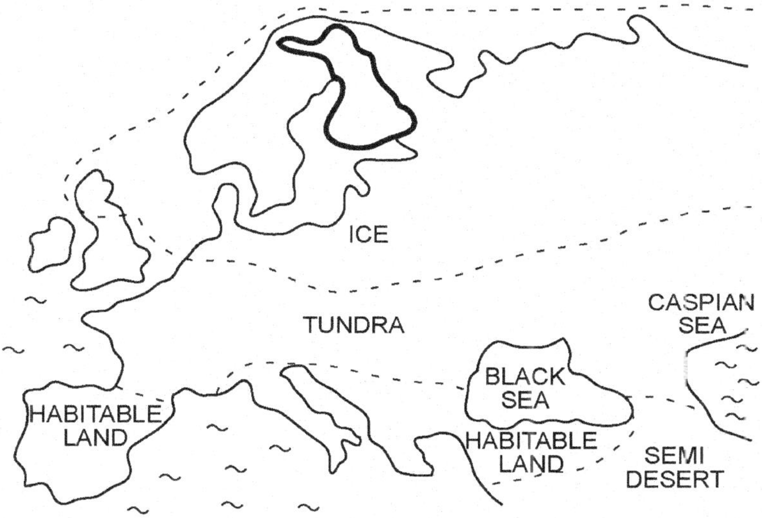

MAP, MIGRATION ALONG DOUBS, SAONE, RHONE, EBRO RIVERS

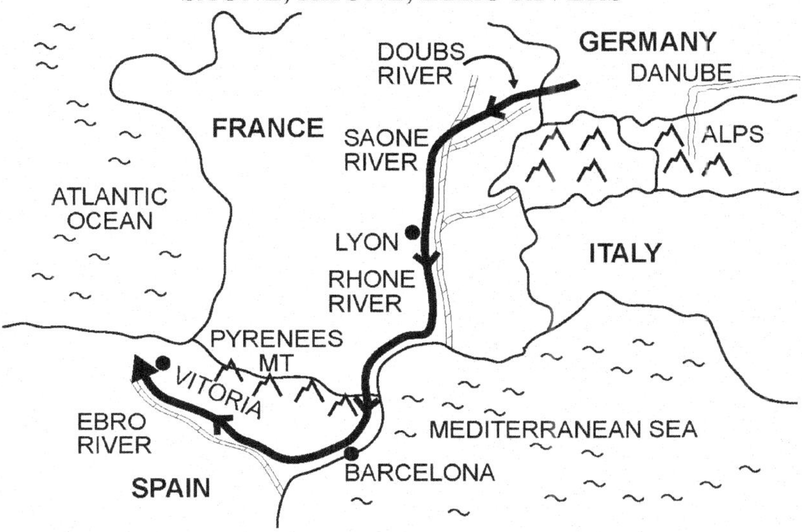

In the morning, Shaman Lisa and several other women scour a nearby valley for edible plants while the men hunt upriver. After several hours of finding many good plants and roots, they hear squealing and turn to see three wolf cubs stumbling from a bush.

"They're so small that they're surely not yet weaned," Lisa says to the others. "We should leave. Their parents are probably nearby."

With their arms and their bags full of plants and roots, the women hasten back toward camp. They are almost there when Lisa hears more squealing. She turns around; the three wolf cubs have followed them. None of the clan has seen wolf cubs so close up. Lisa's daughter, Eva, and the other children rush to pet them, and the fuzzy cubs jump up on their legs. The adults watch, amused, while the cubs and the children play.

Lisa's smile becomes a frown when it occurs to her that the cubs' parents might be tracking them.

"Shoo!" She flaps her hands at them and stomps her feet. The cubs must think this is some new game, because they playfully nip at her bare toes.

She looks back down the hill in the direction of the valley. There is no movement and no sign of angry wolves.

"What will we do if the parents come?" asks an older woman, following Lisa's gaze. "What if they come before the men return?"

Lisa thinks for a moment. Few of the women are hunters, but until the men return, they have to be prepared. "Let's get our spears and watch the hillside."

Weapons in hand, the women sit in a semicircle around

the camp, facing out, waiting. They hear sounds and leap to their feet, spears pointed. Lisa sighs with relief when she sees her husband and the other men coming up the hill.

"What's wrong?" Heikki yells, running to her. "Why do you all have spears?"

Lisa points to the wolf cubs. "They followed us home. We're watching in case the parents come."

The men cast wary eyes at the cubs, but Heikki smiles as he watches them play. "They probably belong to the two wolves we saw a bear kill at the river."

"Oh," Lisa says. "Then can we keep them then? The children love playing with them."

Heikki walks over to the children and runs a hand over the animals' backs, inspecting them. He returns to Lisa. "Well, all right. We had a successful hunt, so we don't have to kill them for meat. Not right now, at least."

Lisa nods. Not ever, she thinks to herself. The hunting is good in the plains within a half day of the river, and they will surely have plenty of deer meat.

The air is cold at night, and Lisa sees the cubs snuggling next to Eva and another sleeping child, their soft fur like warm blankets. The next day she and the other women watch closely as the children play with the cubs, but the cubs don't make any aggressive moves no matter how roughly the children play.

Several moons go by. The cubs grow fast but remain playful and harmless. They wander off the campsite every day but always return. When the children go to sleep, the cubs always snuggle close to Eva and the young son of Heikki's brother Johan.

Still, as the cubs grow, the clan becomes more concerned.

"We should kill them," Johan tells Heikki. "It's dangerous to have them around our children."

Lisa looks up in alarm. "Oh, no! We women will keep an eye on them. I'm sure they won't hurt the children."

"Well . . ." Heikki watches the cubs frolic. He looks at Lisa and then Johan, shrugs, and walks away.

Several years later, the three wolves that came to them as babies are full-grown adults. Johan becomes more insistent about killing them, but Heikki refuses. Eva loves them, and Lisa is fond of them. She has stopped worrying about leaving them alone with the children.

At dawn one morning, while the men are out on a hunt, Lisa leaves camp with the other women to gather plants at the bottom of the hill, keeping a mother's ear attuned to the children's sounds. The sun is high overhead when she hears screams. She freezes.

"The children!" She drops her basket of plants and races back to camp, the other women close behind her. How could she have been so wrong about the wolves?

She is within sight of the tents when she sees the mountain lion. Her worst fear realized.

The children are running toward the tents. The mountain lion lopes after them, comes up on one girl, and drags her to the ground. It is Eva.

"Help me! Help me!" she shrieks.

The mountain lion releases her leg, but only to move to her neck. It opens its jaws.

Appearing from nowhere, two of the wolves jump the beast, knocking it off Eva. The third wolf joins the fight, and all three tear into their prey with their paws and teeth. Two of them rip its neck open while the third bites hard into a rear leg.

A minute later, the mountain lion lies motionless.

When the men return and learn what happened, Johan takes Heikki aside. "The wolves saved Eva. It could have been my son. I was wrong. I want them to stay."

After a successful hunt, the clan holds a special feast. Heikki and Johan personally take pieces of fresh deer meat to the three wolves. Every night after that, the wolves are fed deer meat like everyone else; their place in the clan's life is assured.

The children name the wolves Waa, Wee, and Woo. Clansmen give them bones and meat whenever they respond to their names, and soon the wolves come quickly when called. Johan, now their staunchest advocate, teaches them to fetch bones and sticks. After training them to obey commands, he and Heikki take them on a hunt. They are surprised at how fast the wolves learn to stalk game, help the scouts herd the deer toward the hunters, and chase down wounded animals. While they're out hunting, the men leave one wolf at camp to keep the children safe. With their keen senses of smell and hearing, the wolves know when danger is near.

The wolves still leave the camp each day for a short time, for reasons no one ever learns. Before nightfall, they return and play with the children and snuggle next to them all night. One evening, Waa and Wee disappear for several days, and everybody thinks they are gone for good, but they come back. Later Wee disappears again, this time for much longer. When she returns with three puppies, everyone is surprised and pleased, and the clan celebrates.

Even with the wolves' help, food eventually becomes scarce as time goes on, the deer too sparse to continue feeding such a large clan. Heikki leads the clan west along the big river through vast plains and rolling hills. When the weather grows colder and colder every year, Heikki asks Lisa, "Is the sun god angry at us?"

Germany and Spain

The elders are the first to notice that the days are colder than the days of their youth, in both summer and winter. Chief Heikki ignores their warning that the clan must have displeased the sun god.

"The cold and the white rain arrive each year, old man," he tells one elder. "Yet just as certainly, the days grow long and warm. So it has always been, so it will always be, just as our clan, named long ago for two great leaders, has always been the Hei-Lee clan and will always be."

Still, he knows that it can be dangerous to discount an elder's words, so he directs Shaman Lisa to have the clan pay more respect to all the gods, and then he does his best to put the entire matter out of his mind, even when next year's white rain becomes a series of blizzards the likes of which no elder can recall.

Each year in the fall, the Hei-Lee clan watches flocks of birds fly southwest because they can't survive the bitter cold and snowy winters. Heikki isn't certain, but it seems that in the past few years, when the birds return, it is for a shorter time than in his youth. The ground grows harder and few plants grow. After the next harsh winter, Heikki sends scouts to explore territory far to the southwest, in the direction the birds fly. Two full moons later the scouts return with glowing reports of plentiful deer and relatively flat land between large mountains. Heikki still can't fully credit what the elders said about the sun god, but with hungry mouths to feed, they must move southward now.

Aside from winters almost as cold as in their former home, the new area looks like a good place to live. Heikki and his young boys, Jouni and Tauno, take the clan's two wolf dogs to explore large caves for a possible campsite. Heikki stations Jouni outside a cave that looks promising and goes in with Tauno and the dogs. They are deep inside when they hear footsteps and a grunt. The dogs snarl as a huge brown bear lumbers from the farther depths of the cave.

"Run, Tauno!" Heikki yells.

He turns to flee and trips on a rock. Barking furiously, the two dogs spring toward the bear to protect Heikki. He scrambles to his feet and makes it out of the cave with Tauno. He hears the dogs barking even more furiously, he hears the bear roaring.

Then nothing. Silence.

Neither of the dogs makes it out of the cave.

The whole clan is sad about the loss of their dogs. Heikki announces that they will move on, and no one objects. They begin their first long trek south.

After one moon of journeying through plains and hills, Shaman Lisa's father and mother come to her and Heikki.

"We and six others are too old and weak to travel," her father says. "We need your help to find a cave to shelter us in the coming winter. We will stay here."

Distraught, Lisa turns to Heikki, who stands silent. While

he shares Lisa's feeling, he understands why an elderly couple would tire of what has become a longer, more difficult trek than any of them expected. Finally, he says to the old couple, "We'll find you a safe cave. On a gentle hill overlooking the river, where you can fish and gather plants."

Lisa's father nods to Heikki gratefully and hugs his daughter, trying to soothe her. "It is for the best, my Lisa, your mother and I will do well here."

The clan camps for the night, and once news of the beloved elders' decision is known, there is little talk. The next day, Heikki finds a suitable cave, searches every inch of it to make sure there is no sign of bears, and lays in a stock of deer meat and furs. He knows this will be the last stop for Lisa's parents, and the parting is difficult and tearful. Lisa is nearly inconsolable.

Over the next two years the clan is constantly on the move southward, finding slightly warmer weather and less snow each time they camp. One morning late in the second year, Lisa tells Heikki that her parents visited her the night before. She weeps, and he weeps with her. Both know that if your ancestors appear to you during sleep, it means they have passed from this earth.

Heikki strokes her hair. "What did they say?"

"My mother said to follow the river," Lisa tells him through her tears. "She said that the rivers are the best source of life."

Heikki recalls stories handed down from the ancients that say the same thing. "The river we're on now has many plants to eat, but it will take more than plants to sustain us. If we follow it, will we find warmer weather?"

Lisa nods. "Yes. My parents will always give us good advice."

Heikki puts his trust in Lisa's words. His scouts find more deer farther down the river, but the weather is only a little warmer there. They continue south to where the river meets another river heading south, and they follow it to the sea.

When the coastal area becomes crowded with other clans, the Hei-Lee clan pushes farther south, down the coast, and camps at a big river flowing into the sea. Fish are plentiful, but they miss their deer meat. They move inland along a river where other clans have told them there are deer herds. They follow this long river west to hills and plains south of high snow-capped mountains. They set up a campsite along the river east of some other big mountains. Hunting is good and the river gods are kind. Through the wisdom of the ancestors and Heikki's careful leadership, the clan finds a fine place to live.

The Hei-Lee clan encounters some friendly clans in the area and joins them in their annual summer festivals. Heikki and Lisa meet the other chiefs and shamans at these festivals, and they especially like those from the Basque clans. The Hei-Lee clan moves north to a valley on the east side of a river flowing south from nearby hills, where several Basque clans are camped. They set up on the west side of the river.

One warm summer day, Heikki sends Jouni and Tauno upriver to scout for deer. Half a day out, they cross to the east side at a spot where the river is wide and shallow. They climb to the top of a hill to see what lies on the other side. Three Basque girls at the base of the hill are gathering nuts and berries.

Tauno grins at Jouni. "Let's go down and meet our new neighbors, brother."

As they approach the girls, they notice clouds of smoke rising over a tall hill far to the north. As Jouni is saying, "Brother, what is that?" gusty winds blow from the north, and yellow flames burst over the hilltop. The fire spreads quickly downhill, burning everything in its path.

Tauno and Jouni run to the girls. "Where's your camp?" Jouni demands, and points to the approaching wildfire.

With a terrified expression, one girl points toward the valley. "Over there."

Jouni looks where she's pointing—to a spot directly in the fire's path. "The oldest of you take my brother to your camp and warn them," he says, "and the other two come with me. We have to get away from the fire."

The oldest girl eyes Tauno. "All right," she says.

"I'll meet you and her clan at the shallow place in the river," Jouni tells his brother, and sets off with the two younger girls. As he leads them at a run, one of the girls trips and falls, grabbing her ankle.

"Mari! Help me!" she calls out.

Mari runs back to her. "What's wrong, Mina?"

"My ankle, it's—"

With Mari following, Jouni scoops Mina up in his arms and carries her to the river's edge, then across at the shallow place to the west side. He sits her on a fallen log and turns to Mari. "Gather up some tall dry grass. Quickly!"

She stares at him for a moment as he begins yanking up clumps of grass, and then she pitches in. Soon they have enough for two big bundles. Jouni strikes a flintstone above one bundle several times, and finally a spark hits the grass. He blows it into smoldering flames, puts the second bundle on top until it catches, and hands it to Mari.

"Here, help me light this field on fire."

"Why?"

"Just do it! Start over there."

Soon the field is burning. Driven by the wind, the fire tears across the grass until it reaches a rocky hill and dies down, leaving only wisps of smoke curling up from the scorched ground. Jouni looks back to see Tauno and the girls' clan running toward the river just ahead of the advancing wildfire.

Jouni waves frantically. "Over here! It's safe over here!"

Tauno's group wades across the river as the wildfire continues racing down the east side. Swarms of sparks fly across to the west side, but thanks to Jouni's quick thinking, there is nothing for them to ignite.

A distinguished-looking older man steps from the group, embraces Mari and Mina, and shouts thanks to the sky for his daughters' survival. Mari points to Jouni. "He saved us," she says. "I didn't understand at first, but Jouni told me help him burn the grass on this side."

Tauno gives his brother a proud smile as the man says, "I am Chief Asier, and you, Jouni, are a smart and clever young man."

"I couldn't have done it without Mari," Jouni says, and looks across the river to hide the blush rising to his cheeks. "Your camp is surely gone. Come to ours."

Chief Asier nods sadly. "Yes, we accept your offer."

When they arrive at the Hei-Lee campsite, Jouni introduces Chief Asier to his father and tells him about the fire.

"Your sons are heroes," Chief Asier says. "They saved my daughters and our whole clan."

"Thank the gods they were there," Heikki says. "We would be honored to have your clan stay with us until you find a new campsite. Perhaps we can hunt together. You must know all the best places."

At the evening feast to celebrate their clan's survival, Mari and Mina sit across from Jouni, their bold stares making it clear that both of them are interested in him. For his part, he can't keep his eyes off Mari's beautiful brown face. He notices his father and Chief Asier glancing back and forth between him and Mari from time to time, and when the evening winds down, he hears Heikki say to Chief Asier, "Mari is a charming and beautiful girl."

Chief Asier smiles. "Is she not? She and Jouni would be an excellent match. I have no sons, and if Mari marries Jouni, I will make him the next chief of my clan."

Heikki considers the proposition. "Chief Asier. We will hate to see him leave our clan but it is a great honour for Jouni and our Hei-Lee clan to see him become one of the chiefs in the Basque clan."

11
Northbound

"Can I offer you some dessert, John?" Andy asked.

"Is it another one of your Finnish specialties?"

"Of course. It's Benni and Jerri's." Andy went into the kitchen and returned with an ice cream scoop and a carton of Cherry Garcia.

Lisa passed John a bowl distractedly. "So if the Saami were in Spain, how did they get from there to Finland? Did they sail up the Atlantic coast?"

"No, there were no ships or boats back then, only wood rafts used to cross rivers."

"Did they ride horses?"

"No, no horses to ride. Clans were still hunter-gatherers and didn't start to domesticate animals and cultivate crops until about ten thousand years ago."

"So you mean . . . you mean they walked all the way?"

"Yes," John said. "They walked all the way from Spain to Finland, following close along major rivers. They walked everywhere, just as all their ancestors before them did millennia ago after they left Africa and slowly migrated to Europe, Asia, and the Americas. Hang on a sec." He got up from the table and returned with another map showing the southward route he'd traced earlier, but in reverse.

"But how did they know to go north and what paths to take?"

"Good question, Lisa. So let's say you're in central Europe during the end of the last ice age, and the climate is warming, and the permafrost and glaciers are melting, and plants are growing back on land that's been frozen for thousands of years. Animal herds begin heading north and clans follow them, trekking along the same big rivers their ancestors had taken south during the beginning of the ice age."

"Was the famous blue Danube one of those rivers they travelled north along?" Eva asked.

"No, the Rhine, Rhone, Saone, and Mosel were the main rivers to follow north, but the Danube played a significant role in migrations too. At the end of the last ice age, a rare and amazing natural event occurred to change the source of two of Europe's most important waterways, the Rhine and the Danube. Before the last ice age, the source of the Rhine was in the hills on the western side of Germany's Black Forest. After the last ice age, the Rhine's new source was high in the Swiss Alps, at the Rheinwaldhorn Glacier near Andermatt."

Eva's spoon stopped in mid-air. "How on earth did that happen?"

"Toward the end of the last ice age, warmer weather rapidly melted many of the Alps' mountain glaciers, creating the Rhine's new starting point and a strong water flow down to Basel, Switzerland. From there the Rhine flowed north along the French-German border and then into Germany and finally up into the Netherlands and the North Sea. As for the

MAP, MIGRATION ALONG RHONE, SAONE, MOSEL, DOUBS AND RHINE RIVERS

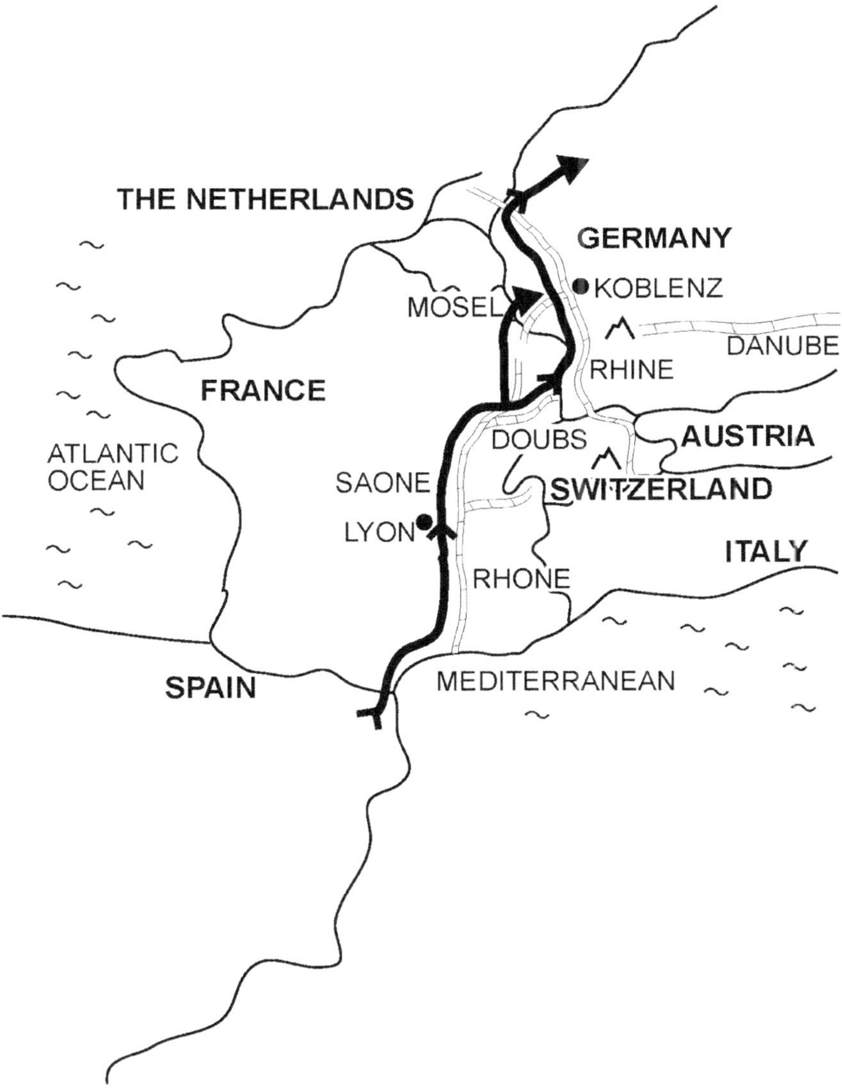

Danube, its source before the last ice age was in the north side of the Swiss Alps, and afterward it started in the eastern hills of the Black Forest. The sources of the two rivers had switched locations, a truly unusual feat of nature, and these two major changes influenced the migration paths of many clans moving back to central Europe. If a clan crossed the Rhine and headed east, they would likely find the Danube and migrate to eastern Europe instead of northern Europe, but the Rhine is a very wide and deep river, and most clans approaching it from the west would have turned north and followed it up to western and northern Germany, which was where massive deer herds were going. The Mosel River in France, which joins the Rhine at Koblenz, was another major river the clans used to migrate to Germany."

Eva sat there trying to take it all in. "Well, shut my mouth," she said.

***

12,000 Years Before Present, Spain

Weddings in the Hei-Lee clan are always much-anticipated events, but Chief Heikki needs two more bear teeth. Sari, his oldest daughter, is ready to marry the clan's best hunter, Tauno, and the sacred tooth necklace is needed for the wedding ceremony, but three of the clan's four necklaces are full, with twenty dangling teeth each, the maximum number according to clan tradition. The fourth necklace has only two teeth, from a very large dead bear found long ago in the foothills of a big mountain range, but each has fifty cut marks, and there is no room for more. One new cut mark is required for the mingling of blood, but the clan can't find another bear. Fearing the gods' wrath if they fail to keep the sacred tradition, the clan searches far and wide for several moons until they find a bear carcass at last. The fourth necklace is strung with two new teeth, and the wedding feast ensues.

The clan has mastered using animal furs and skins for clothing and shelter, and has learned to make tents that can be quickly struck for ease of moving to better grounds. More and more, that is necessary as the deer herds thin around each new campsite. Hunting is poor where they are now, and Heikki takes the clan north, where they find deer with thick coats developed over many years of living in cold weather.

The move doesn't ease their lot. After another spring of poor hunting, Heikki sends out scouts who find huge herds of deer moving in two different directions, some farther north and some to the east.

After the scouts return, Chief Heikki's younger brother, Teuvo, comes to him. "We should go up the big river to the north," he says. "I'm certain the deer will be more plentiful there, enough to feed our clan until the end of time."

"No, I have given this much thought. We must take the river to the east."

Teuvo argues with him, and the conversation's ugly turns convince Heikki of what he has suspected for some while. Teuvo is smart, well liked, ambitious, and a strong hunter. He doesn't want to take orders from Heikki; he wants to be clan chief himself.

"There are too many of us here," Teuvo says. "We have to split up." He holds up two fingers. "In two days I'll lead a new clan north. Each family can decide whether to join me or stay with you."

"It saddens me to see you leave our clan, Teuvo. And it's not wise, especially with such haste."

"For once I'm not doing it your way."

Teuvo turns on his heel and walks away. He spends the rest of the day talking with other clan members. Most of them choose to remain with Heikki, but by the next day, two cousins and their families join Teuvo, along with one of the smaller clans in the Hei-Lee cluster. The following day Teuvo's new clan sets off, and Heikki's heart tells him that he will never see his brother again.

Teuvo leads his clan up the river to the north, toward its source in the hills west of the mountains. The plains give them a variety of edible plants and some large deer herds, but they have few hunters. The deer continue to move north, and Teuvo's clan follows them to a second large river, this one flowing from the mountains' northern hills. Though the weather is warming, the winters are still bitterly cold, and the clan lacks sufficient fur for clothing and shelter. Life is a constant struggle, and Teuvo comes to regret leaving his brother's clan.

Years later, when Teuvo dies, his son Paavo becomes chief. The clan continues journeying along the big river as it winds north through small valleys and steep hills on both sides. The clan crosses back and forth often, trying to find level ground more favorable for gathering vegetation and hunting. Each time, they become more adept at maneuvering log rafts across the river.

One summer day, they are crossing the river at a sharp

bend where the current can easily push their rafts to the other side. Chief Paavo and his sons, Teuvo and young Erik, are on the last raft, along with his brother Johan and Johan's six-year-old son Zak and a few other clansmen. Halfway across, the raft hits a hidden boulder, spins around, and sends the two young boys flying into the water.

"Help!" they yell as they drift away from the raft, flailing their arms. Neither of them can swim. Johan, Paavo, and Teuvo jump into the river screaming the boys' names. Johan swims toward where he saw Zak sinking, and after moments of frantic searching, he spots an arm, grabs it, and pulls his son up.

Paavo sees a head bob out of the water a little downstream and swims toward it with all his strength. He reaches Erik and tows him to shore against a strong current. "No!" he cries as he pulls his son's limp body from the water. He drops to his knees and weeps.

Death is not new to Paavo and his clan, but this is the most grievous loss he has suffered. From that day on, he decrees, the clan will never cross the river again.

After his brother leaves, Chief Heikki's clan cluster follows the deer herds up the river to the east between two imposing mountain ranges. As Heikki had envisioned before Teuvo forced the clan to split, the hunting is good, but the deer keep moving upriver, and the clan keeps following them, until they reach the river's easternmost point, where it makes a hairpin turn southwest toward steep mountains.

When the deer once more become scarce, Heikki sends scouts east across an expanse of flat terrain. The land has warmed and is fertile again. Fertile land brings plants and trees, and these bring deer to forage. Heikki's scouts find deer near a wide river that flows north. They follow the river.

The clan sets up a large campsite south of where the river meets another large river. It has now been many years since the Hei-Lee clan split up. The time is approaching for Chief Heikki and Shaman Lisa to pass the leadership of the clan to Tauno and Sari, who will become the new Chief Heikki and Shaman Lisa, as tradition dictates.

One morning, Heikki and two scouts set out from the camp in search of deer. Torrential rains pour down for several days, and they do not return. Over many moons, the clan expends every effort to find them, until they have to accept that Heikki and the scouts are gone forever. Tauno becomes the new chief, and Sari the new shaman, with her mother serving as second shaman. Tauno and Sari decide not to take the traditional names out of respect for Lisa, and in their continuing hope, however faint, that one day Heikki will return. When their first son is born, they name him Heikki, in honor of his lost grandfather.

Nine years later, on a warm summer morning, young Heikki and two cousins go off to play hide-and-seek outside the campsite. The cousins watch him run across a narrow valley into a forest of tall pines. They run after him, but he is nowhere to be found among the trees. They search everywhere, calling his name, but he doesn't answer.

They run back to the campsite yelling, "We can't find Heikki!"

Once Sari is certain that the children aren't playing a trick on her, she panics. Tauno and most of the men are away on a hunt, and will not return for two days. With her mother's help, she recruits a search party of women and old men to look for her son. His two older sisters beg her to let them go along, but she is too afraid of losing them too, and she tells them she needs them at the camp.

The search party returns after dark. With pain in his eyes, one old man tells Lisa, "We scoured the forest and the valley. We had no success."

Another Heikki is now missing. Lisa can't stop weeping, and Sari is frantic with fear of what might have happened to her only son.

Heikki is determined to hide so well that his cousins will never find him. He moves deeper into the forest and crouches behind some boulders. He listens. No one is calling for him, and there is no sound of footsteps. He waits a while longer and then starts back through the forest toward the campsite.

He walks along, pleased with himself, but soon the trees and vines and boulders begin to look unfamiliar. Shouldn't he have reached the campsite by now? He finally comes to a clearing he thinks he recognizes and walks on, telling himself that he'll spot the clan's tents any minute, but nothing is familiar now. He is lost. He yells and yells. No one answers.

He walks toward the setting sun. Far ahead he sees a river. Ah, it must be the one his clan is camped on! He runs to it, but this part of the river doesn't look anything like where the campsite is. It's dark now, and he has no food. He curls up under a tree and tries to sleep, but hunger pangs and the noises coming from the bushes keep him awake.

Follow the river, his parents had always told him. That's what he decides to do the next morning. He walks the entire day, but he can't see anything that looks like home, and he hasn't encountered a single person he can ask for help. In his nine years of life, he has never been alone.

In the fading daylight, he suddenly sees campfires ahead. Relief floods him. He breaks into a sprint. He can't wait to see his family.

He stops short. It's a camp, but it's not his. Maybe it belongs to one of the smaller clans in the Hei-Lee cluster, he thinks. Yes, surely that's it.

Hunger propels him forward, but as he nears the camp, he doesn't recognize anyone. At all. The strangers sitting by their fires stare at him.

A woman stands up and comes to him. "Who are you, child?"

Heikki doesn't want her to think he's a scared baby, but he can't help himself; he starts to cry. "I'm lost," he says through his tears.

As Heikki hastily wipes his face with the back of his hand, the woman leads him to a campfire where an old man is eating. "This boy just wandered in from the trees, Chief. He says he's lost."

"He speaks our language?"

The woman nods, and the chief dismisses her. He looks Heikki over. "What's your name?" he asks gruffly.

Though intimidated by the old man's stern gaze, Heikki squares his narrow shoulders and puffs out his chest as he has seen the men of his clan do. "My name is Heikki."

The woman returns with a piece of roasted deer meat. He thanks her and eats it, thinking that he has never tasted anything quite so good.

The chief leans forward. "How long have you been away

from your clan?"

Heikki swallows the bite he's chewing. "Two days."

"And from which direction did you come?"

Heikki points north. "I've been walking along the river. Our camp is near a river."

The chief nods. "I'll send scouts tomorrow to find your clan."

The next morning, and for two days more, the scouts search north along the river but find no clans. Heikki cries himself to sleep that first night, and every night after, waiting for word that never comes.

One night as he lies on his sleeping mat crying, the clan's shaman comes to him and puts her arms around him. She hums a soothing song, and after a moment, he smiles and starts to hum with her.

She stops humming and looks at him in wonder. "How do you know this song?"

"Everyone in my clan knows the Lee hum song."

"What? Teuvo, come here!" she calls to her husband.

Chief Teuvo rouses himself from the fireside and walks over, a question in his eyes.

"Heikki knows the Lee hum song. He must be from the Hei-Lee clan."

"Oh my," Teuvo says softly, as if to himself. "My grandfather Teuvo left the Hei-Lee clan many years ago. Our clans went in different directions. This is wonderful news." He looks at Heikki kindly, his sternness gone. "Our ancestors have smiled on us. We must find your clan now."

Not wanting Heikki to endure a long search that might yield only disappointment, Chief Teuvo leaves him with

Shaman Maria when he sets out at daybreak with several scouts. They follow the river north again, this time to where it joins another big river. They move south along the other river and finally see a large campsite. They approach it cautiously, stopping when several clansmen look their way.

Chief Teuvo cups his hands around his mouth and yells, "Are you the Hei-Lee clan?"

"We are," a man yells back.

"Where is your chief?"

"I'll get him."

Wary glances greet Teuvo's group as they walk into camp. Moments later, a man appears from a tent.

"I am Chief Tauno," he says. "Who are you?"

"Chief Teuvo. I'm your cousin. I found your son."

Tauno gasps. "My son? Can it be? Where is he?"

"At our camp. He came there five days ago."

Tauno turns toward the tents. "Sari! Sari! Come! They found Heikki!"

Sari comes running. "Where is he?" Hearing that her lost son is safe at another camp, she bursts into tears.

Shaman Lisa wants to accompany them to Teuvo's camp, but she has to acknowledge that the journey might be too long for her aging body. If she stays, the clan will still have leadership in the absence of its chief. She asks Heikki's sisters to stay with her, and though they long to see their brother, they agree out of love for her. Tauno and Sari quickly pack some food and set off with Teuvo and his men, discussing how the families separated all those years ago. Sari tells Teuvo about her father and how they all feared that another Heikki had gone missing forever.

"I'm overjoyed to have my son back," she says. "I still miss my dear father. If he were here, I know he would be so happy to see you and your clan. After all, we're family."

Days later, the two clans meet at the Hei-Lee campsite and feast on roasted deer. They enjoy many nights of storytelling about their separate journeys. One moon later, they join as one big clan. "By helping us find what was lost, both now and so long ago, our ancestors have truly smiled on us all once again," Teuvo says, and each member of the newly reunited clan seconds his words.

12
Gift of the Sun God

Dinner with John Anderson became a regular event in the Koskinen household as Lisa and her parents grew more and more absorbed in finding out all they could about the history of the tooth necklace. Tonight they were continuing their discussion of the Saami migration to Finland over Chinese takeout John had insisted on bringing.

"If the Saami went from Spain up the Rhine to the Netherlands like you told us last time, didn't they have to cross the North Sea to get to Finland?" Lisa asked.

John retrieved another of his seemingly endless supply of maps from his briefcase. "You'd think so, wouldn't you, but during the last thousand years of the last ice age, the North Sea between Germany and Norway was still land. The ice glaciers in Norway, Sweden, and Finland were the last to melt, and the clans followed the deer herds north up Norway's western coast all the way to Lapland in northern Norway and Finland."

Andy helped himself to an egg roll. "So how long did it take them to walk from Spain to Finland?"

"Two or three thousand years, and it was during this time

MAP, MIGRATION SPAIN TO FINLAND, END OF LAST ICE AGE

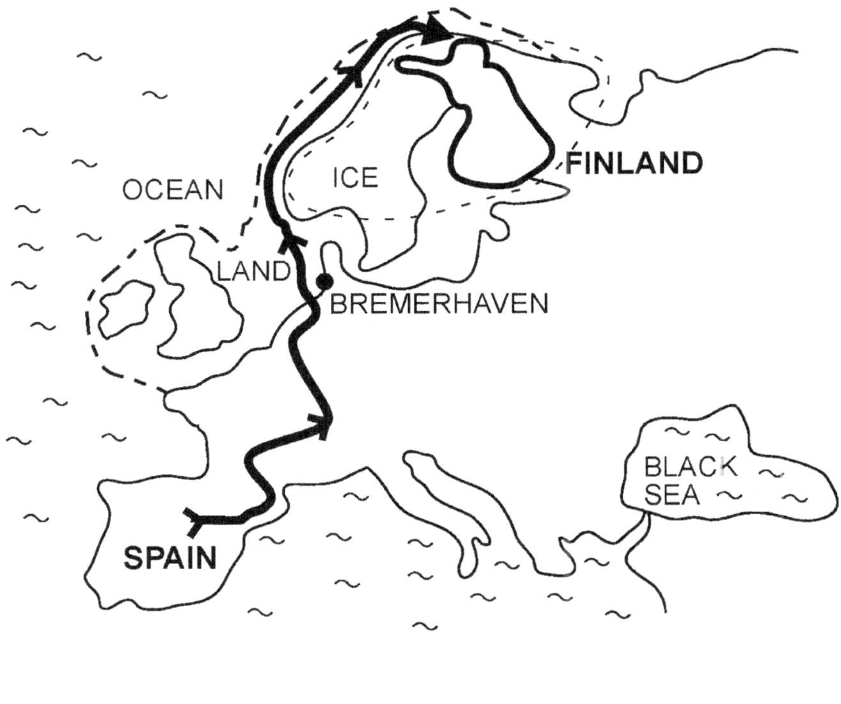

that skin color slowly changed from light brown in Spain to pale white in the far north. Hair and eye color also changed dramatically in some cases, from brown to blond and blue."

John paused long enough to take a few bites of General Tso's. "After the clans arrived in Lapland, they struggled to endure the long, dark winters but thrived during the warm summers. None of the Saami clans who first arrived there knew it, but this was their last stop. These courageous hunter-gatherer clans became the first settlers in Norway, Sweden, and Finland. The Saami are one of the oldest, largest, and most successful indigenous tribes in the world. Today they number about one hundred thousand, and continue to live in Lapland, which comprises the northern parts of Finland, Norway, Sweden, and Russia."

"Your food's getting cold, John," Eva said, ever the attentive hostess.

He smiled at her. "Is that a hint to shut up? Just when I'm getting to the good part?"

"No, of course not," she said. "I want you to go on, I just don't want you to starve."

"No worries there, I'll polish this off before you know it," he said, picking up where he left off. "After the Scandinavian glaciers and permafrost melted and the land became habitable, some Saami tribes slowly trekked southward inside Finland. They traded with other clans, and some intermarried with the Finns, who migrated into southern Finland from Russia about four thousand years after the Saami arrived in northern Finland."

Andy grinned. "Hey, like my ancestors!"

"Right," John said. "The Saami became part of the Finnish

culture's fabric and contributed to a unique shared language that is part of the Finno-Ugric language group today. This group's primary languages aren't part of the Indo-European language group most Europeans speak. Only three countries in the world speak Finno-Ugric languages: Finland, Estonia, and Hungary."

"What's the connection between Finland and Hungary? They're so far apart."

"Good question, Lisa, as usual. The location of these three countries has been of great interest to those who study the history of languages. While Estonia is across the Baltic Sea from Finland, Hungary is indeed far away in central Europe, yet the root language of all three countries is the same. Scientists are still trying to determine the language's origins and the connection between the Finns and the Hungarians. Although there are linguistic similarities, the Finnish and Hungarian languages are distinct. And another interesting point. It's common to see blue-eyed blonds in northern Europe, but Hungary is the only central European country with an abundance of them."

"These days the Finns and Hungarians treat each other as long-lost cousins," Andy added. "The Finns cheered for the Hungarians at the 1952 Olympics in Helsinki, and when Finns go to Hungary on vacation, they're treated like family."

* * *

Northern Europe, 10,000 Years Before Present

On a cool fall day, several clanswomen help Shaman Lisa deliver her first child. When they put the baby girl in her arms, she gasps. "Her eyes! Is she blind?"

Her sister Eva takes a closer look. "Why, they are the color of the sky!"

"And her hair! It's so different! It's white!" Lisa brushes the tufts on the baby's head apprehensively.

"She is a beautiful baby," Eva says comfortingly. "The sun god wanted you to have a child of the sky, with blue eyes and golden hair. This is a special omen."

Lisa stares at her blue-eyed baby, and her worry evaporates, replaced by delight. "Yes, she's beautiful."

Her husband isn't so sure. "She isn't like us," he says. "What will the clan think?"

"You are their chief, Heikki. Tell them our daughter is a special gift from the sun god."

They name her Saami. The whole clan comes to see her and is enthralled. As the years pass, her golden hair lengthens, and everyone who meets her marvels at her sparkling blue eyes and fair skin.

When Saami grows up, she becomes an especially caring member of the clan. She loves learning, especially when Lisa teaches her how to find plants and herbs to help heal sicknesses and wounds. She grows up wanting to help people, just like her mother.

When it is time for Saami to marry, Chief Heikki and Shaman Lisa select a distant cousin named Tauno, the clan's smartest scout and best hunter, to be her husband. The couple binds themselves to the Hei-Lee clan by pricking their fingers and adding their blood to a new cut mark in the sacred tooth necklace. When Saami becomes shaman, nobody in the clan wants their sky goddess to change her name, so Tauno keeps his own name too.

During their first winter as the Hei-Lee clan's new leaders, many people in some of the smaller clans become sick. Their skin turns yellow, and several die. Shaman Saami learns that they are only eating deer meat—vegetation is scarce in the long cold winters—and she manages to find some plants for them to eat. When their health improves, they all speak of how their sky goddess saved them.

Tauno and Saami have three children, all blond-haired and blue-eyed. Several children of Saami's younger cousins also have blue eyes and blond hair. Soon clan members come to Saami wanting her to ask the sun god to give them children like hers. When many get their wish, they credit their children's blond hair and blue eyes to Saami's entreaties to the sun god on their behalf.

Word spreads to other clans, and they too appeal to Saami to help them have blond-haired, blue-eyed children. Enough such children are born to convince many clan members of Saami's special abilities.

Every summer the Hei-Lee cluster joins other clans for festivals and hunts. Deer are plentiful and times are good. Once word spreads of the Hei-Lee clan's successes, more clans come to the area.

One summer, after several major attacks on deer by clans competing for their meat and hide, the animals seem to sense they are in peril. The deer herds split into three groups. One goes north, one east, and one southeast up a big river. The clans in the Hei-Lee cluster argue about the choice of direction and split into three groups too. Most go north along a long coast with the Hei-Lee clan following the largest deer herds. Four cousins and a smaller clan go southeast, and two cousins and another small clan go east.

The main Hei-Lee clan prospers, finding excellent hunting around their northernmost coastal campsite. One clear fall night, as they are enjoying a big feast, the sky lights up with shimmering green and red colors.

"What's happening?" one frightened clansman asks Shaman Saami.

She stares up at the awesome display. "The sky god is welcoming us to this new land," she says.

* * *

"Pass the fortune cookies, Eva," John said, pointing at his empty plate. True to his word, he had finished his dinner in record time.

Lisa was still digesting everything he'd told them. "Dad, when do you think your mother's Saami ancestors and your father's Finnish ancestors first met?"

"Nobody in our family really knows, or they just don't want to talk about it. I think it may have been more than a hundred years ago. For a long time, many Finns thought the Saami were primitive and uneducated and that it was not socially acceptable to marry them. Just like it was frowned upon until recently for whites to marry blacks."

"Was it still like that when you and Eva married?" John asked. "How did you two meet anyway? I'd love to hear the story."

"Next time," Eva said. "I'm feeling a little tired, and I've got an early day tomorrow."

Andy shot her a worried glance as John looked at his

watch. "Yikes, I had no idea it was so late. I need my beauty sleep too," he said, rising from the table. "Night, all."

Lisa walked him to the door. "Thanks for the Chinese. And everything else," she added shyly.

* * *

Finland, AD 1200

Matti and his two sons go north from their small farm outside the city of Oulu, near the Kemi River, to clear land. Matti is expanding the farm so he can grow more crops and have more cows, but he continues to hunt deer to provide his family with their favorite meat, just as his An-Eva ancestors did before him. He knows that his boys—Heikki, eighteen, and Antti, sixteen—are eager to join the hunts.

In preparation for the fall's last big hunt, Matti sends the boys out four days in advance of the main party to scout. It's the first time their father has allowed them to do this, and they're proud. After a half-day hike, they reach the family's hunting cabin on the Kemi, which flows all the way from Lapland to the Kemi trading post and into the sea, Matti has told them. After a night's rest, they leave the cabin and hike north to scout the valleys and rolling hills. Matti will lead the hunt after they find a herd.

The weather is clear and pleasant until the second evening out from the cabin, when black clouds approach from the northwest as they're setting up their tent. During the night, Heikki hears sounds on the tent and peeks out to see heavy snow coming down. He doesn't think much of it; snow is a fact of life, and he and Antti have often camped in deep snows. He is more concerned in the light of morning: several feet of snow surround them, and dark clouds hover over them as far as he can see.

"We've got to get back to the cabin," he tells Antti. "Fast. It'll snow again before evening."

They strike their tent and head out, but his calculations are off. Before they are anywhere near the cabin, a blinding snow begins to fall. They can't see where they're going, but they trek on, knowing that to stop will mean death. They climb a hill hoping to spot the river and get their bearings.

"This area doesn't look familiar," Heikki says, "and I can't see the river." The snow has let up a bit, but there is no sun to give them direction.

Antti points ahead. "Let's climb that hill over there. It's taller and maybe we'll see the river on the other side."

They trudge across a narrow valley, through a pine forest, and up the hill. No river. They cross another valley and climb another hill, but still no river. Neither brother can ever recall not being able to find the river.

"I don't know which way we're going now," Heikki says at last, "and I'm getting tired. We'll have to stop."

Antti is quiet. He knows the risk, but no alternative presents itself. "All right," he says finally.

They clear an area big enough to pitch their tent on, but another heavy snow falls that night. In the morning, the snow is chest-high. He and Antti discuss their options. They have a little food left. Should they stay put until they can see the sun for direction? Or should they go on and hope they stumble onto the river?

Two men lie in the snow semiconscious, and from the state of their clothing, on the way to freezing to death. Unable to draw a name from either man, Tauno's hunters put them on sledges and take them back to their camp. Tauno's Saami tribe has recently migrated south to this area from northern Finland's Lake Inari, seeking new hunting grounds.

The Saami put the two men in a tent, remove their wet clothing, and cover their bodies with deer furs warmed by the fire. One of the Saami calls to two young girls to bring hot soup. If they are to be saved, he thinks as he looks at the men's frostbitten faces, it will take warming them fast.

Hours later, Heikki peers up from his bed, his mind clouded. His eyes refuse to focus. Is that his father bending over him? No, it is a stranger.

The effort of keeping his eyes open is too much to sustain. He dozes off again. Sometime later, he can't tell how long, he wakes and sees that he and Antti are in a big tent with many people milling about talking to each other. But what are they saying?

Pretending he is still unconscious, he eyes the strange people. His father has told him stories about tribes different from most Finns, strong tribes in the far north that live in tents and hunt deer for most of their food and clothing. Can this be one of those tribes? He has never seen people who look and dress this way, and their speech is definitely different from his and Antti's, yet it has a familiar sound. Listening hard, he finds he can understand much of what they say. They are talking about a dog named Nair, killed the day before in a bear attack. The adults are trying to comfort two girls who grew up with the dog and miss him terribly.

Heikki hears Antti stir beside him. The girls see that they're awake, bring them bowls of soup, and spoon it into their mouths.

An old woman approaches. "Ah, you are awake now." She dabs a wet cloth on Heikki's face as she turns to the girls. "So handsome!" she says. "Both of them. Why, I believe your father brought them home just for you."

The girls blush, and Heikki hears laughter that seems to echo around him.

A burly man steps close, smiling and holding up an open hand in friendly greeting. "I'm Chief Tauno. Welcome."

"You saved us," Heikki says weakly. "Thank you."

A startled look crosses the chief's face. "You speak our language?"

"Well, I—a little bit. Mostly, I guess."

"What is your name? Have you been with our people before?"

"I'm Heikki, and my brother there is Antti. No, we've never met your people, but we've heard what good hunters you are."

Chief Tauno doesn't reply, and Heikki can tell he's thinking. After a moment he says, "Your names are similar to some of ours, and you can speak our language. Where did you learn it?"

Heikki smiles. "It's our language too. We live south of here, near the Kemi River. I don't know why our languages are so much alike. That's . . . interesting to me."

"And to me. But let me introduce my family. Here is my wife, Sari, and these are our daughters, Lisa and Eva." Tauno nods toward the soup girls and proceeds to name all the other people gathered in the large tent.

Heikki turns his gaze to the girls. Now that he can see better, he is surprised to find that they have blond hair and blue eyes, just as he and Antti do.

When it is time for the main meal, Tauno has his daughters serve Heikki and Antti roasted deer meat. The girls sit nearby while they eat, whispering and stealing glances at their guests. From time to time, Heikki hears one of them giggle and the other one shush her.

After the meal, Tauno comes over to Heikki and Antti. "Do you have wives and children?" he asks bluntly.

Antti clears his throat. "No, we're not married."

In his side vision, Heikki sees Lisa and Eva smile.

"Where do you live?" Sari asks.

"On our parents' farm, near the Kemi trading post on the river," Heikki says.

Tauno frowns. "The big river? That's about half a day from here. What were you doing so far from home?"

"We came to scout deer for our hunters. The storm caught us and we got lost. We must have gone the wrong way."

"We're lucky you found us," Antti says.

"The sun god helped us," Tauno says. "And maybe my daughters are lucky we found you too."

Lisa leans forward. "Would you like more hot soup, Heikki?"

He nods. "Yes. Yes, I would."

Lisa leaps up to refill his bowl, and Eva follows her with Antti's bowl. They are back in seconds.

"You need rest, Tauno says. "Stay a day or so to gain your strength, and then I'll guide you back to the big river. Your family must be very worried."

Lisa spoons up some soup. "Yes, *please* stay," she says, and Heikki thinks he hears an echo again, but it's just Eva saying the same thing to Antti.

Tauno observes his daughters. "You know, I'd planned to go to Kemi next summer to trade furs."

Heikki swallows a spoonful of soup. "I saw some nice furs at the trading post last year, and I heard they came from your people. My family sells farm goods there, mainly cow milk."

Tauno laughs. "Cow milk? How does *that* taste?"

"Good," Antti says. "We drink it almost every meal."

Eva giggles. "Father, can we go with you to Kemi to . . . to try the milk?"

"Surely, daughter, you and your sister too. You can help carry the furs."

Two days later the storm has passed, leaving a sheet of white under the clear morning sky as far as the eye can see. Tauno sets out early with Heikki and Antti after the girls bid them a reluctant farewell. At the edge of the camp, Heikki turns back and calls, "See you in the summer!"

They have been walking for several hours when they hear yelling.

"Heikki! Antti! My sons! My sons!" Matti can't believe his eyes. He and his hunters have been out searching high and low since the storm abated, and have all but given up hope.

After introductions and rejoicing, the boys recount the story of their rescue, and Matti insists that Tauno come to the hunting cabin for a lunch of hot stew. They sit talking around the fireplace in the warm cabin, and after Matti thanks Tauno for the fifth or sixth time, Heikki says, "Chief Tauno would like to trade deer furs at Kemi come summer. Can you help him, Father?"

"With utmost pleasure. My cousin Johan owns the place, and I'll make sure he gives you a good bargain."

"My thanks," Tauno says. "I must go now, but I will bring more than furs with me when I return." He winks at the boys.

"Until summer, then," Matti says. "May you have a safe journey."

On a warm, sunny day, Tauno, his daughters, and three Saami hunters arrive at the Kemi trading post, the packs on their backs loaded with all the deer hides they can carry. The hunters leave their hides and set out for home.

As soon as Tauno and the girls enter the store, Johan welcomes them. "Matti told me you were coming. Let's see what you've brought me." After inspecting the furs, he says, "They're of excellent quality, I'll buy them all. And I'll take those too." He points at two pairs of deer-hide boots in the load.

"Oh, no!" Lisa says, blushing. "These are for . . . for special friends."

Tauno slowly walks around the store. "You have much here I like, Johan. Those metal pots look well made. And these large knives . . ." He picks one up and tests its blade on his thumb.

Lisa and Eva are making their own tour of the store, wide-eyed. "Look, Father," Lisa says. "Look at all this wool and cotton material. Colors like I've never seen."

"And the sewing needles," Eva chimes in. "So fine and sharp! And the threads in so many colors. Mother will love these."

"We will return later to buy before we leave," Tauno says. "Now we must put up our tent. I saw a clear field just north of here. All right to camp there?"

"Absolutely not," Johan says. "You are not permitted to camp there."

Tauno looks at him in surprise.

Johan grins. "You are to stay at Matti's farm. It's only about an hour from here, and easy to find."

Lisa and Eva whisper and giggle all the way to the farmhouse. As they near it, Tauno calls out to announce their arrival.

Heikki and Antti are inside repairing an old pair of boots. "That's Tauno's voice," Heikki says as he and his brother jump up from the worktable. "Antti, they've come!"

"Boys!" Their mother looks up from her sewing. "We are civilized here. We will greet them properly."

The brothers follow their parents to the door. When his father opens it, Heikki peers around them and sees Tauno and his daughters. His heart leaps into his throat.

"Welcome to our home," Matti says. "This is Sanna, my wife, and I believe you already know my sons."

"Thank you for inviting us to stay with you," Tauno says. "Such a nice house. Made of wood and all."

"Our house is yours," Sanna says, ushering them in. "I understand you live in big tents and move often. I can see why this is so different for you."

"Yes, it is different," Tauno says, looking around admiringly.

"Why, Matti, they're such handsome people." Sanna turns to Tauno. "Your daughters are beautiful, and—why, Tauno, you look a lot like my husband. Don't you think so, Matti?"

"Well, perhaps he does look something like me."

"Why, I just can't get over it. You—"

Matti touches his wife's shoulder. "We and our guests can chat later on, Sanna. Perhaps Heikki and Antti will help me show them around."

During the tour of the farm, Heikki enjoys watching the girls' eyes light up as they see many things they have clearly never seen before. The barn is new to them, and certainly the herd of cows mooing and chomping in the barnyard. He can't wait to show them how to milk the cows—that will be a real experience they can share when they return to their camp.

Back at the house, everyone sits around the big kitchen table while Sanna moves about clanking pots and pans as she prepares dinner. The girls offer to help, but Sanna declines, preferring to be in charge of her own kitchen. Matti and Tauno are soon engaged in trading stories. Occasionally one of them uses a word unfamiliar to the other, but their languages are so similar that they have no trouble communicating.

Heikki turns to the girls. "We have something for you," he says.

"Oh?" Lisa and Eva exchange glances.

"Wait here, and close your eyes."

"Tighter," Antti says. "No peeking."

The brothers leave the room and return moments later with two puppies. "Now hold out your hands," Antti says.

The girls feel the puppies' warm weight and open their eyes. "Oh! Thank you! Thank you!" they exclaim at the same time, turning to Tauno. "Can we keep them?"

Tauno watches the puppies squirming and wagging their tails. "This is unexpected, but . . . well, of course. Maybe they can help us hunt when they're bigger."

"And we have something for you!" Eva says, handing her puppy to Lisa. She fetches the package they wrapped at the trading post and holds it out to the boys, who unwrap it eagerly. Two pairs of leather boots tumble out.

"We made them from deer hide and decorated them," Lisa says. "I hope you like them."

"Antti, let's try them on," Heikki says, and then, moments later, "They're wonderful! They fit very well."

"And they feel great," Antti says. "Oh, and we have something else for you. Fresh cow milk!"

Tauno and the girls laugh.

"We'll have some with dinner," Sanna says. "Roast cow meat, gravy, mashed roots, green peas—and all the milk you can drink. Believe me, we have plenty."

They stay up late after the meal, enjoying the warm summer night and the full moon. In the morning, Matti and the boys show their guests around the farm again. Matti explains that most of his crops are grain, some for the cows and some for making bread. Tauno declines to help milk the cows, saying he'll leave it to the experts, and watches while Heikki and Antti undertake the chore with Lisa and Eva's dubious assistance.

"I'm amazed how gentle and cooperative these big animals are," Tauno says to Matti.

"Yes, they're very tame."

"Do you think I could tame deer?"

"Well, we've tamed many different animals, cattle, horses, pigs, dogs. Why not deer?"

"How about bears?"

Matti laughs. "I wouldn't want to try."

Tauno enjoys learning about farming, and Matti tells him that he admires how the Saami live off the land, how they can move around and live anywhere. The two men get along like brothers. Privately, Matti tells Sanna he likes Tauno's curiosity and sharp mind, thinking it odd that his wife's reply, while civil, doesn't hold the enthusiasm he feels.

Late the next morning, Heikki finds Matti and Tauno in the barn. "Father, may Antti and I take Lisa and Eva out in the rowboat to fish?"

Matti nods and looks at Tauno, who smiles and agrees.

The fish are plentiful on the nearby lake, and that evening Sanna allows Lisa and Eva to help prepare a dinner of fresh fish, followed by sweet blueberries for dessert. Once the evening chores done, they all go outside, and the boys take the girls for a short walk. Matti notices that Sanna seems less talkative once they've left.

When their guests say their goodnights and go to sleep, Matti and Sanna sit by themselves under a bright moon and a pale blue sky, listening to the cows low. Matti stretches out in his wooden chair.

"They're nice people," he says.

"Hmm."

"Make nice neighbors."

Sanna says nothing for a while but finally turns to him. "I like them. But I don't want the boys to get involved with Saami girls."

Matti raises his eyebrows. "Oh? Why not?"

"Well . . . what's wrong with the girls around here? There are some very nice girls on the farms nearby. The boys should marry them. They share our customs. It doesn't seem right for our boys to marry girls who don't. We always marry among our own people, you know that. And both those girls are used to moving about, they've been doing it all their lives. What if they grow restless years from now? We might lose our sons, and any children they might have, if the girls decide to just pull up their tents and leave us!"

She pauses, breathing in the farm odors that waft by on a soft breeze. "I'm glad they live so far away," she says, and in her mind, that ends the matter for good.

Heikki and Antti go to the Kemi trading post with their guests the next morning to see them off after they pick up the goods they traded for.

"We hope to visit you when we go on our first fall deer hunt," Heikki says to Tauno.

"I'd like that." He gives Heikki a sly smile. "So would my daughters, I expect."

During each of the three big fall hunts, Heikki and Antti stop by Tauno's camp to see Lisa and Eva. After returning home from the last one, they sit down with their parents.

"I'm going to marry Lisa," Heikki says. "And Antti's going to marry Eva."

Matti and Sanna are quiet for several moments. Sanna's gaze travels from Heikki to Antti, who nods to confirm what his brother said.

Heikki tries to gauge what his mother is thinking. For another endless moment, she sits motionless, staring ahead. "I love you boys," she says finally. "If that's your wish, I respect it."

The next summer, Matti and Sanna prepare for a double wedding and feast. They invite the local farmers and send word to all their relatives. Some relatives will travel from a distance, set up tents, and stay for several days. Tauno and his family will stay at the farmhouse.

The night before the wedding, with the cows milked and the dinner dishes washed, the boys take Lisa and Eva for a walk. Tauno and Sari are sitting at the kitchen table with Matti when Sanna comes in with a leather pouch. "It's time," she says. "We have a special ceremony, and we'd like you to join us in it."

With secret pride that his wife seems to have overcome her conflicted feelings, Matti empties the pouch onto the table to reveal a tooth necklace. Tauno and Sari gape.

"Where did you get this?" Tauno asks.

"It's been in our family forever," Matti says. "It binds us to our ancestors when there's a marriage."

Sari rubs her hand slowly over her mouth. "Tell us more, please."

"We pass the necklace on to our oldest son when he marries," Matti says. "See these cuts? Each has the blood of the new couple and the son's parents, to cement the bond to the ancestors. The necklace is worn only for marriages and other special occasions."

Sari lets out a long breath. "I can't believe it. You see, we have a similar sacred custom in our Saami family."

With that, Tauno takes his own leather pouch from his pocket, pulls out his own tooth necklace, and lays it carefully next to the other one.

Sanna and Matti are speechless.

"We also have a bonding ceremony," Sari says. "It is almost the same as yours in the way we treat the cut marks and the blood, but in our family, we give the oldest daughter this sacred tooth necklace."

Happy tears fill Sanna's eyes as she looks directly at Sari. "Then this was meant to be. In this strange way, it seems, your family is already connected to ours."

Sari fingers the new necklace. "Let us all put our blood in the cut marks on both sacred necklaces," she says wonderingly.

Matti nods. "Yes, and why don't you and Tauno give your necklace to Lisa and Heikki, and we'll give Antti and Eva ours. That way, both families will be bonded forever."

Sanna is lost in thought. "Our necklace is one of two in our family. The other has twenty teeth, not twelve like this one. Your necklace has fourteen teeth."

"Yes," Sari says, "and I didn't think to mention it before, but ours is one of four. The other three have twenty teeth."

"Four old necklaces? Then your family must be twice as old as ours!" Matti grins at his wife. "Why, Sanna, that means we're just youngsters."

The room fills with easy laughter, and in this moment Saana sees the Saami in a completely different light. Now she knows they are family.

The double wedding ceremony takes place on summer's longest night, under a cloudless sky of light blue. Everyone stays up late, even the tiniest of the children. Several of them huddle next to Lisa and Eva, and when they become restless, the sisters start humming a song.

"I see Heikki and Antti taught you our song," Sanna says.

"No they didn't," Eva says. "It's always been in our family."

Sanna looks at Matti in disbelief, but he only shrugs. "Just another one of those family things," he says, and he and his wife join in the hum song until every child has been lulled to sleep.

After five years of marriage, Heikki and Lisa have three children, but Eva and Antti have none. Sanna's heart aches at their disappointment, and one day she tells her visiting sister from Oulu about the situation.

"Take me to them," Aila says. "I can solve their problem."

No matter how often Sanna asks, Aila won't divulge a single detail of her plan, but knowing of her sister's giving and helpful nature, Sanna arranges the visit anyway. When they arrive at Eva and Antti's house, Aila asks Eva without preliminaries, "Do you know about the blueberry god?"

Taken aback by such a question from a relative she has only just met, Eva says, "No, I've never heard of him. Or her, or—"

"No matter." Aila holds out the big basket she has carried all the way to Eva's house. "Here. Eat a bowl of these every night before you go to bed with Antti."

Sanna looks into the basket. "Blueberries?" she says, narrowing her eyes at her sister. "That's your big secret?"

Aila gives an offhand wave. "You'll see."

Ten months later, Eva gives birth to a healthy boy. She continues to eat blueberries for many years. She and Antti eventually have seven more children, all with blond hair and blue eyes, and whenever she meets a young wife who can't get pregnant, she tells her to eat blueberries just before bed.

13
Golden Gophers

John sat in an easy chair in the Koskinen family room eating popcorn and watching a track meet with Andy, Eva, and Lisa. During a commercial, Lisa said, "Dad, mute that, will you? I want to ask John about the Saami migration from—"

John held up a hand. "No Saami today. I want that story you promised me, Eva."

"Story?"

"About how you and Andy met."

"Oh, gosh," Eva said. "You don't really want to hear about all that old stuff."

John took a big handful of popcorn and settled into his chair. "You bet I do."

"Me too," Lisa said. "Hang on a sec, let me go get my notebook."

* * *

Minnesota, 1977

On a clear Saturday morning in September, two days before the start of classes, Andy is out for his regular run at the

University of Minnesota campus track. He sees a black woman in white shorts and a red top running ahead of him and smiles at her as he passes her. After he circles the track once more, he stands on the sideline and watches her run three more laps, then head for a bench at the track's edge. He walks over to her.

"Hi, I'm Andy. You're new around here, aren't you?"

Oldest pickup line in the book, Eva thinks, but she smiles at him as she towels off. "Yes, this is my first—"

"Eva, over here! I'm in a no-parking zone." A blond woman is waving from one of the stadium exits.

"Well, that's my ride." Eva gets up to leave.

"Hope to see you again," Andy says, and watches her jog to her friend's car, mentally kicking himself for not asking if she's going to run again tomorrow. The next day, she isn't there, but on Monday, on the way to his first class, he sees her walking ahead of him, and his heart flips in his chest.

"Hey, Eva, it's great to see you," he says, catching up to her at the classroom door.

"Hi. Andy, right? Are you in this class too?"

"I am," he says as he opens the door for her and follows her in. Eva takes a seat in the front row, opens her notebook, and pats the empty seat beside her.

"I already have an assigned spot," he says. He turns, walks to the podium, and waits while the class settles down. "Welcome to advanced microbiology. I'm Professor Andy Koskinen."

Eva covers her mouth with her hand to hide her surprise.

After his lecture, Andy walks briskly up the aisle after her and invites her for lunch in the faculty dining room. "Meatloaf today, I think," he says.

"Great. My favorite basic food group."

He laughs and starts to take her notebook to carry it for her, just like in high school when he had that crush on Sandy Beckham. He decides against it. What is happening here?

They go through the food line, and Andy leads the way to the only open seats he sees, at track coach Bill Erickson's table. "Coach," he says, "this is—"

"—Eva Jefferson, the best woman runner I've ever seen. Great to have you here, Eva. I heard you opted for a medical fellowship instead of the Olympic track team tryouts. It was the Olympics' loss, if you ask me."

"The Olympics?" Andy says.

She shrugs. "I love running, but a woman can't make a living running track."

"Sad but true," Coach says. "What kind of doctor do you want to be?"

"Oh, I don't want to practice. I want to do medical research."

Andy swallows a bite of meatloaf. "What area?"

"Genetics, DNA research into diseases. It's a young field, but it's fascinating. Well, it is to me. Oh, before I forget, can either of you recommend a good department store? I'm a Mississippi girl, and I don't have any clothing that's warm enough for Minnesota."

"Not me," Coach says. "Wife does all the shopping." He picks up his tray and walks off as if the very idea of himself in a department store affronts his manhood.

"What a coincidence," Andy says. "I'm going to go buy myself some socks right now. Would you like to join me?"

"I'd love to. Excuse me, I have to visit the ladies' room first."

While he waits for her, Andy's mind drifts back to his

senior year at the university and the terrible Sunday when his fiancée was killed in a car crash on her way back from her parents' home in Duluth. That afternoon he'd just returned to his apartment from a track meet, in high spirits because he'd broken the school record for the two-mile race, when the phone rang. "Linda's dead," her father said, sobbing.

All Andy can remember after that is slumping to his knees and screaming "No!" over and over again, as if that will turn back time. Since Linda's death, his life has consisted of research, teaching, and running track. The biology department dean's wife keeps trying unsuccessfully to fix him up with dates. He attends a party once in a while but goes home early and alone. His only entertainment is watching sports on TV, going to Golden Gophers games at the school, and taking in an occasional Vikings game. Sports distract him from the pain of losing Linda. He runs several miles nearly every day and drinks too much at night.

As he waits for Eva, Andy wonders if he's at a turning point in his life.

Andy drives across the Mississippi River into downtown Minneapolis and takes Eva to several department stores. At one store, Eva steps out of the dressing room in purple wool pants and a white cable-knit sweater. "What do you think?" she asks Andy.

He looks her up and down slowly and smiles.

"You look terrific in that outfit," the saleslady says. "I think your boyfriend really likes it."

It's almost dark when they return to St. Paul. A few blocks from her apartment, Eva points to a busy supermarket. "Would you mind stopping here for a minute? I'm about

out of food."

"Sure," Andy says.

At the apartment, Eva deposits her shopping bag on a chair and thanks Andy for carrying in the groceries. "Would you like to stay for dinner?" she asks, peering into one of the sacks. "Let's see, how about fried chicken, mashed potatoes, and gravy? And those Le Sueur peas you recommended?"

"Sounds delicious."

"By the way, I'm curious. What kind of food do Minnesotans usually like?"

He's never thought about it before. "Well, we're mostly farmers from the Scandinavian countries. We eat a lot of roasted meat—beef, pork, ham, or chicken—with mashed potatoes and gravy and a vegetable. Your dinner menu fits right in."

Just then an attractive blond appears from the hallway. "Annie, this is Andy," Eva says. "Andy, this is my roommate."

"Pleased to meet you," he says.

"Same here, but I've got to run. I'm going to Darren's for pizza and Monday Night Football, Eva. You're right, though, he sure is good-looking," Annie says as she flies out the door.

Eva blushes and goes into the kitchen. Andy joins her and watches her make dinner from his barstool. "Can I help you with something?"

"No, just sit there and relax. You can help me set the table after I fry the chicken."

"So, what does your family eat?"

"A lot of this." She jabs at the chicken, which is sending off a wonderful aroma. "And pork and fish, served with rice or potatoes with gravy. And vegetables—corn, black-eyed peas, cauliflower, collard greens—and of course grits."

"What on earth are grits?"

She laughs. "You've never heard of grits? It's ground corn that looks like cream of wheat. We eat grits at breakfast, with sunny-side-up eggs and bacon, or maybe ham and biscuits. And the South is famous for desserts too. Peach or apple cobbler, eaten warm, with vanilla ice cream."

"My mom makes a mean blueberry pie," Andy says. "And she serves it warm, with vanilla ice cream."

"Another coincidence," Eva says, turning over the chicken. "Would you like a beer? Or some wine?"

It's the first time in the years since Linda died that Andy hasn't wanted a drink before dinner. "No thanks. But please help yourself."

After the meal, they sit in the living room with their coffee. It is quiet except for an occasional car passing by outside.

"Where's your family from?" Eva asks.

"They were dairy farmers in Finland," he says. "They came over in the late 1800s." He tells her the highlights of his family's history after coming to the United States, and she tells him some stories about her parents and grandparents and the founding of Mound Bayou, Mississippi.

"My folks were resilient," Andy says. "They had to be. Minnesota winters are brutal, and there was no electricity back then. My father and mother got married in Hibbing, Minnesota, and later moved to Moose Lake, where I grew up."

"Moose Lake? That's an interesting name. But wow, it sounds like a tough life. Now look at you, a college professor!"

"We all have our burdens to carry," he says, "but my mine don't compare to yours, what with your slavery background and the civil rights struggle. I read about school integration in Mississippi years ago. How is it now? Things any better there?"

Eva looks away suddenly and stares out the window.

"It's okay," Andy says. "I understand if you don't want to talk about it."

She turns back to him. "Some whites murdered a relative of mine because he was going to marry a white girl."

"My God."

"It's getting better, but there's still segregation, and there's still plenty of racism. My parents are worried about me going to a mostly white university, but so far it's been okay."

"I think you'll find most people here friendly and tolerant," Andy says. "That's generally true of Scandinavian people. And color's never been an issue at the university as far as I know."

They continue talking about their families, her interest in genetics, and whatever else comes to their minds. Finally, Andy glances at his watch.

"Good Lord, it's ten o'clock. I have to finish my lecture notes for tomorrow." He stands. "This has been a great day. Thanks for everything."

"Thanks for the peas," Eva says, squeezing his hand.

That night Andy falls asleep thinking about Eva, and he wakes up thinking about her too, and that feels good.

Eva is nervous about seeing Andy this morning. Will it be awkward for him to have her in his class? She takes a seat in the back, trying not to call attention to herself, but she hangs on every word of his lecture.

Andy puts down his notes and leans forward on the podium. "Dean Peterson is having a barbecue on Saturday," he says. "Teachers, staff, and grad students are invited. If you need a ride, see me sometime this week."

After class, he stops Eva as she's leaving. "Can I give you a lift to the barbecue? I hope I'm not being too forward."

Too forward, she thinks, delighted. What a charming, old-fashioned way to put it. "Not at all," she says.

"Great. I'll pick you up at eleven."

As Eva walks down the hall behind two of her female classmates, she hears one say to the other, "Did you see that? Maybe Professor Koskinen is finally breaking out of his shell."

Eva wonders what that means, but it doesn't stop her from feeling good for the rest of the week. When Andy arrives at eleven sharp on Saturday, she's wearing her new purple pants and white sweater.

"How many other students are you picking up?" she asks as she gets into his car.

He grins. "None."

At Dr. Peterson's lakeside home, they're greeted by his wife, Suki, an attractive Asian woman. Andy introduces himself and Eva, and Suki leads them through the spacious house, across a manicured lawn, to a plump man wearing Bermuda shorts who turns out to be Dr. Peterson. He raises his glass and salutes Eva.

"Glad you're here, glad you accepted the fellowship, must've been a hard choice."

"I beg your pardon?"

"You know, between Good and Evil. Between the scholarship and the Olympic team."

Eva laughs, and Suki takes her around to meet the other guests, many of them professors and department members.

With all the attention from the dean's wife, Eva feels like a princess. When they rejoin Andy, Suki suggests that the two of them go for a scenic boat ride on the lake with two other couples, and by the time they return, most of the guests have left. Andy goes over to talk with Dr. Peterson while Eva helps Suki collect used paper plates and plastic glasses.

"You know," Suki says, "you remind me of myself years ago, when I met my husband."

"Oh?" Eva chases down an errant glass and tosses it into the trash barrel.

"Sit down," Suki says. "I have a story to tell you. When I got here from Hong Kong, straight off the boat, I enrolled in the university, and Jimmy"—she casts a fond eye at her husband—"was my freshman-year biology professor. He was so handsome, and I adored his class, and we fell in love, but because I was his student, we kept it secret."

Eva thinks she sees where the conversation is heading. She's afraid that Suki is about to tell her to stay away from Andy. With all her heart, she hopes not.

"You really like Andy, don't you?" Suki says.

Eva's breath catches. "Yes, I do. I think . . . I think I'm falling in love with him."

"I think he's falling in love with you too, Eva, and that makes me happier than I can say. Andy's fiancée was killed in a car accident five years ago, and I don't think he's dated anyone since. Don't be afraid to take the first step."

Back at Eva's apartment building, Andy escorts her to the door and says good night, but he's clearly not ready to leave her.

Don't be afraid to take the first step. "Would you like to come in?" Eva says.

Andy and Eva spend every day together for the next four weeks. One Saturday morning, over a breakfast of grits and eggs at Andy's house, he says, "Move in with me, Eva."

She gets up and sits on his lap. "I'll start packing right now," she says, running her fingers through his hair.

He kisses her neck and slides his hand under the waistband of her flannel pajamas. "Not right now, wait until after morning dessert."

It's Thanksgiving break, and Andy has invited her to Moose Lake. They take off the next day, the brisk air clouding with snowflakes on the drive up. Snow is a scarce commodity where Eva comes from. She watches out the window as it bathes the land in white.

"I'm worried," she says, turning to Andy.

"Worried? Why?"

"What if your parents don't like me? And the whole town is white, isn't it?"

He strokes her arm. "It'll be fine. Everyone will love you. And my parents have been downright eager to meet you since I told them about your vast intelligence and your fabulous personality. I poured it on thick. Mom asked me to send photos of you, and the next time I talked to her, she said you were gorgeous, a real beauty, and Dad said you looked like a movie star. We'll have a great Thanksgiving, and then you'll owe me one."

"Owe you?"

"Well, it stands to reason. You visit my parents, I visit yours."

"No!" She grips his knee hard. "Andy, we can't go to

Mississippi, it's not safe, you don't know how it is down there. They'll run us out of town when they see us together."

"Hey, this is America, how bad can it be?" Andy says, hoping she can't hear the trepidation in his voice. They drive in silence until they reach his parents' house.

Eva holds Andy's arm as they walk up the front steps, recently cleared of snow. She is hesitating at the door when Andy's father flings it open. "Welcome, Eva!" he says.

"Thank you, Mr. Koskinen."

"Thomas. And this is my wife, Amanda."

"Come in, Eva. Did you have a nice trip?" Amanda asks.

"I'm so happy to meet you," Eva says, touched by their genuine warmth. "Andy has told me wonderful things about you and your family."

She and Andy get settled in their rooms and then join his parents in the living room.

"So, the buzz around town is that Andy has a black girlfriend," Amanda says. "Everyone wants to meet you. Why, you're the first black person ever to visit Moose Lake."

Eva's stomach lurches and drops back down with a thud she is certain everyone can hear.

"Mom, you told the whole town about us?"

"Of course, Andy. In fact, go put your coats on again. We're meeting some people at Hart's for dinner. Henry and Barbara and the kids are there already."

"My brother and his family," Andy says to Eva.

Eva tries not to show how nervous she is as they pile into Andy's car and drive along the lakeshore, crossing a bridge where the lake flows down rapids into a river. The restaurant is right on the lake, surrounded by pine trees. Andy holds the door for Eva, and she steps into a sea of ruddy white faces sipping beer from frothy mugs. He introduces her to Henry and Barbara and some of his friends.

"I hear you're a runner," Henry says.

"Oh, uh, yes. And I hear Andy was a good athlete in high school, track and basketball."

Andy's cousin Mert winks at him. "Did he tell you he once played for the Lakers, Eva?"

Astonished, she punches Andy's arm. "You never told me you played professional basketball!"

He laughs. "Well, Mert, now you have to tell the rest of the story."

Mert wipes beer foam from his mouth. "The Los Angeles Lakers weren't the first or only team to be called the Lakers."

"Right, I remember, originally they were the Minneapolis Lakers, weren't they?" Eva says.

"Very good. But there was another Minnesota team that had the name first. Drum roll, please. It was . . . the Moose Lake Lakers!"

Andy and Mert clink mugs amidst chants of "Lakers! Lakers! Lakers!"

Eva relaxes, realizing that her fears were pointless.

Later that night, she is in the kitchen helping Amanda with Thanksgiving preparations when she hears humming from down the hall. She listens, entranced. "That's a beautiful song," she says.

"It's Barbara singing her kids to sleep," Amanda says.

"Is it a Finnish lullaby?"

"Yes, a very old one. Maybe Andy can teach it to you."

***

Eva smiled, remembering. "And he certainly did teach me that song."

"I still love hearing you sing it to the rug rats, Mom," Lisa said.

"That's no way to refer to your brother and sister. They're ten years old, and they've just about outgrown lullabies."

"What happened next?" John asked.

"Aren't you all tired of listening to me run my mouth?"

"Are you kidding? I can't wait to hear the rest. Pass the popcorn," John said.

Eva sighed. "Well, if you're going to know the whole story, guess I'd better tell it."

***

Mississippi, 1978

Back at the university, Andy keeps bugging Eva about taking him home to meet her family. She always finds a way to change the subject until he gives her an actual date: June 11, when his classes are over and he has a couple of free weeks before teaching a summer course. He is so insistent that she doesn't put him off, doesn't tell him that it isn't safe or that she's talked to her parents about it and they agree.

They cross the Mississippi border south of Memphis and keep heading south on Highway 61. Andy keeps an eye on his gas gauge and stops in a small town when he sees he's running low. He gets out of the car, starts the pump, and goes into the station to use the bathroom.

Eva sits staring at her hands, wishing he hadn't left, trying not to worry, forcing herself to listen to the soft dinging of the gas pump. It clicks off, and a shadow falls over the dashboard. Someone taps on her window.

She looks up to see two white men in ragged T-shirts with cigarette packs rolled up in the sleeves. The taller one smiles at her with brown teeth. "Afternoon, ma'am."

Where is Andy? She stares past them to the station and sees him coming out the door. The two men see him too. *Andy, be careful, please be careful.*

Andy steps briskly toward them. "Can I help you?"

The taller one grins and takes a swig from a wrinkled paper sack. "Why, lookee here. You got a pretty nigger in your car. Are you a nigger lover?"

"Watch your language," Andy says angrily.

As he starts around the car, the shorter man steps forward and swings at him. Andy blocks his fist and throws a hard right punch, striking him squarely in the nose. The man falls to the ground groaning. The second man comes at Andy from the side, and Andy lands a powerful punch to his stomach. The man doubles over in pain.

The station attendant, an old man wearing a frayed blue shirt with the gas company's name stitched over the right pocket, runs from the building. "I called the *po*-lice," he says. "I seen it all."

Andy is relieved, but Eva grits her teeth, her fear rising.

Siren wailing, a police car pulls in from the road. A young officer steps out and surveys the two men. "What happened here?" he asks.

"I seen it all," the attendant repeats. "I was lookin' out the window and seen this man hit them. He didn't give them no warnin' at all."

My God, it's happening. History repeats, again and again. Eva sits frozen, watching the scene unfold as if it is some sick stage play and she has a front-row seat.

"No, they started the fight," Andy says.

The officer demands his driver's license, and when Andy hands it over, he stares at it, then back at Andy, then back at the license. His face loses its scowl.

"Andy Koskinen? The Flying Finn from Moose Lake?"

Stunned, Andy can only manage, "I beg your pardon?"

The officer points to the name tag on his uniform. "John Makinen. Used to live in Minnesota, in Carlton. You don't remember me, do you?"

"Well . . . no."

"I ran against you in high school, right before you won the state championship, and I followed your career as a Golden Gopher and then a Big Ten champion runner."

"You know, you do look familiar," Andy says.

"What's a fellow Finn doing in Mississippi?"

Andy nods toward Eva. "My friend and I are headed to her parents' home in Mound Bayou."

The officer turns to Andy's attackers and the station attendant, all standing there in disbelief. "You two guys move on up the road," he says. "I ought to cuff you and take you in, but I didn't see what happened, and I can't trust the witness. There's no way Andy Koskinen started that fight."

"But how did you end up in Mississippi, John," Andy asks as he puts his driver's license away.

"Hey, it's only a short boat ride down the river from where we grew up. I was stationed here in the air force, and I married me a southern belle when I got out. Minnesota was too cold for her, so I joined the Mississippi State Highway Patrol. We live in Cleveland now, that's where she's from."

Eva leans out the car window. "Cleveland? I might know your wife. What's her name?"

"Imaya. Half Choctaw Indian."

"I had a good friend named Imaya at Cleveland High School. Class of seventy-three?"

"That's her. What's your name?"

"Sorry, John, I should have introduced you," Andy says. "This is Eva Jefferson."

John's eyes open wide. "Eva Jefferson! Another track star. Imaya talks about you a lot. Wow, this is crazy, meeting both of you here in Mississippi." He opens his wallet, pulls out a business card, scribbles on it, and hands it to Andy. "Here's my home number and the Highway Patrol dispatch number. I'll tell Imaya we met. She'll be really happy to see you again, Eva. And look, call me if you have any more trouble."

When Andy and Eva drive up to her parents' farmhouse, he's as nervous as she was back in Moose Lake, but the welcoming hugs from her father and mother and assorted aunts, uncles, and children put him at ease. Within minutes she can tell he feels like a long-lost relative finally returning home.

"Well, can't stand around talking all day, time for me to start dinner," her mother says.

"Anything I can do to help, Mrs. Jefferson?" Andy asks.

"Yes, you can stop calling me Mrs. Jefferson. Everyone calls me Oni. Now you two run along."

Eva takes Andy for a walk around the farmyard, and she points out all the things that bring memories from her past: a barn with broken door hinges, a chicken house that's still full of cackling white hens, the lane that runs between the cotton fields and disappears into a small woods. She sits in the tractor-tire swing and he pushes her, listening to the squeak of the chain and the cawing of a crow in the distance.

"I was surprised by how warm your parents were to me," he says.

"Well, what did you expect?"

"I don't know. I guess I just remember those stories about the past."

She puts her feet out to stop the swing. "Mom and Dad know how much I love you. That means a lot. And I told them about the reception your parents gave me in Moose Lake and said I wanted them to treat you the same way. You are probably the first white person they've ever hugged." She shrugs. "Hey, it's a start."

Andy laughs and kisses her hard on the lips.

That evening, after a delicious dinner of fried chicken, they take another walk around the farm. Everything is quiet, as if the world has already gone to sleep for the night. They walk through a cotton field, between rows of green plants that throw long shadows onto their legs. Andy stops and puts his arms around her.

"I'm glad we came," Eva murmurs into his chest.

"Me, too." After a moment, he releases her, reaches into his pocket, and pulls out a tiny box. He opens it and holds it out to her. "I want to spend the rest of my life with you," he says. "Will you marry me?"

"Oh, Andy. My mother has always told me that when I meet the right man, I should follow my heart. Well, I have, and I will." She slips the ring on her finger.

In late August, before school starts, they return to Mississippi and are married in Mound Bayou. Andy's family and friends from Minnesota attend, and so do John and Imaya Makinen. When the newlyweds head back north, John provides them with a special escort to the Tennessee border.

Three years later, Eva graduates from the University of Minnesota with a PhD in microbiology, and they move to San Francisco when she gets a job with a start-up biotech company. Andy easily finds a position as a biology professor at San Francisco State University.

* * *

"And you were born the following year," Eva said, smiling at Lisa. "So there were plenty of happy endings from that trip to Mississippi. Now can we get back to the track meet?"

"Mom, it ended hours ago!"

14
Clan Splits

The Saturday before Christmas, John turned up at the Koskinens' door with his omnipresent briefcase and an armload of packages.

"Well, what a nice surprise," Eva said. "Come on in. Down, Sukie!"

"Guess I should have called, but things have been crazy, and I thought I'd take a chance on catching you at home."

"You're in luck. We're watching the Forty-niners game."

"How's it going?"

"The Panthers are creaming them."

John reached down and scratched Sukie's ears. "Man, the Niners have been biting it ever since Steve Young got that concussion and had to sit out the rest of the season."

"Yes, a darn shame," Eva said, "but come join us, unless you'd rather go upstairs and watch cartoons with the twins."

"The game can't be worse than SpongeBob—or can it?" he said as he followed her into the family room

"John! I thought you'd already left for the holidays." Andy hauled himself out of his recliner to greet his guest as Lisa waved from the couch.

"Not yet, but I'm just about to take off, and I wanted to stop by first," John said, depositing his packages on the coffee table and sitting down next to Lisa. "I have some news."

Lisa turned to him expectantly. For the last week, she'd been itching with questions about the Saami.

"I'm getting married."

There was a moment of stunned silence before Andy said, "Well, I'll be. We didn't even know you were dating. Who's the lucky girl?"

"Her name's Daphne, and I met her two years ago at an anthropology conference. She teaches at UCLA, so we don't see each other much except on breaks, and we're tired of being so far apart. I've taken a leave of absence for next semester, and I'm moving down there to look for a job. Professor Rutherford was awfully nice about it."

"We wish you nothing but the best, John," Eva said, "but we're certainly going to miss you, aren't we, Lisa?"

"Yes, we are," Lisa said forlornly.

John flashed her a smile. "Before I migrate to L.A., I've got some other news. Based on language and genetics, I think the Finns and the Saami lived together way back in time."

"What?" Andy said. "You mean before they hooked up in Finland six thousand years ago?"

"*Way* before." John pulled three maps from his briefcase. "I'm talking before the start of the last ice age twenty-four thousand years ago. For more than ten thousand years before that, there was a major warming of the climate that created good habitable land all across most of Asia and Europe. The Finns and the Saami probably lived together around the Caspian Sea or the Black Sea during this time. Modern man

MAP, HABITABLE LANDS, 32,000 YEARS BP

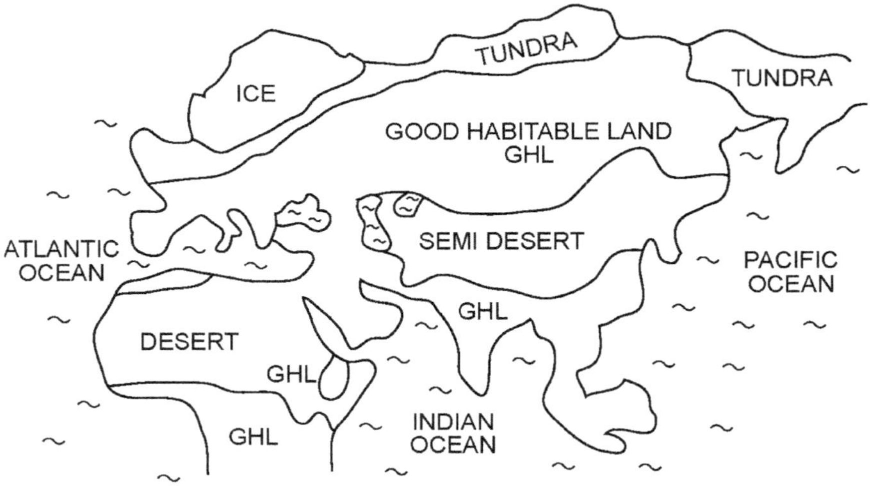

MAP, VOLGA AND DANUBE RIVERS

MAP, MIGRATION ALONG DANUBE RIVER

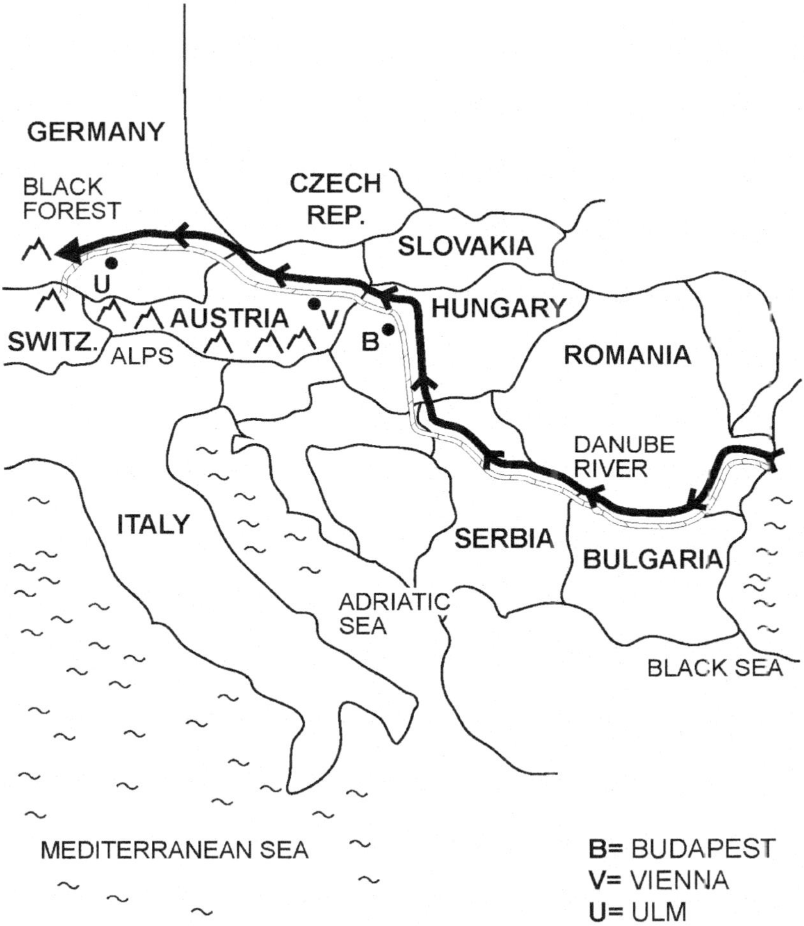

first migrated into Europe to these two areas after the long journey from Africa. Then, when the Finns and the Saami split up, the Finns would have headed north up the Volga into central Russia, and the Saami would have gone east along the Danube to central Europe. During the last ice age, the Saami would have retreated southwest, eventually reaching Spain, and the Finns would have retreated back down the Volga until things warmed up enough for them to head north and meet up with the Saami again."

"It's almost impossible to comprehend these vast spans of time and distance," Eva said. "What was the world like before the last ice age?"

"A global warming of the climate started about thirty-five thousand years ago and lasted until the beginning of the last ice age. Conifer woodlands spread from the Pacific Ocean in Asia to the Atlantic Ocean in Europe. Vegetation, animals, and human life flourished for more than ten thousand years across Asia and Europe. There were bountiful herds of woolly mammoth and deer in the Great Kirghiz Steppes in southwest Kazakhstan and in southern Russia around the Volga Delta, where the river flows into the Caspian Sea. Rivers grew larger as ice and snow melted on mountains everywhere. Like I said before, the Volga and the Danube became major migration paths. They're the two longest rivers in Europe."

While John was speaking, Lisa had recovered from her shock at his announcement, giving herself a stern internal lecture about the foolishness of her crush on him. Resolving not to let her feelings get in the way of her interest in his work, she asked, "What were the people like then?"

"Well, it was a little before my time, but I have a pretty good idea. Many different clans left Africa and walked to Asia and Europe over the course of thousands and thousands of years. Members of the same clan and clan clusters were connected to each other through their common language and need to survive. Smaller and less resilient clans that could not survive on their own joined larger clans and learned their language. The larger clans did not typically merge with other large clans, sometimes because of language differences, and sometimes because they simply wanted to determine their own destiny. Eventually, after migrating far north of the equator, people absorbed significantly less of the sun's ultraviolet radiation than their ancestors had in Africa, and their skin color slowly changed from black to brown, and often their hair and eyes got lighter too."

"That's just what you were telling us a while ago, Mom," Lisa said.

"Yes, but I still haven't gotten much further with my research, so I'm glad we have an expert to fill us in, even if not for long. How big were these clans, John?"

"The successful clans and clan clusters probably ranged from one hundred to two hundred members. Greater numbers made it easier to hunt large animals and herds but at the same time made it harder to keep everybody happy with all the decisions that were necessary. Remember, they were still hunter-gatherers then, and they had to move constantly. The task of the clan chieftain and shaman became increasingly difficult when the clans were too large."

"Shaman? Is that like a witch doctor?" Lisa asked.

"No, more like a healer and spiritual guide."

"Our team could sure use a shaman." Andy pointed to

the TV, where the scoreboard was showing the final game results: Panthers 41, 49ers 24.

***

South Russia, 32,000 Years Before Present

Seven-year-old Saa and her twin sister Eva are playing the game of round stones with Anni and another older girl when Anni asks suddenly, "Why does everyone in your family have such short names, Eva?"

"Our mother says that's the way we honor our ancestors," Eva replies.

"And they're easier to say," Saa adds.

"Well, they sound funny," Anni declares. "Whenever someone calls your father 'Hei,' it sounds like grunting." She and the other girl laugh.

When the game is over, Saa and Eva pick up their round stones and go home. They find their mother, Shaman Lee, gathering plants, and they tell her what happened. "Why can't we have longer names like the others?" Saa asks.

"We have always taken the names of our parents and grandparents," Lee says. "I'm proud of them, and you should be too. Our Hei-Lee clan is named after our ancestors from long, long ago."

That night, after the girls are asleep, Lee tells Hei and his brother, Tau, about the teasing. "Saa wishes she had a longer name."

"You know, I did too when I was young," Hei says. "I never mentioned it because I didn't want to upset my parents, but maybe it's time."

Lee frowns. "It would be hard to change our names after so long."

Tau shrugs. "We won't change them, we'll just add to them."

"Yes," Hei says, "I agree with brother Tauno."

"No!" Tau says.

"That's it!" Hei says, "Tauno!"

Tau considers. "I like it. Tauno sounds good, like a chief's name."

"And I will be Heikki, and you, my dear wife, will be Leesa, and Saa will be happy to be Sari, and Eva—"

"Will have ideas of her own," says the newly christened Leesa.

Eva does. She likes her name and keeps it. "It's short, but it already takes two beats to say it, and I'm sure Ann-*ee* will approve," she tells her family to general laughter.

Soon other clan members are trying out longer names and adopting those that sound good to them. Lee's sister Ee becomes Ena, and her cousins Joh, Tu, and Ou become Johan, Tulli, and Outti, but the Hei-Lee clan name will stay the same, she and Heikki decide. It is part of their identity, and surely changing it will displease their ancestors.

Years later, it is time for Heikki and Leesa to choose husbands for Sari and Eva. Because the Hei-Lee clan cluster is so large, there are many fine young men to choose from. The difficulty is in deciding which daughter and her husband will become the next clan shaman and chief. Should they choose one of the twins as the next shaman and then choose a husband and future chief for her? Or should they choose the best young man and then decide which daughter will marry him?

They settle on the last course and narrow the field to two strong candidates, Tauno and Antti. Young Tauno is a distant nephew of Heikki's brother. Antti is the son of Aman, who is Heikki's close cousin and has been openly campaigning for his son. Heikki knows that Aman doesn't care which daughter his son marries; he just wants Antti to lead the clan. After much discussion, Heikki and Leesa choose Tauno to be the next chief and Sari to be his wife and shaman. Eva is disappointed that she will not be the clan's shaman someday, but she resigns herself to the decision, knowing that Sari will fulfill their mother's role with diligence and honor.

Aman isn't resigned at all. The night after the announcement, he stalks over to Heikki's tent, jaws clenched. "My son would be a much better chief than Tauno," he says. "Antti is a much closer relative, and he would be much more loyal to the clan."

Heikki shakes his head. "The decision has been made and announced. Tauno will marry Sari, and he will become the next chief. You will accept my choice—"

"I will not!" Enraged, Aman turns as if to leave, then turns back with a knife in his hand. He thrusts it deep into Heikki's chest, and with a loud groan, Heikki falls to his knees.

Leesa bolts from the tent and sees Aman running away. She looks down. Heikki lies there bleeding, the knife protruding from his chest. She drops to his side and pulls it out, pressing her hands to the wound as hard as she can and calling for help.

"Heikki, don't leave me," she whispers into his ear.

He looks up at her and tries to speak but only manages a

gargling noise. His eyes close.

As the clan members arrive in response to Leesa's cry, Eva and Sari come rushing up from the riverbank and stare at their father's body in horror. When Leesa tells them what happened, all the hunters set off at a run.

They track Aman down and kill him.

In the wake of her father's death, Sari wants to postpone her wedding, but Leesa insists that the clan must carry on. Sari marries Tauno, but they decide to wait before following the tradition of taking the names of their predecessors. When Eva comes to Leesa tearfully and says that she loves Antti despite his father's unthinkable act, Leesa looks past her deep grief and allows the pair to marry. Antti and Eva become chief and shaman of a small new clan in the Hei-Lee cluster.

While most of the clan feels that justice has been served by the killing of Aman, his children and relatives suffer from lingering ill feelings. Not long after his marriage, Antti goes to Chief Tauno. "It is too painful for us to stay here. Eva and I will move north, up the river that flows here into the sea, and we will start a new clan with those who want to go with us."

Tauno sits silently, looking out at the bustling activity of the camp. He knows of the pressure Antti is under, unfair pressure, but the clan will never forget the murder of their beloved chief. And Antti's offer can solve another dilemma; the clan cluster has grown too large to manage easily, and is certainly large enough to split into two.

"I understand, Antti," he says slowly. "You and Eva may form a new cluster, and the rest of the clan will decide whether to go with you or stay with me."

That summer, each Hei-Lee clan member announces his

or her choice. It is a difficult decision, since all the clans share relatives and friendships. In the end, Tauno's clan cluster keeps more than half of all the members, but Antti's new cluster is big enough to hunt large herds.

The day before Antti and Eva are to start their journey north up the big river, the two clan clusters meet for a festival and a feast of deer meat. In the evening, as the fires built for cooking and to keep predators away are blazing high, Leesa takes her daughters and their husbands aside. She turns to Eva. "It is time for you to have your own necklace," she says, smiling. "It will continue to bind all our family together."

Tears come to Eva's eyes. She doesn't want to leave her mother and her sister and her clan, but she understands Antti's difficult position, and given the sad circumstances surrounding their departure, she has never expected to be honored with a necklace. By tradition, her father would have made the new necklace for her, but Tauno will assist Shaman Leesa tonight.

Leesa leads them all to a quiet glade outside the campsite and directs Tauno and Antti to build a small fire. They sit around it, and Leesa takes three sacred tooth necklaces from their leather pouches. Two of them have ten pairs of bear teeth, and the third has four pairs. With Tauno's help, she removes two teeth from the leather thong of the third necklace and strings them on a new thong. There is room for a few new cuts marks on one of the teeth, and Tauno takes a sharp flint and makes a careful, precise groove. Leesa watches, wishing her beloved Heikki were here to perform the sacred bonding ceremony.

"Heikki and I will be with all of you forever," she says,

fighting back tears. "Sari, Eva, I know your father is proud of you." She performs the ceremony by herself, cutting Eva's index finger, then Antti's, Sari's, Tauno's, and her own, and pressing each into the groove on the tooth to mingle the blood. Then she puts the new necklace around Eva's neck.

"Your new clan shall be known as the An-Eva clan," she says. "I wish you a safe journey up the river, and every blessing in the years to come."

The next morning, the An-Eva clan parts from the Hei-Lee clan and heads off to forge their own destiny, with promises to meet again someday.

Many moons later, a violent flood forces the Hei-Lee clan to move. With the big river overflowing its banks, they cannot join the An-Eva clan in the north. When scouts tell Chief Tauno that the deer herds are moving toward another sea far to the west, he decides to follow them.

After Leesa dies, Sari grieves deeply but takes comfort from the thought that her parents are together again. "Mother said when she visited me last night that it is time for us to take our traditional clan names," she tells Tauno, "and that if we keep sight of the sun as it disappears every day, we will always have food."

Sari and Tauno become Shaman Leesa and Chief Heikki, and over the next several moons, they and their clan follow the setting sun and the animal herds migrating west. The hunting is good, and the clan prospers. They eventually meet several other big clans at a river that flows south into another sea. These clans speak and completely different language, but through crude sign language, Heiki learns that they came from mountains to the south. Because they are so hard to communicate with, the Hei-Lee clan mostly leaves them alone.

Some of the cluster's smaller clans want to travel north upriver in search of deer, but Heikki remembers what Leesa's mother told her in her dream. Trusting his wife's words, he wants to cross the wide river and continue to follow the setting sun. He sends out two scouts who swim across and soon return with reports of big herds of wooly mammoth and deer in the plains just west of the river.

Heikki stands on the riverbank and peers across at a thin line of trees. Yes, they must go to the other side, but how? Most of the clan can't swim.

He finds a sharp bend in the river where it seems the crossing will be easier. Recalling stories of the ancestors who crossed rivers, he directs the clan to build big rafts from fallen trees and branches, tying them together with strips of animal hide. Several good swimmers board the first raft and use branches as paddles to help them find the river's current and drift over to the western shore. Once the whole clan is safely across, they keep going west until they reach a sea and camp beside it. Then, moving south along the seacoast, they reach a large river flowing from the west.

Leesa's parents still visit her dreams occasionally. Whenever her mother appears, she says that Leesa and Heikki and their clan must continue to follow the sun and the rivers, because they are the sources of life.

* * *

Danube River (Serbia, Hungary, Austria, and Germany), 30,000 to 24,000 Years Before Present

Chief Heikki leads his clan and a cluster of smaller clans away from the sea, following a big river west between mountains and gorges toward the setting sun. The weather is warm in the summer and mild in the winter. They see many other clans journeying west along the big river.

One summer Heikki tells his cluster of four small clans to set up separate campsites, each a long walk from the main Hei-Lee camp and from each other. He wants to make sure that there is plenty of open land for the women in each clan to forage for edible vegetation. Though the clans live at a distance, they meet at each full moon for joint deer hunts and festivals.

A few days after the new camps are established, Chief Hannu of one of the small clans comes running into the Hei-Lee camp in great distress. "A strange clan kidnapped three of our women while they were out gathering food," he tells Heikki. "One is my brother's wife. A fourth woman escaped by hiding in the bushes."

"Do you know where they took them?"

"Yes. Two of our scouts followed them to their camp on a hill not far from ours."

"How many in the camp?"

Hannu opens and closes his hands two times. "Men." He opens and closes his hands once. "Women and children."

Heikki nods and looks at the sky, which is darkening into night. "They probably need women for their clan. We'll scout their camp together tomorrow and then decide what to do."

They set out at daybreak, stopping first to check on Hannu's camp. As they approach cautiously, they see black smoke rising above the hill, and when they reach the top, they behold a terrible sight.

The camp is on fire. Men, old women, and children are lying on heaps of smoldering ashes, and the air is permeated with the foul smell of burnt flesh and death. Seeing the brutally murdered corpses of people he knows and loves, Hannu falls to the ground and weeps. Heikki weeps too, but his are tears of anger.

Hannu finds his brother Gan dead in a pool of blood. His wife and three more young women are missing. "I want my wife back," he shouts, "and I want to kill all of them."

"We will, Hannu, I give you my word. Show me where their camp is."

Hannu points to a hill in the near distance, and Heikki frowns. "Perhaps it isn't only the women they want. They probably didn't want you so close to their hunting grounds."

Two days later, Heikki leads all the men of the Hei-Lee clan cluster to the base of the hill where the raiders are camped. He quietly directs some to go with Tauno to the right, some to follow Kan to the left, some to stay with him, and the rest to go with Hannu. He meets Hannu's eyes, and they carry a resolve that matches his own.

"It is your job to find your women and guard them during the attack," he says, and watches the resolve in Hannu's eyes turn to bald hate.

It is a clear moonlit night. Heikki and the other three groups climb the hill and quietly surround the camp. He motions for the men to kneel. In the silence around him, he can hear the savages talking and laughing. Moments later, he stands and raises his long spear. "Strike! Strike!"

While Hannu and his men run to find the women, the rest of the men rush forward from every side and unleash a volley of spears at the unsuspecting enemies sitting around their fire pits. Screams of pain erupt as a second volley of spears strikes home.

Hannu finds the women's tent and leaves his men to guard it while he joins the fight. "Kill them!" he screams. "Kill them all!" He and Heikki and their clansmen make short work of the surviving savages with their knives. The surprise attack doesn't last long; soon it is quiet.

All the men of the enemy camp are dead except for one who escapes down the hill into the forest. Hannu's wife and the women of his clan are all safe. He and Heikki find other women and children hiding in a tent.

"What do you want to do with this clan's women and children?" Heikki asks.

Hannu confers with his wife for a moment, then says, "Our clan is gone. We'll take them and start a new clan if you'll help us."

Heikki nods. "Yes. Of course we will help you."

When Heikki is sure that Hannu's new clan is well established, he leads his own cluster on a trek up the blue river as it turns north in an area of fertile plains and large deer herds. His skilled hunters easily kill twenty deer in a joint hunt. Shaman Lisa and the clan's stronger women help butcher and transport the slain deer.

Chief Heikki and Shaman Lisa have always revered their ancestors and the sun, but now they worship the rivers and the deer as sources of life. They continue to move north and camp on hills overlooking the deep blue river that weaves past tall green trees and grassy plains.

One cold winter day, Shaman Lisa and her younger sister Ena are heating water in a big turtle shell so the mothers of the clan can bathe their babies and children. Lisa knows that if the water stays on the fire too long, it will boil and disappear. She dips a finger into the water to test it. Too hot. She takes a wooden cup and adds some cold water and keeps testing it until it is safe for the little ones.

The clan has many children, so the heating, testing, and cooling requires several cycles. Tired and hungry by the time they finish, Lisa and Ena sit down to a dinner of deer meat left over from the previous night. The meat is hard, tough, and cold because of the freezing weather.

Ena points to the turtle shell. "Let's heat more water and put the meat in to warm it." Lisa nods, and they have just finished cutting the meat into pieces and dropping them into the water when they hear a woman scream. They run to her and see that her little boy has fallen and cut his elbow badly. Lisa wraps leaves around the wound and tells the mother to press tight until the bleeding stops.

By the time they return to the campfire, the water is boiling and has turned brown. Fearing disaster, they scoop the meat out with their wooden cups, and when it cools enough, they taste it.

"Mmm, it's good," Lisa says in wonder. "The meat is juicy, and it's easier to chew." As she takes another bite, an idea occurs to her. She goes to a covered pile of frozen roots, grabs a few, and throws them into the shell, adding more water and meat.

"That smells good," Ena says when the water comes to a boil again. Scooping out a cupful, she blows on it, takes a taste, and grins at her sister. "Try it!"

Lisa and Ena experiment with different roots and plants, and soon the tasty new hot meal becomes a favorite in their camp.

The Hei-Lee clan keeps moving, living in tents and caves along the blue river and adapting to the long, cold winters. Deer hunting is good, and the clan cluster grows larger.

Early one summer, Chief Heikki's cousin Johan, who is chief of his own small clan, comes to him and says, "There are too many of us. I want to find another river."

Heikki thinks for a moment. "I don't usually like to split up the clan, but in this case, you're right. With so many people, it's hard to get everyone to agree on decisions about new camps and joint hunts. Much as I don't want you to go, it might be better for all of us." He puts his hands on Johan's shoulders. "You will be missed, but not forgotten."

"May I ask if any other clans want to join me?"

This idea isn't as palatable to Heikki, but he agrees. "As long as you don't steal all my best hunters and scouts," he says with a laugh.

Before Johan and his new clan depart, Lisa teaches them how to cook the new meal of meat and plants in hot water.

Heikki's clan continues west along the river toward the setting sun until they reach the foothills of high snow-capped mountains to the south. They find two limestone caves that are too small for a clan the size of theirs, so on a patch of flat ground they erect big warm tents made of deerskins, tree branches, and woolly mammoth tusks.

In the evenings at their hillside camp, they can see fires in the distance where other clans must be cooking their evening meals. On nights when their campfires dim and the skies are cloudless, they spend hours watching the thousands of bright stars, tracing different shapes and figures. Adults and children alike peer at the moon, which they call the night sun, until they are sure they can see the features of a face on the bright golden circle. Long ago they have learned that the night sun changes shape slowly, on a regular basis, and that the full circular shape always returns. They use this time interval as their calendar, and they know that the warmer weather of spring comes after every twelve full night suns.

The many bushes and trees in the foothills of the high mountains provide the clan with a variety of edible vegetation. Colorful flowers appear in the summer, including a attractive plant with white petals in a star pattern and a yellow center, which Shaman Lisa uses as medicine to relieve stomach pains.

Times are good. Nightly, the Hei-Lee clan gathers around the campfires after dinner to hum their children to sleep. Each family has its own humming songs, but everybody's favorite is the Lee hum song passed down from the ancestors. All the mothers and young women learn it, and many men join in humming it.

As the seasons pass, more and more clans begin hunting nearby, and the deer herds move west along the river. Chief Heikki knows it is once again time for the clan to follow them.

After they settle in their new camp, Shaman Lisa discovers a tall green plant, and Heikki discovers that its flower adds a pleasantly bitter tasted to the traditional brew he makes for special occasions of celebration or mourning, or for ritual observances to the sun, river, and deer gods, and to their ancestors.

Before one such occasion, a hunter kills a large bird that is cooked over the campfire, cut up, and passed around for all to enjoy. Heikki chews on a long leg bone, sucks the marrow out, and blows into the bone, which produces a strange sound that makes everybody look at him in surprise. He blows into the bone again, and the same sound comes out. Lisa takes the bone and inspects it, noticing that there are a few holes in it, probably from Heikki's teeth. She puts her finger over one of the holes, blows, and makes a different sound. She keeps the bird's other leg bone, and the next day she and Ena make holes in it with a sharp rock. They take turns putting their fingers over the holes and blowing until they learn to produce melodic sounds. From then on, they collect as many bird bones as they can find, poke them with holes, and sometimes play them while the other women hum to the children.

But even as this new tradition is forming, another one, central to the clan's identity, becomes imperiled.

One evening, Lisa is sitting with Heikki beside their campfire as he tells her about the day's hunt, but she is preoccupied and barely hears him. She gets up suddenly and goes into their tent, returning with the sacred tooth necklace. "Look at this," she says, holding it out to him.

"At what?" he asks, puzzled.

"There's no room on any of the teeth for another cut, just look. Our daughter is marrying at the next full moon, and we need two more bear teeth to start a new necklace for her. We must perform the blood-bonding ceremony, for surely the ancestors will be displeased if we do not."

Heikki inspects the necklace and sees that she is right. "Yes," he says, "but I haven't seen a bear, dead or alive, in many moons."

"Then look harder," Lisa says. "Either find a dead one or kill a live one. We must have those teeth."

Is she serious? Heikki hasn't been strictly truthful with her—for the last few days, he and his scouts have seen a bear coming down to the river to fish—but in his whole life he has never heard of anyone killing a bear. Deer are safe and easy targets, but anyone who attempts to kill a bear will more likely lose his own life.

Heikki thinks about his dilemma overnight, and a plan evolves. In the morning he goes to his cousin Tauno, who is sitting on a log sharpening a new spearhead.

"That bear we've seen down by the river?" he says. "We have to kill it. We need its teeth for the sacred necklace."

Tauno stares up at Heikki. "Impossible. You can't kill a bear, it will kill you first."

"But the bear always comes down from the same place and goes back to the same place. You'll think I've gone mad, but I have an idea."

Tauno considers the plan Heikki outlines. "It's risky, but it might work. When do you want to try?"

"Tomorrow. The bonding ceremony is soon. There is no time to spare."

Well before dawn, Heikki, Tauno, and a party of hunters collect several wooden shovels fashioned from logs, along with as many mammoth tusks as they can carry. They find a rock-free area behind a bush near the bear's regular path, and they use the tusks to break up the soil as they dig a pit as deep as a man is tall. They make stakes out of sturdy branches sharpened to a fine point, and they embed them firmly in the ground at the bottom of the pit. Then they cover the pit with branches and leaves, lay a big hunk of fresh deer meat on top, and retreat to the bushes to hide.

"There, there he is," Heikki whispers a short while later as the bear lumbers toward them, pausing to sniff the air. Heikki feels a spike of fear, but then the bear moves off the path, lunges for the meat, and falls into the pit.

Heikki signals his hunters, and they run to the pit to see the bear thrashing on the stakes, roaring so loudly that Heikki feels the earth tremble under his feet. They hurl their spears and rain big rocks down on the beast until at last it lies motionless.

"We did it! Heikki yells. "He's dead!" Whooping, he jumps into the pit, pulls his knife from its sheath, and claims the teeth, and the story of the bear and the pit becomes legend in the Hei-Lee clan.

***

"So that's how the Saami and the Finns started out together tens of thousands of years ago and found each other again millennia later," John said, "and that's the end of my lecture. I'd better get going, it's a long drive to L.A."

"But it's not the end of the story," Lisa said. "What are we going to do without you?"

John took one of the packages from the coffee table and

handed it to her. "Why don't you open this now?"

"Okay," she said, "if you want me to." She unwrapped the package methodically. "It's a book. It's . . . *your* book. *Prehistory Human Migration from Africa to Europe,* by John Anderson. Oh, John, that's awesome. Thank you."

"An advance copy, hot off the presses." John stood and picked up his briefcase. "Enjoy it, Lisa. It will take you all the way back to the beginning."

15
Black Skies

Over the holidays, Lisa spent every spare minute reading John's book. Whenever she finished a new chapter, she reported on it at dinner, causing the twins to roll their eyes and bolt from the table even faster than usual.

A few days after John's departure, Lisa came downstairs with the book and sat down at the kitchen table while Eva and Andy were fixing dinner together. "I know where the Finns and the Saami were before they got to the Caspian and Black Seas," she announced.

"Where?" Andy asked.

"The Indus River Valley. John says that early migration out of Africa was mostly eastward along the coast of the Indian Ocean toward India and Asia, but then there was this totally dramatic event that forced some of the clans to head north into the Indus Valley."

"I guess that's my cue to ask what happened," Eva said.

"Just trying to build a little suspense, Mom. What happened was that the Toba volcano in Sumatra, Indonesia, erupted about seventy-four thousand years ago, and it was the largest volcanic explosion in the last two million years. Winds blowing northwest carried volcanic ash high and dropped it in a carpet that was several feet thick and covered all of India, though it spared Thailand and most of the Malaysian Peninsula. It took hundreds and hundreds of years for India to recover." Lisa opened the book to a map that showed the area of coverage and read a paragraph from the facing page.

"'Clans that had migrated along the western coast of India and into the interior were buried under ash—scientsts have found stone tools under the ash layer—and the volcano's toxic gases also spread, killing humans and animals alike. But winds blowing south from the Himalayas and the Hindu Kush Mountains, along with eastward winds from the Sulaiman range in Pakistan, prevented the Toba ash from reaching the Indus River in central and northern Pakistan. Animals fleeing the falling ash found refuge in the Indus Valley, providing good hunting for the clans that survived. The numerous rivers flowing into the valley from the Himalayas made it a fertile haven for modern man.'"

"How big is the valley? And how many people lived there?" Eva asked, taking the book from Lisa to study the map.

"It's several hundred miles long, but John says that back seventy-four thousand years ago there were probably only ten to twenty clans with maybe twenty-five to a hundred members each. These clans prospered as they slowly migrated north up the Indus River, and some moved to a large area east of the river called Punjab, which means 'land of five rivers.' The clans that continued north encountered colder winters as they neared the foothills of the Himalayas, and they learned to use narrow strips of hide to sew clothing, boots, blankets, and bedding out of animal furs and skins. They also

MAP, TOBA EXPLOSION,
AREA COVERED BY ASH, 74,000 BP

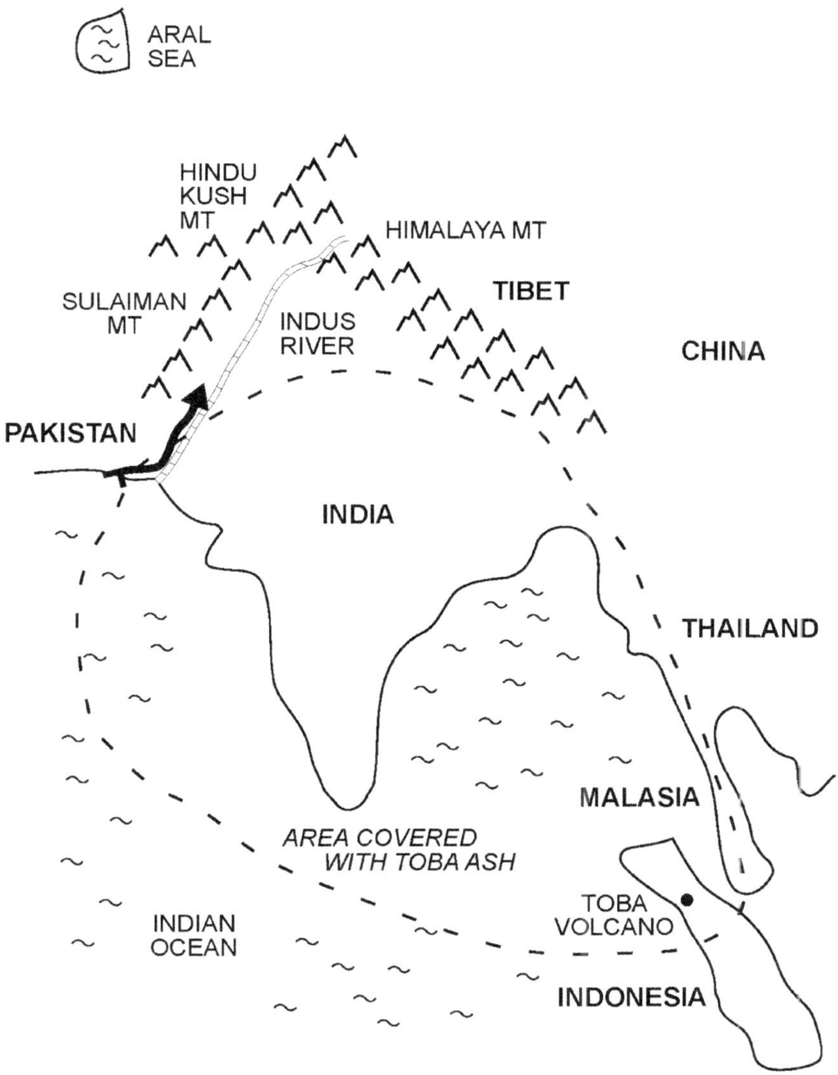

learned how to make their knives and spears stronger and sharper, and how to build enclosed lean-to shelters, and then big cone-shaped tents that gave them greater protection from the elements."

"You're a regular encyclopedia, aren't you?" Andy said. "What else do we know about these people? Anything about their religion?"

"John thinks they worshiped their ancestors, because many indigenous tribes still do today. After the Toba explosion, the sun and the rivers may have become gods for many of the clans. The sun gave them warmth, and the rivers gave them fresh water, fish, vegetation along their banks, and herds that came to drink. Shamans who had been praying to the ancestors probably started praying to the sun and river gods to bring their clans good fortune. The clans had shamans who were their spiritual leaders and prayed to the ancestors on the clan's behalf."

"Were these shamans men or women?" Eva asked, handing the book to Andy.

"Probably they were the wives of the clan chiefs, chosen because they were smart, clever, wise, and caring."

"Just like you, Eva," Andy said as he turned a page. "Hey, here's more about the shamans. 'The clans of that time depended heavily on animal meat and fish,'" he read, "'but many plants and trees in the fertile Indus River Valley provided valuable nourishment. Shamans learned which plants were edible, becoming experts through years of trial and error and passing their knowledge down to the next generation of shamans. They discovered a wide range of edible vegetation in the Indus Valley, including tree bark, twigs, leaves, cones, and seeds; many types of berry, such as chokeberries, raspberries, gooseberries, and mulberries; lichens and mosses; the seeds of various grasses; wild rose, cattails, and water lilies; fireweed, milkweed, thistle, and dandelions; and a variety of nuts and plant roots that they ate raw, mashed, or roasted over an open fire. The shamans also learned which plants could be used for medicinal purposes and became doctor/pharmacists to their clans. The shaman's multiple roles as spiritual leader, nutritionist, and medical guide became increasingly important as hunter-gatherer clans moved into diverse landscapes and weather conditions.'"

"Maybe I'll be a shaman when I grow up," Lisa said. "Can we have some roasted roots for dinner?"

* * *

Pakistan, 74,000 Years Before Present

"Hei! Come quickly! There is no sun!" Shaman Lee cries.

Her husband rushes out of their lean-to and sees her pointing at the horizon to the southeast of their camp in the wide valley near the big river. It is early in the morning, and the sun should be rising, but instead the sky is blackening.

Hei stares as other clan members run from their tents and crowd around their chief and shaman. "What is wrong? Have we angered the sun god?" an old man wails as the sun comes up, glowing red through the ominous clouds relentlessly advancing toward them.

Shaman Lee raises her arms to the sky and begins a guttural chant. When she finishes, she turns to the terrified clan members. "The sun god says we must go upriver, away from the black clouds."

"Then we will obey. All of you gather your children and all the provisions you can carry. We leave now," Hei says, but he lingers for a moment, gazing east and thinking of his brother, Joh. Many seasons ago, when the clan was camped near the delta of the big river flowing into the sea, food became scarce as more and more clans arrived. Hei decided to take the clan north up the river after the herds, but Joh protested, saying that the clan had always thrived by fishing along the coast and moving east when necessary. After a bitter argument, Joh announced his intention to keep to the coast, and half the clan chose to join him. Hei knew that the dispute had little to do with fishing and everything to do with the fact that his brother resented him and wanted to be chief of his own clan, but he loved Joh and was pained to see him go. Now, as he watches the black clouds claim the sky, he fears that they are blanketing Joh and his clan.

"Hei, help me with the children," Lee calls, snapping him out of his reverie, and he pulls himself together, assembles his clan, and leads them north up the river under the black sky.

***

Indus River, 72,000 Years Before Present

Shaman Lee wakes up smiling. Her parents have been dead for many years, but her mother visited her again in her dreams last night, looking as she did when Lee was young, and saying that the clan must always follow the rivers, the source of life. Yes, the sacred tooth necklace has bonded Lee well to her ancestors.

She glances at Hei lying beside her, and then at her twin girls asleep on their pallets. She knows that there are clans that don't look kindly on twins and sometimes give one away to another clan, or even kill it if food is scarce. The Hei-Lee clan cherishes their twins and all their children, and all the women help raise them. Children are not a burden, her mother has told her, they are a blessing. She thinks back fondly to when Saa and Sai were babies and she sang them to sleep with a melody she created by imitating the sounds of the winds and rivers. Now all the women sing Lee's hum song to their children.

Saa and Sai have grown into smart, strong, and beautiful young women. Lee has taught them what a shaman needs to know, and both are well qualified to succeed her when the time comes, but only one of them can receive the sacred necklace and become the next shaman. She and Hei have been wrestling with this dilemma for months and have finally made their decision. A week from today, Saa will marry Tau, the clan's smartest and strongest hunter, and they will become the next shaman and chief in due time. Sai will marry Jaa, another excellent hunter, from a smaller clan in the cluster.

When the girls wake and go off to forage for plants, Lee says to her husband, "I have been thinking about the sacred necklace. It will not be fair to give it just to Saa. We should give each girl part of it, create two necklaces where before there was one."

"We should and we will," Hei says, and watches as Lee

fetches the leather pouch, takes out the sacred tooth necklace, and removes two bear teeth, leaving two pairs of bear teeth and one of lion teeth on the thong. She strings the teeth on a new thong and hands it to Hei, who solemnly makes a cut mark on the tooth that still has room. The night after the double wedding, Hei and Lee preside over the blood-bonding ceremony, giving the original necklace to Saa and the new one to Sai.

"Saa, your necklace is older than Sai's," Hei says, "but both have the same significance. You and Tau will become our clan's next shaman and chief" — he turns to Sai and Jaa — "and because the clan is growing, you two will be shaman and chief of a new clan that will remain part of our cluster."

He nods to Lee, and she repeats the clan's age-old injunction. "You are married. Our blood and yours binds you to the Hei-Lee family forever. You will pass the necklaces on to your oldest daughters, and in turn they and their husbands will add their blood to new cut marks, and in this manner our family's spirit will live on until the end of time."

A few weeks later, the Hei-Lee clan cluster is migrating up the big river's west bank when scouts spot a deer herd moving north on the east bank. Sensing an opportunity, Jaa volunteers to take his clan across the river after the herd. He has his men build log rafts, and they ford the river and trek on until they find signs of the herd at a smaller river flowing into the big one. They follow the herd along the smaller river until darkness falls and they have to make camp.

Overnight, heavy storms set in, and it rains for five days, making travel impossible. On the fifth morning, Sai wakes to see the river lapping at the campsite. The clan hurriedly moves the camp to the top of a rocky hill.

It rains for two more days. The next morning, Sai looks out at the river, now partway up their hill, and hears her stomach growling. Her practiced eyes scan the water's edge. Vines. That means food.

"Come help me gather berries," she calls to Jaa's younger sisters, Kai and Mai.

They inch down the slippery hill, holding on to trees and rocks, until they reach a pool of water slowly swirling around trees that were once on dry land. A big vine, partially submerged, is caught on a branch, its red berries beckoning.

Kai and Mai wade a few steps into the water and grab the vine. As they pull it toward them, Sai hears a hissing roar and turns. Water is rushing toward the girls in a white wall of fury.

"Run! Run!" Sai screams, but it's too late. The rushing river sweeps Kai and Mai with it, arms flailing, and then they are gone.

Sai scrabbles up the hill and finds Jaa outside their lean-to. She falls to her knees and covers her eyes in anguish. "Kai and Mai are . . . Jaa, the river took them. It was my fault," she sobs.

"What? What do you mean?" Jaa says in shock, looking toward the river as if he will surely see his sisters coming up the hill, but there is no time for explanations, and there is no time to mourn, for water is surging toward them. "Get up, Sai! We must alert the others. We must move right now."

Abandoning their campsite, the entire clan runs down the other side of the hill and starts across a narrow valley. Clutched in Sai's hands is a hide mat wrapped around the leather pouch containing the sacred necklace.

Without their lean-tos, the clan spends the night huddled under trees that do little to protect them. When dawn breaks, the sun stays hidden behind huge dark clouds that rumble and drop a heavy downpour on them.

Jaa leads the clan east, Sai trudging along beside him in blind grief, pressing the necklace pouch to her breast, feeling the lumps of the teeth against her fingers. She longs to go back and rejoin the Hei-Lee clan, but floodwaters cover the land to the west, and going west would mean death.

Shaman Lee is up early, cooking breakfast for her family. As she has done every morning for many days now, she turns to the east and stares into the distance. She has had quite enough of the dark days and gloomy skies, which only add to her worries about what has become of Sai and Jaa. They are still so young, and their clan is so new. Every day she looks across the wide river and prays for the sight of rafts bearing them home. Every night she waits for her parents to visit her dreams with reassuring words, but they don't come to her.

Hei and his scouts search for Jaa's clan for several full moons, until finally they are forced to go north after the herds without them. Lee keeps looking south and east, her hopes gradually fading.

One morning, thinking of how Sai and Jaa might be faring, she picks up a stick to throw on the fire and pauses as a fleck of white lands on it. More flecks appear on the ground all around her. She looks up.

"The sky is falling!" a woman cries from a nearby campfire.

"Come see!" cries another. "The clouds are dropping white rain!"

Lee turns her palms up and watches the flecks of white hit them. They are soft, and they turn to water when they touch her hands. She doesn't know what they are, but she's certain that the sky isn't falling on their heads, and she tells the women so. Before long, all the children are running through the white rain, laughing and trying to catch it as their parents look on, smiling. Soon it stops falling and melts away.

Why has the sun god sent them white rain? Shaman Lee ponders that question over the next several days, during which time the white rain comes down again and is quickly gone. "My mother has never spoken to me of white rain," she tells Hei. "I think the sun god is sending us a message, but I don't know what the message is."

"Maybe it's a gift," Hei says, "something to make us happy, as a gift does."

"Perhaps you're right. It's pretty, and it does no harm, and all the children love it."

The occurrence fades from memory until the following winter. The clan has been moving steadily north, and one day they see tall mountains in the distance, their peaks covered with white rain. Soon after, the white rain comes again, but this time it doesn't melt. It keeps falling, harder and harder, bringing bitter winds along with it. Lee comes to believe that the first white rain was a warning.

The clan struggles in the years to come. They learn how to make clothing and blankets and boots using crude bone needles and thin strips of hide. They build big cone-shaped tents, cover the walls with hides and furs, and learn how to light small fires safely inside. Some of the clan doesn't survive, but those who do gradually increase their knowledge of how to live in such a harsh, frigid climate.

Lee pines for her lost daughter, wondering if that first white rain carried an even darker message. Will she and Sai ever see each other again in this lifetime?

16
Waterfall

"Mom, Dad, aren't you dying to know what happened to the clans in the Indus River Valley?" Lisa asked, reaching for John's book as the twins fled the dinner table.

"As a matter of fact, we are," Eva said. "We were talking about it last night before bed."

"Well, they stayed in the valley for tens of thousands of years because it was so fertile, like the Great Rift Valley was before climate change caused the droughts that precipitated the historic migration out of Africa. But the Indus Valley was even better because of all the rivers coming down from the Himalayas, plus there were far fewer dangerous predators like lions and hyenas, so the clans didn't start heading northward from Pakistan into Afghanistan until thirty-five or forty-five thousand years ago."

Andy grinned at his daughter. "You know, it's almost like John never left," he said. "So when did people start settling down and growing crops?"

"*Homo sapiens* were still hunter-gatherers back then. They didn't grow crops or domesticate animals until about ten thousand years ago. Until then, they kept moving."

"Where to?" Eva wanted to know.

"Eventually to southern Europe." Lisa opened the book and read a passage. "'Clans that came from northern Pakistan into Afghanistan later trekked through the Hindu Kush mountain passes north to the valleys near Kunduz. West of Kunduz they would find the Amu Darya River. When worldwide climate warming began thirty-five thousand years ago, ice and snow in the Pamir Mountains west of the Himalayas melted rapidly, feeding the Panj and Vikash Rivers, which grew stronger as they flowed west into the Amu Darya, turning the area northwest of Afghanistan, previously desert, into a flourishing landscape of trees, bushes, and vegetation. Deer herds grew larger in number along the river in Turkmenistan and Uzbekistan, and the Amu Darya became another of the great migrations routes, flowing west all the way to the Aral Sea.'"

"But that's a long way from Europe, isn't it? A map would help right about now," Eva said.

"No, not that far. Mom, look at this map. Here's the Aral Sea, which isn't too far east of the Caspian Sea, which is only a relative hop, skip and a jump from the Volga in south Russia, which is technically part of Europe."

"You make it sound so easy," Eva said.

***

MAP, INDUS AND KABUL RIVERS

MAP, MIGRATION IN AFGHANISTAN AND AMU DARYA RIVER

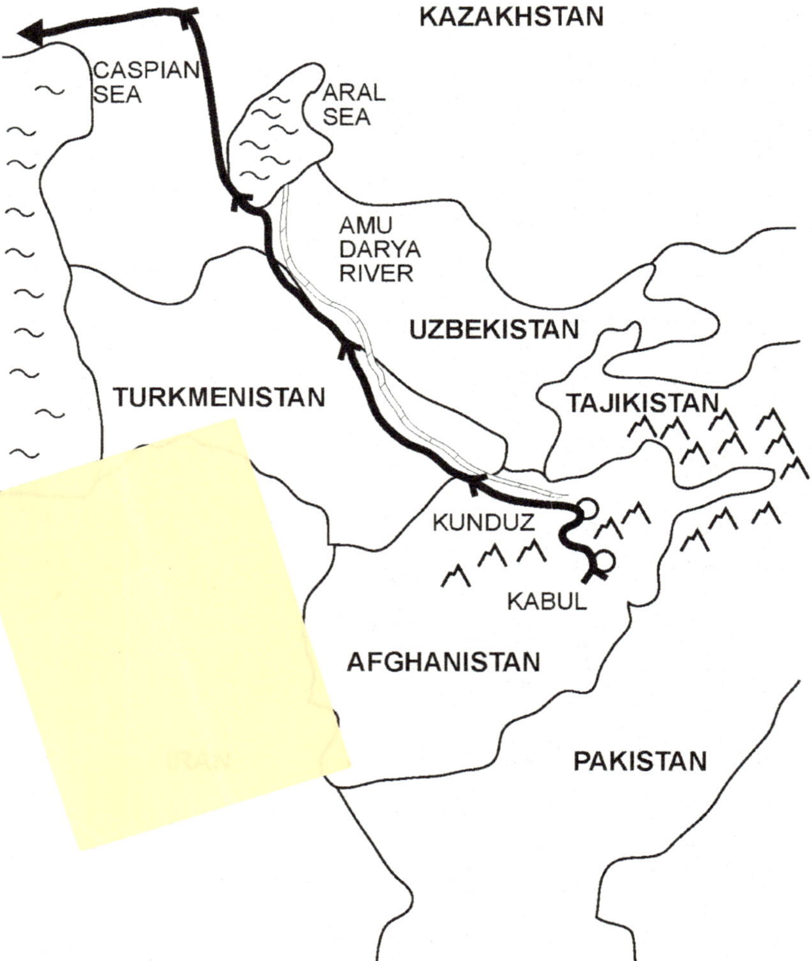

Pakistan, 45,000 Years Before Present

Lee is expecting her third child. She misses Hei, who went off on a hunt several days ago. There is much to oversee in his absence. Their clan has about fifty members, and three smaller clans with about twenty members each have joined them in their northward migration. The other clans have adopted the Hei-Lee language and customs, and the Hei-Lee children have begun to intermarry with them, which means that family connections often aren't as close as they used to be. Still, life is good, and will be better with Hei back at her side and their new baby in her arms.

For many seasons now, the clan has been following the herds north along the big river and the mountain range to the west, and Hei has been saying that it will soon be time to move on again. The river has been good to them, but Lee has begun to wonder about the wisdom of continuing north. It has been some time since her parents visited her dreams to give their advice, but she remembers many stories of the ancestors telling that every time the clan moves north, the weather seems more miserably cold.

Lee hears footsteps and squints into the spring sunshine to see the four scouts who left with Hei approaching. She squints harder, thinking that Hei must be right behind them. Tau, his younger brother, comes out to greet them, looks past them, and voices the question forming uneasily in Lee's mind.

"Where is Hei?"

There is a long silence, and then one of the scouts steps forward, his face a mask of sorrow. "Our chief is gone. He was swept over a waterfall trying to save another clan's hunter from a bear. He died a hero."

Lee screams, "NO ! My Hei. NO !"

After the ritual three days of mourning, the clan's elders choose Tau as the new chief, and he seeks Lee out. "By tradition, my wife will be clan shaman," he says, "but you would do me honor by remaining shaman alongside Saa."

"The honor is mine," Lee says. "I accept, and I thank you." With Hei gone, it is fitting that Tau and Saa lead the clan, but she takes solace in continuing as second shaman. She loves Saa, and she will gladly teach her everything she knows to help her in her new role.

"And out of respect for Hei, I will not take his name," Tau continues, "and Saa will not take yours. He will always be our Hei, and you will always be our Lee."

The next morning, Saa goes to confer with Lee, saying that she thinks it is a bad omen to continue to the north, where Hei met his death. Lee confides her own misgivings about the northward course, and when they take their concerns to Chief Tau, he agrees. He sends out scouts who soon find another river flowing into theirs from the west, with many signs of herds.

Tau sets a westward course following the new river, and they trek along it, winding through mountains on both sides. The journey is difficult, but the deer are plentiful, and after struggling through an arduous mountain pass for two moons, they reach an expansive plain.

"This place is good," Tau says. "We will stop here. We may be the first to have traveled through this pass, and there are no signs of other clans, so we'll have the hunting to ourselves."

Hearing this, Lee's heart lifts for the first time since Hei's death. He is gone, but their children and their clan will survive. She settles into the tent the clansmen build for her, and it is not long before she gives birth to a son, attended by Saa.

"He is strong, just like his father," Saa says. "I felt his strength as I brought him from you."

"Yes," Lee says, holding her baby close, "and he will be named for his father, and he will continue Hei's line.

Afghanistan, Ten Years Later

"An! Eva! Hei! Come here!" Shaman Lee watches her children run toward her, proud of what she sees. Eva is smart and beautiful, Hei and An are handsome like their father, and all of them are strong and healthy. Hei is still quite young, but soon, too soon, An will go with the hunters and scouts, and she will need to keep her eye out for a suitable mate for Eva. Thoughts of their leaving her give her a pang of regret, but so has it always been.

"Are you ready to go, children?" she asks.

"Yes!" they exclaim all at once, and she shoos them off affectionately, watching as they race each other down the trail, giggling with excitement. She follows, wishing she had half their energy, because she can hardly wait herself. Since the loss of her husband and Hei's birth ten summers before, the clan has moved farther west from the mountain pass, and other clans have moved in behind them. Now they are returning to a campsite near the pass for a summer festival and hunt. It is good to visit with other clans, and Lee relishes each opportunity.

They arrive during the festival's second week, after most of the hunters have gone north in pursuit of huge beasts Lee has only heard of, beasts that are said to have thick, shaggy hair and long curved tusks. The hunt is to last three days. Chief Tau directs the clan members to set up camp outside the festival area, and soon they are joining in the footraces and spear-throwing contests and the seemingly never-ending feasts. Lee is looking forward to meeting with shamans from the other clans and introducing Saa as the official new shaman of the Hei-Lee clan.

After they settle themselves in at the campsite, Lee and Saa ask where the shamans are meeting, and are directed to a group of women sitting around a campfire near the racecourse. As they approach, Lee spots An among the runners, and she and Saa pause to cheer him on loudly as he crosses the finish line in first place.

The shamans are engaged in a lively discussion of the medicinal properties of various plants. "In our clan, we chew a type of bark that relieves headaches and pains," one is saying. "It's from a tree that grows along our river, with long branches that bend to the ground as if they're weeping."

Lee steps forward. "Excuse us, may we join you?" she asks, introducing herself and Saa. The other shamans welcome them warmly, and they take seats around the campfire. As the discussion continues, Lee notices an attractive woman about her age staring at her from the other side of the fire. She has eyes of a color Lee has never seen, a green as bright as budding leaf, and those eyes hold a startled look, as if she knows something about Lee.

When the shamans take a break to stretch their legs, the woman comes to her. "I am Zee," she says. "Was that your son who won the race?"

"Yes, that was my An," Lee says, her pride overcoming her reluctance to talk to this strange woman.

Zee opens her mouth and closes it again, as if she doesn't want to speak. Finally she asks, "Is . . . is your husband well?"

What a strange question. Lee doesn't want to answer it, but she does. "My husband was killed many years ago in an accident."

Zee fixes Lee with those intense eyes. "Do you have a girl named Eva?"

Though the day is warm, Lee feels a chill rising from the base of her spine. How on earth does this strange woman know her daughter's name? She hesitates, but something in Zee's gaze prompts her to say, "Yes, and I have a younger boy named Hei, after his father."

With a soft cry, Zee bows her head and covers her eyes.

"What's wrong?" Lee asks, baffled.

Zee raises her head with what seems like great effort. "Will you walk with me? I have something to tell you," she says, and leads Lee away from the campfire to a fallen log. They sit down, and Lee waits, swatting a fly.

Zee takes a shuddering breath. "Ten years ago, my clan was camped near a waterfall that fell from a high hill. While my sisters and I were gathering plants one morning by the pool at the base of the waterfall, my husband and my brother went up the hill to hunt. They hadn't been gone long when we heard screams and looked up to see two men and a bear tumbling down the waterfall into the pool. We swam in hoping to save our men, and when we got close enough we saw that the bear had crashed onto an outcropping of rocks and was dead. My husband's broken body lay next to it, and I knew he was dead too, but my brother was still moving. We swam to him as fast as we could, and when we turned him over . . . Lee, it wasn't my brother."

"Then who—" Lee breaks off as those green eyes bore into hers.

"Lee, the stranger, that fallen man—it was Hei."

Lee recoils as if Zee has slapped her. "What? Is this some cruel joke? Hei? My Hei? He's alive?"

"Yes, Hei is alive. He and my husband were trying to save my brother from the bear, but he was the only one to survive," Zee says, and Lee knows from her grave tone that it's true. Day after day in the throes of her grief she had beseeched the sun god to bring her dead husband back to her, and now this green-eyed woman has answered her prayers.

She jumps up from the log and hugs Zee. "Where is he?"

"He's on the hunt, he'll be back tomorrow. He went looking for you the minute he recovered, but your campsite was deserted. For months he searched far and wide, but he couldn't find you."

Lee nods. "Yes, after his scouts returned without him and told us he was dead, we decided to go in a different direction. We went west along a new river, through the big mountain pass. We had to find food, we didn't know—"

"How could you have known?" Zee says. "He searched for you every spring, but—well, the years passed, and he was sure he'd never see you again. He stayed with our clan and became our best hunter."

Lee stares in the direction the hunters have gone, as if she can see him in the distance.

"When our chief died five summers after what happened

at the waterfall," Zee continues, "we asked Hei to become our chief." Her face clouds over, and she looks away from Lee for the first time. "It is our tribe's tradition . . . if he agreed, if he became chief, he . . . he had to choose a wife. He—"

Lee grips Zee's arm hard, her mind racing to a conclusion. "Go on."

"I wish there was another way for you to know these things, but yes, he helped me raise my children after my husband died, and he knew I cared for him, so he asked me to be his wife, and we have two more children now. I only hope you can forgive me."

Lee covers her hand with her mouth, afraid she's going to be sick. She forces herself to breathe in and out slowly. At last she says, "So . . . Hei has two wives."

"Yes. What are we to do?"

Lee gathers herself. "He is alive. Nothing else matters. Thank you for saving my husband's . . . our husband's life."

Despite the gravity of their situation, they laugh. Neither speaks for a moment, and then Zee says, "I have thought so often of you and your children. Tell me about them. Are they all well? Is Hei strong and handsome like his father?"

"Yes. Yes, he is," Lee says, serious again. What will Hei do when he sees his children? How will they react when they see him? Which family will he remain with?

She and Zee worry over that question until the sun sinks and long shadows fall over the assembled clans. "We both have much to think about," Lee says, "and we must both go to our families."

"Yes," Zee says, and they part with an embrace.

The next day, Lee and her children stand at the top of the

hill staring into the valley. Tau and Saa stand next to them, still trying to absorb the incredible news.

Lee is the first to see him in the distance. Crying out his name, she runs to meet him, the children right behind her.

Hei looks up and drops the load of meat and furs he's carrying on his shoulder. "Lee?" he says wonderingly as she leaps into his arms. "My Lee? I thought—" He is too overcome to go on. He holds her tight and sees his children staring up at him. His children. Two of them haven't seen him for many summers, the other, not at all. They smile at him shyly. It will take time, he thinks.

Lee turns and glances up the hill to see Zee waving. She takes Hei by the hand and says, "Come, I have much to tell you."

"And I you," he says, his gaze shifting to Zee. "So much has happened—"

"A lifetime has happened," Lee says in the measured, calming tone he knows so well and has missed so much.

At the top of the hill, after a joyous reunion with his brother and Saa, Hei turns to Lee with a question in his eyes. "I don't know—"

She puts a finger to his lips and calls to Zee, who walks over to them slowly, her green eyes traveling from Hei to the children and family he had before the waterfall.

"Have you decided?" Lee asks her.

Zee nods and says softly, "I don't want to live without Hei, and I don't want my children or yours to be without their father."

"Then it's settled," Lee says. "We will both be your wives, Hei. Our children will have one father and two mothers."

Relief washes over Hei's face but soon gives way to a frown of concern as he thinks through the implications of the arrangement. "Your decision brings me great happiness," he tells them, "but how will we choose which of our clans to live with?"

"There will be no need to choose," says Tau, who has been silently watching this drama unfold. "We will join our clans, brother, and you and I will share the duties of chief."

Days later, as the summer festival winds down, the two clans celebrate their union with a feast of deer meat from the hunt. When the feast is over, Lee takes her family to a secluded spot and brings out the sacred necklace. Hei incises a mark in the newest tooth, and they all cut their fingers and press them to the tooth, Zee intermingling her blood with the blood of her new clan and binding herself to them for all time.

* * *

36,000 Years Before Present, Northern Afghanistan, Amu Darya River

On a particularly warm midsummer day, Chief Hei's scouts return to the campsite shouting about hundreds of deer only half a day away.

Hei chooses forty hunters to surround the herd, and four women to help cut up the animals and carry back meat and fur. One of them is his younger daughter, Dee. "You will come with us," he tells her. "We will need you if the gods grant us a big kill."

They find the herd at the end of a valley blocked by steep rocky hills, a perfect trap. Hei splits his hunters into three groups, one going to the right, one to the left, his own going straight ahead. They advance quietly.

When Hei gets closer he gives the signal, throwing a short spear high into the air. The hunters raise their spears and run toward the deer, who sprint in all directions, but mostly to the right, toward Kan's group.

Kan is cousin to Hei, and chief of one of the smaller clans joined with Hei's. He has two sons, Raa and Taa, and they are with him now, all of them racing toward the deer and trapping them against the rock wall. They thrust their spears into the animals' necks, felling ten. With strong, true throws, Raa and Taa bring down two more who are trying to flee.

Once the kill is over and the numbers are totaled—twelve for Kan's group, thirteen for the other two—Chief Hei turns to his cousin. "Twenty-five! That is more than ever for one hunt. You did well."

Kan grins.

"So well that this is too much to carry back in one trip, even with the women to help. We will cut up fifteen deer now, and you will take them back to camp. I will guard the rest until your return tomorrow. Take Raa with you, leave Taa."

Kan nods.

After Kan departs with his hunters, Hei's men move the ten remaining deer to their campsite for the night, circling it with fires to scare away predators and scavengers. Hei watches Taa cut up a deer for Dee to roast for the evening meal. Taa is a good man, he thinks, perfect for his older daughter, Ee.

The feast that night is a fitting celebration of the clan's biggest kill. As it winds down, Taa and Dee go for a walk, stopping many times to look up at the bright stars and talk about the patterns they make and what meanings the ancestors have given to each pattern. Taa looks at Dee and feels something stir deep inside him. They find a quiet place to lie down together.

Later at their camp, in their tent, Hei lies down with Lee. Afterward, he tells her that Ee is of an age to join with a young man and that Taa is the best young man in all the clans. Lee does not disagree, but she says that Raa is a good man too, older and more mature.

"Ee likes Taa," Hei says.

Lee laughs. "So does Dee. All the girls like Taa."

"Did all the girls like me?"

Lee laughs again and gives him a playful punch on the shoulder.

He takes her hand. "Tomorrow I will speak with Kan. He will be especially happy with our choice because Taa will become the next chief of our clan."

In the morning, after consulting Kan, Hei says to his daughters over a breakfast of leftover deer, "Your mother and I have made a decision."

Dee and Ee glance at each other warily but remain silent.

"It is your time to take a man, Ee. You will go with Taa. He is a good match for you."

Dee gasps and runs from the campfire, followed by Lee.

"As you wish," Ee says solemnly, but her eyes sparkle.

Women, Hei thinks to himself as he goes off to look for Taa. He finds him cleaning a pelt with a stone blade just outside the camp.

"I have spoken with your father," he says, "and we agree that you will take Ee for your wife."

Taa looks startled—does Hei see a shadow of a cloud pass over his face?—but then says quickly, "I like Ee. We will be good together."

Hei nods and walks with Taa back through camp to Kan's tent. Taa goes inside, and a few moments later Raa storms out.

Hei returns to his own tent and finds Lee drying some medicinal plants for storage. He tells her what happened. "Surely we made the right decision," he says, "but now Raa knows that Taa will be the next chief. It will be hard for him to take direction from his younger brother." He sighs. "And where did Dee run off to?"

Lee shakes her head. Men, she thinks.

Dee watches Taa court Ee and attends the sacred marriage ceremony. What choice does she have? She can't tell her sister about her brief encounter with Taa and her feelings for him, but the pain she feels in seeing them together grows greater each day. She knows what she must do. For her sister's happiness and her own, she must leave the clan.

She joins a small clan that has recently been traveling with the Hei-Lee cluster. Within months, she realizes her terrible mistake. Unlike her parents, the chief and shaman of the new clan are stupid and unreasonable whenever she offers an idea or disagrees with them in any way. But how can she return to the clan of her birth when the man she loves has married her own sister?

One year later, at the big summer festival, Dee gets drunk on her clan's special brew and picks a fight with a girl from Chief Kan's clan. Raa, who is also drunk, comes over to watch and roars his approval when Dee bests her opponent.

"You are prettier than Ee and tougher," he slurs. "I like

that."

Dee crawls up off the ground. "You do?" She knows he's as drunk as she is, but she's drawn by his fine body and his directness. She doesn't know that he's the only clan member who suspects the source of her rebelliousness and bad behavior.

"Do you have any more brew?" she asks.

"In my tent. Come."

Dee and Raa spend the next three days in his tent, laughing and drinking and sleeping together, with occasional breaks to swim in the river. The following week, Dee joins Chief Kan's clan. Raa sees that her physical strength and defiant spirit can be an asset to his clan. He teaches her how to throw a spear and takes her on a hunt, and from then on she goes on all his hunts. He avoids the larger hunts with the Hei-Lee clan, preferring his excursions with Dee. Besides, he wants to keep Dee away from his brother in case Taa's eyes stray to her.

One day on a hunt, Dee is ahead of Raa as they cross a shallow stream. Raa sees two bears appear from a stand of trees directly in her path. She is looking to her right, she doesn't see the bears. Raa shouts a warning.

Dee freezes as the bears rush toward her. Raa runs to her, grabs her, and bolts back across the stream. He lifts her onto a big boulder. *I almost lost her, almost lost her*—the words circle through his mind again and again.

The next day he goes to his father. "I want to take Dee as mine," he says.

Kan smiles. "And so you shall. I told Hei a year ago that you two would be a good match, but I did not think it would take so long. And another thing. I am ready to cede my position as chief to you once you and Dee marry. Your mother will help Dee learn everything she must know as shaman, and perhaps help you to keep Dee's impulsive nature in check."

Raa is surprised but pleased that his father approves his union with Dee, and this commitment seems to soothe Dee's restless spirit while giving full scope to her athleticism and fearlessness.

Hei is pleased too. So has it always been with his clan, since time long before his birth, the elders looking after the next generation and protecting the clan from the perils of harsh weather, predatory animals, and the threats posed by other clans greedy or desperate for spoils.

Over the course of the next year, the deer herds become sparse again. Chief Hei and his clan talk about whether to follow the big river west over vast plains or head north along the western foothills. Scouts have found animal herds in both directions, but the river route is warmer. Since the clan has always thrived when it follows the rivers, Hei and Lee choose to go west.

As the time to leave approaches, Chief Raa and Shaman Dee go to her parents. "We will go north," Dee says, "and two other clans will go with us."

Lee frowns. "Do not leave us, Dee. We will never see you again."

"Come with us," Hei says.

Dee casts sad but resolute eyes from one beloved parent to the other. "Raa and I have consulted the sun god and the ancestors, and we will go at the next full moon."

"You must do what you must do, as you always have,"

Hei says.

Lee says nothing. It is all she can do to hide her grief over her daughter's decision. When Raa and Dee leave, she loses herself in thought about her family.

That night she says to Hei, "The sacred necklace always passes to the oldest daughter and stays with our clan, but with Dee leaving, we must find a way to bond her to us forever. We must make a new necklace for her."

Hei considers her words for some while. At last he says, "You are wise, Shaman Lee. We will perform a sacred necklace ceremony before Dee and Raa depart."

The ancestors had long ago decreed that twenty teeth was the maximum for one leather thong, so the sacred necklace has by now become two thongs with ten pairs of teeth each, as well as a third thong with three pairs. Lee takes the outside pair from this third thong and strings them on a new one.

At the ceremony, Hei and Lee prick their index fingers with a knife and pass it to Dee and Raa, who in turn pass it to Ee and Taa. They all rub their blood into a new cut mark on one of the teeth in the third necklace, and then into an old cut mark on a tooth in the first necklace. Dee bows her head to hide her tears as Lee presents her with the new necklace. Hei watches, praying to the ancestors that the cleaving of the necklace will preserve the family bond and that they will someday meet again.

17
The Beginning

The Saturday after New Year's, Lisa came bouncing down the stairs from her room waving John's book. "I finished!" she called. "Where is everybody?"

Eva poked her head out of the family room. "The twins are out playing with friends, and your father and I are in here catching up on some reading, but we're not as caught up as you are. I guess you know the end of the story now, so come tell us."

Lisa settled herself on the couch next to her mother. "Probably the simplest thing is if I just read it to you," she said, opening the book to a page toward the end. "'Through an analysis of DNA data, human population genetics shows that *homo sapiens* originated in Africa more than two hundred thousand years ago. They had brains about the same size as ours today, and their vocal cords were as capable of speech as ours are. For the most part, they lived in the fertile Great Rift Valley in Tanzania and Kenya, and by eighty thousand years ago, the population had grown to about thirty thousand. As hunter-gatherers, they moved around constantly for the next seventy thousand years in search of plants and animals. Deer and antelope were their major source of protein and a high percentage of their diet, but hunting was dangerous because they had to compete with lions, leopards, and hyenas.'"

"Is that why they left Africa?" Eva asked.

"No, it was climate change." Lisa resumed reading. "'About eighty thousand years ago, a major world climate change caused a severe drought in Africa, turning the Great Rift Valley into a near desert. Most animals died, and those that didn't moved north from Kenya into Ethiopia in search of rivers and lakes. Clans followed them, journeying along the Omo River and then the Awash River to Djibouti and the west coast of the Red Sea at the Gate of Grief, named for the difficulty of navigating it with the crude rafts of early times. See this map how they journeyed up from Kenya to the Red Sea.'"

"So that must be how they eventually got to Europe," Andy said. "They crossed the Red Sea and went north until they got to the Mediterranean, right?"

"Nope." Lisa was relishing her role of channelling John for her parents. "Here, listen. 'After African clans crossed the Red Sea to Yemen and Arabia's southern coast, some tried to go inland, but they were stopped by the vast Arabian Desert. They trekked east along the coast instead, constantly moving because of stiff competition for food, until they reached southwestern Iran. Some clans continued eastward along the southern Persian coast, fishing and searching for edible vegetation, and some went north inside Iran to hunt animals in the hills and valleys of the Zagros Mountains. See the second map how they moved east along the coast.

MAP, MIGRATION KENYA TO DJIBOUTI

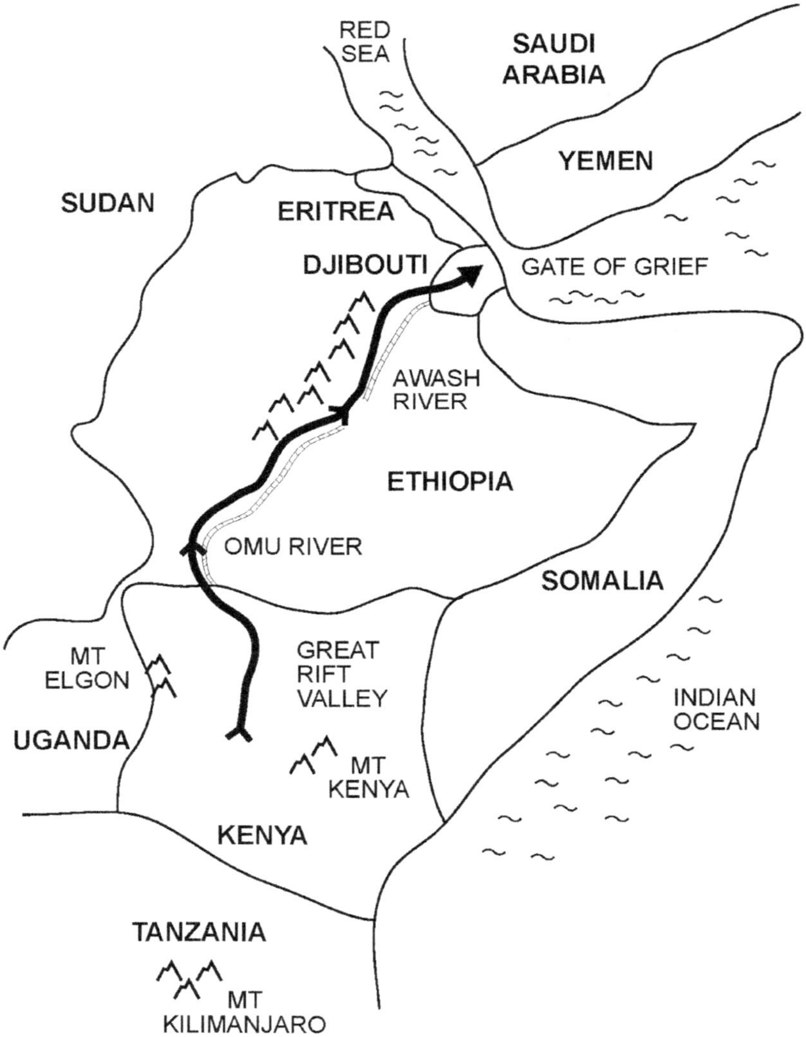

MAP, MIGRATION OUT-OF-AFRICA, SOUTHERN ARABIAN COAST 80,000 YEARS BP

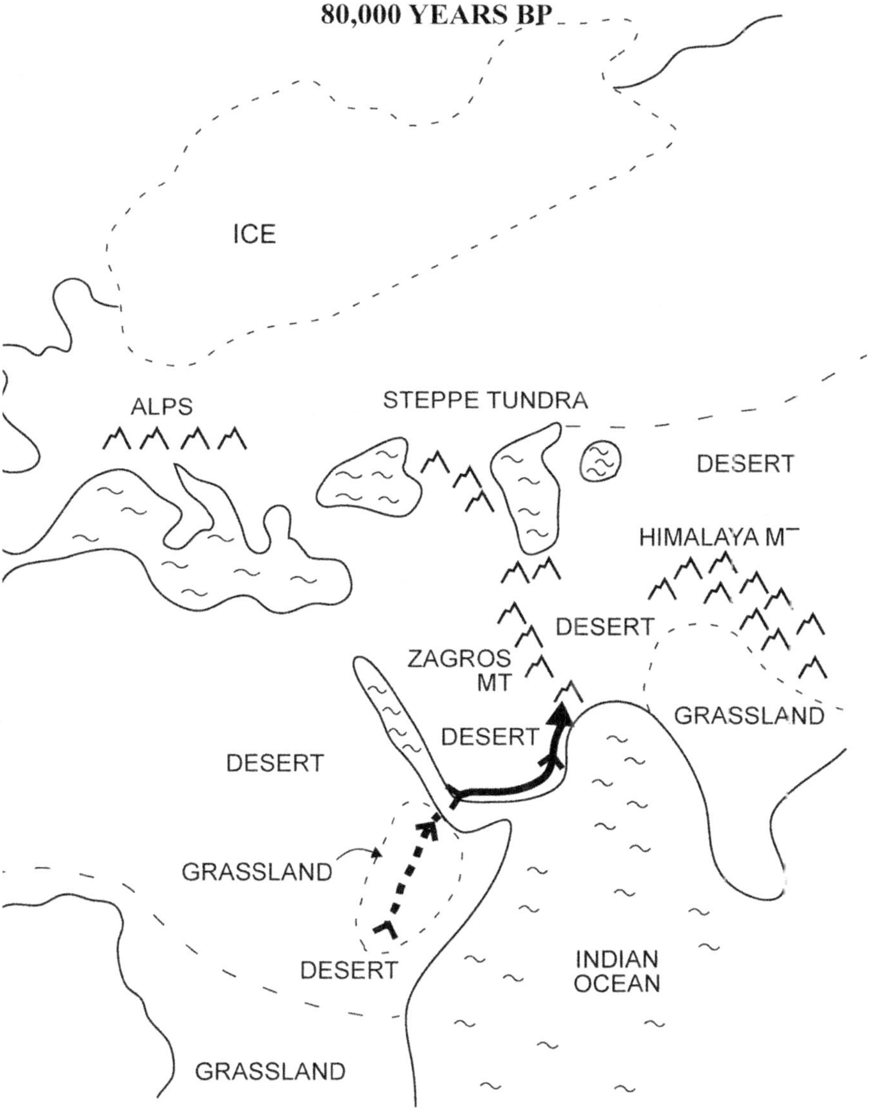

It wasn't until some fifty thousand to thirty-five thousand years ago that the land to the north became habitable and the clans could start moving toward the Caspian and Black Seas. The most successful migration path for clans leaving Africa was east along the coast of the Indian Ocean toward India and Asia. These were the clans that would later move up the Indus River before and after the Toba eruption and would live in the Indus Valley for tens of thousands of years before migrating to Europe.'"

Lisa paused and looked at her mother. "Remember what John told us about everyone alive today being descended from forty women in Africa?"

"I remember," Eva said, "and I've been thinking on it."

"Well, here's what John says about it. 'By using maternal DNA, or mitochondrial DNA, scientists have developed what they call ancestor trees showing that all humans living today are descended from forty or perhaps fewer women who lived between eighty thousand and sixty thousand years ago. Their descendants had many daughters who helped form resilient clans. Descendants of the many thousands of other women living eighty thousand to sixty thousand years ago, at some point, did not have daughters, or their families did not survive over time, so there is no maternal DNA linkage today from them.'"

Eva sat back, reflecting. "My maternal DNA showed that my mother's ancestors came from the Yoruba tribe in Nigeria. I'll bet they were descended from one of those forty women."

"I'll bet we all are," Andy said.

* * *

Kenya, 80,000 Years Before Present

Lost in thought, Chief Paa leads his hunters across a wide valley near their hillside camp. Yes, he has made his decision. He drops back and falls in step with Hei and Han, sons of An, the clan's best scout and hunter until his death.

"Hei, you have seen fifteen rainy seasons, and Han, you have seen thirteen. You are the strongest, fastest, and smartest hunters we have, even better than your father, and you have both reached the age to take a woman. Our clan is small, and there are no suitable mates for you. We must look for someone in another clan."

Hei stares down at his feet, thinking of Kee, the girl he'd wanted to marry. Kee died two summers ago from snakebite, and he has had little interest in girls since then. He glances at his brother. Han looks uncomfortable too; he has a girlfriend in the clan, Yee, but she is too young for marriage.

"Thank you, Chief," Hei says, "but—"

Screams pierce the air, women's voices. That morning, the women of the clan had gone out into the valley to gather nuts, berries, and plant roots.

Chief Paa grabs Hei's arm. "Go, both of you. Hurry!"

The brothers sprint across the valley, hardly noticing the sticks and rocks beneath their calloused feet. Paa and the other hunters follow as fast as they can. When Hei and Han spot several terrified women running from a copse of thick bushes, they raise their stone-tipped spears and race past the women into the copse. They stop.

In a small clearing ahead, a snarling pack of hyenas is mauling two women, their necks snapped and their throats spouting blood. Their bodies flail limply as the hyenas rip them apart. Hei recognizes one of the women: Chief Paa's wife, Zaa. He see his brother slump to the ground—only last year, lions killed their mother—but this is no time for grief. Hei fears that these hyenas may not be the entire pack, or that other packs have heard the screams and smelled the blood and are stalking the surviving women.

"Come, brother," he says. "We will mourn later, but now we must make haste."

Back at camp, all the women are sitting on pallets of hide or fur or grass, huddled around cooking fires with their children and the men too old to hunt. There are no hyenas in sight, but Hei looks downhill and sees Paa and the rest of the hunters running toward the campsite. Are they being pursued by hyenas or something equally dangerous, or are they just speeding back see if their women are safe?

"What happened?" Paa yells as he nears Hei.

"Chief, there was . . . there was a pack of hyenas, and—"

His next words go unheard. The women run to their men, crying, and two of the chief's children clutch at his legs.

"My Zaa?" the chief says as the entire clan kneels around him in his grief. He takes his children in his arms, collects himself, and says, "Such is our life, such are our deaths. We must go on."

Two nights later, Hei and the other hunters gather around Chief Paa's campfire. Like the rest of the clan, the chief wears only a short leather skirt, and sweat glistens on his chest. He tosses a branch on the fire and says, "Food is scarce both for clans and for animals. That is why more of us are getting killed. The hyenas and lions attack us because we are easier to catch than animals."

"But what can we do?" asks Joh, the chief's brother.

"We have no choice. We must hunt animals for food, and the women must gather plants. We must do both."

Joh frowns. "We should send hunters out with the women."

"Yes. We will do that, because the women are afraid to leave camp, but we can only do it for a short time. We must have meat. All our hunters must be free to hunt."

There is silence except for the night sounds from the bushes. Hei sits still, waiting, knowing the chief must be the one to speak.

Paa scans the circle. "Some of us will search for deer herds, and the rest will stay with the women, children, and old men. When we find a herd, we will send back a runner, and more hunters can join us for the kill. Joh, you will come with me tomorrow, and you too, Hei. You are our fastest runner."

Hei nods and looks at Han, sitting next to him. Though his brother is only thirteen, he is a smart scout, like their father was before a leopard killed him three seasons past. He turns to Chief Paa. "Can we bring Han?"

"Yes, and Jaa will come with us too."

Jaa, the husband of the other woman killed by the hyenas, shakes his head. "No. My little boy has no mother. I will stay with him."

Hei holds his breath, knowing that the chief can order Jaa to go. After all, Paa will also be leaving his motherless children, for the good of the entire clan. He can also issue a rebuke that will find its way to the ears of the most distant clan in the region. Hei has heard a few of those from Paa.

The chief does neither. He stands and says with rocky

calm, "So be it. You will stay, Jaa, and we will go. The lakes and rivers are drying up, and it will be hard to find a herd. We must be gone for as long as it takes, so you men going with me must bring as much food and water as you can." Paa turns to his other brother, Poh. "Help the women to gather plants until we come back."

Poh scowls, and Hei smiles to himself. He doesn't like Poh, who never accepts his suggestions about hunting. With suppressed eagerness, he waits for Poh to refuse and bring down the chief's wrath. One refusal Chief Paa might accept, but Poh doesn't have Jaa's excuse. To Hei's amazement, Poh accepts the chief's order with a simple nod.

In the morning, Hei and Han check their water pouches, lined with deer bladders, and fill them from a nearby stream. They replenish the supply of dried meat and nuts in their deer-hide bags, sling them over their shoulders with the pouches, and join Joh and Paa at the chief's campfire. None of them take their deerskin sleeping pallets; on such a long hunt, they will sleep as best they can wherever they can.

The four men travel north for two days, finding nothing but the bones of a wildebeest on a hillside. Late on the third day, as they descend into a great valley, Hei spots movement ahead. In the distance, two young deer are nibbling on bushes. The hunters advance quietly. Paa points toward the closest deer and they all throw their spears. Two find their mark in the deer's neck and flank, but it manages to stagger to its feet and run off with the other deer.

"Hei, Han," Chief Paa shouts, "follow it!"

The brothers know that if they don't find their wounded prey quickly, they will lose it, or another predator will get it. They take off into the valley and soon come upon the fallen deer, motionless but still alive. Sensing Hei's approach, it fights to rise, but Hei drives his spear into its neck.

At Hei's call across the valley, Paa and Joh arrive shortly. They cut up the deer and carry it up a hill to a vantage point where they can watch for predators intent on taking their kill. Hei's stomach rumbles as he starts a fire to roast the first fresh meat they've had for many days. They wrap the leftover meat in deerskins and cover the skins with dirt to protect the meat from vultures and scavengers during the night. It will be enough to sustain them for a time.

"Those two small deer must have come from a larger herd," Chief Paa says, hopeful. "Tomorrow, we will search the entire valley."

Early the next morning, the four hunters begin a long jog toward the rising sun. When they stop to rest in a stand of trees at the top of a hill, Hei climbs one to look for deer but sees nothing. Chief Paa sighs, and they all advance down the other side of the hill, Hei and Han in the lead. Near the bottom, they hear a rustling in the bushes and turn to see two lions springing toward them. The wide valley affords no boulders or other protection, and their spears and stone knives are no match for predators like these.

"Back to the trees! Run!" Paa yells, but he and Joh soon fall behind. Hearing a cry, Hei and Han turn to see the lions streaking toward the older men.

"To the trees!" Paa yells again as one of the lions pounces on him and mauls his chest.

The brothers run back to him and hurl their spears at the lion, but they glance off harmlessly. In the next moment, the second lion clamps its jaws around one of Joh's legs. "Help me!" he screams, but Paa manages to cry out, "No, boys, keep running!" Those are his last words before the lion snaps his neck and the other one makes short work of Joh.

Stunned, Hei watches the lions pull the bodies down the hillside to begin their grisly feast. In his mind, all he can see is his poor mother brutalized in the same manner. He sees Han's horrified expression and averts his eyes, feeling too sickened to offer his brother comfort.

Retreating to the hilltop, Hei and Han climb a tree and remain there until the sun is high overhead and the lions have disappeared. Then they retrieve all the spears and jog northward along the rocky hillside, glancing often over their shoulders. That night, they camp on a hill with several tall trees they can climb for safety. Hei starts a small fire to ward off predators. There is nothing left to do but sit close to the weak flames and wait for morning. He puts his head between his knees and weeps for his mother, for Chief Paa and his wife, for Joh, and for his own helplessness. On that cloudless night, bright stars and a crescent moon fill the sky. Exhausted, Hei falls asleep dreaming of hunting deer with his father.

At dawn, he shakes his brother awake and they silently break camp, continuing north for several hours but finding no sign of deer. In his heart, Hei fears that the dry seasons have been too long upon them. They come upon a great barren valley and stop to rest in the shade of a spindly tree. There is no wind. It is hot, and getting hotter. All is quiet. They sip water and jog farther across the valley, toward a hill topped by several massive boulders.

Han points. "Look!"

Two girls are climbing toward the boulders. A third girl is on the hillside below them, gathering nuts and berries. Hei has not often encountered members of other clans, but he remembers his father saying that most clans are friendly. "Let's go talk to them," he says to Han. "Maybe they'll tell us where their clan hunts."

As they approach the girl picking berries, she looks up, startled. Hei smiles to reassure her, noting that she has a pretty face and nice breasts. His smile freezes when he glances up the hill and sees a lion slinking from the bushes, crouched low.

"Lion," Hei yells. "Lion!"

She stares at him warily until he yells again and points behind her just as the lion breaks into a lunging run. She gasps and sprints toward the big boulders on the hill, running faster than any girl Hei has ever seen. The lion ignores him and chases the girl, gaining on her.

Hei races after her, his spear cocked by his ear, Han right behind him. The other two girls have climbed the tallest boulder and are shouting, "Lee, up here, up here!" She scrambles toward them, and just as the lion is upon her, they reach down and hoist her onto the boulder.

The lion leaps onto a smaller boulder and then up onto the big one where the girls are huddled. Lee puts her hands out to defend herself, and the lion claws her arm with a huge paw. As she steps back toward the edge of the boulder, Hei appears behind the lion and thrusts his spear hard into its flank. The lion roars and stumbles forward into Lee, and they both fall over the side and crash to the ground.

Knife in hand, Hei jumps off the boulder after them. He

lands on the lion and plunges the knife deep into its neck. The beast goes limp. Han jumps down beside him, his own knife at the ready. He lands hard and his legs give out from under him. He tries to get up but falls to his knees. "It's just my ankle," he says to Hei. "Is the lion dead? Is the girl . . ."

Hei thinks the lion is dead. It isn't moving. Lee is lying next to it, her arm bleeding, but she's moaning, which means she is alive. With Han crawling after him, Hei moves her away from the lion, wraps his hands around her wound to stop the bleeding, and speaks to her gently to comfort her, as his mother once spoke to him. When he looks back at the boulder, he sees the two girls clambering down. One approaches while the other takes off running. Hei hopes she's heading to her clan's camp for help.

"Did you see any more lions?" Hei asks the girl coming toward him.

"No," she says. "I think we're safe for now." She runs over to a bush, rips off some leaves, and comes back to tie them tightly around Lee's arm. Lee opens her eyes, sees Hei, and faints.

Before long, a throng of clansmen comes sprinting toward them. A tall man nudges the dead lion with his bare foot, then moves to Lee and removes the leaves to inspect her wound. He places his hand under her head tenderly, and she opens her eyes again.

"Are you all right, Lee?"

"My arm hurts." It is barely a whisper.

The other girl points to Hei. "He saved her. He leaped from the rock and stabbed the lion."

The man nods and returns to comforting Lee. Hei notices

that her wound is not as deep as he first thought and that it has stopped bleeding. She smiles at the man, who seems reassured. He stands and says to Hei, "I am Tau, chief of my clan. You were very brave to save my daughter. What is your name?"

"I am Hei."

"Well, Hei, you must come back to camp with us. My wife will want to thank you."

Hei turns to Han, who is still sitting on the ground holding his foot. He reaches down and helps his brother up. Han takes one small step, and only Hei's quick steadying prevents his fall. "This is Han, my brother," Hei tells the chief. "He injured his ankle. He can't walk."

Chief Tau points at a huge man. "Mo, carry him back to our camp." Mo easily picks Han up and throws him over his shoulder as if he were a slab of deer meat.

Tau lifts his daughter in his arms. "Cut up the lion for meat," he says to the other clansmen. "I want his two big front teeth. Cut them out and bring them to me."

When they reach the camp, everyone rushes toward them excitedly. Tau lays Lee on a pile of deer furs next to a woman who leans over her and strokes her forehead gently. She applies a poultice to the wound and says, "You must sleep now, my child."

Lee looks past her at Hei, then back at her mother. "He saved me. He killed the lion," she murmurs as her eyes close.

The woman stands. "I am Eva, Lee's mother. Thank you for saving her," she says gravely.

"You and your brother will share our dinner of deer meat tonight," Chief Tau says, "and tomorrow we will celebrate with a feast of roasted lion after we hold our traditional games. Will you participate, Hei?"

Hei hesitates. "Yes, but we can't stay any longer than that." He explains that he and Han were searching for deer when the lion attacked Lee, and that it is urgent that they find fresh sources of meat for their clan.

Chief Tau listens carefully. "You cannot leave until your brother heals. If he rests, perhaps it will not take long. Eva is our shaman, and she knows a great deal about healing. While you wait, I will tell you all I know about how to find the herds."

The next morning, the whole clan gathers in a big field. Hei looks up at the sky and smiles. Clear, no wind, a good morning for throwing spears.

Chief Tau steps forward. "The first contest is for distance," he says, "and the second for accuracy. Each man will throw three spears for each contest."

Hei looks around at the assembled clansmen and tries to remember the names of those he met the night before. He spots Chief Tau's cousin Tan and his two sons, San and Nee. San is short and stocky, with little hair on his head. Nee is tall, with a sleek muscular body like Hei's own. San is the clan's best spear thrower, according to the chief, and Nee the best runner. Nee had spent most of last night attending to Lee's every need, and Hei feels a pang as he wonders if they have been promised to each other.

He turns to Chief Tau. "May I go last? I'd like to see how the others throw their spears."

Tau nods. "As you wish. You're our guest."

One by one, the clansmen run up to a line drawn in the

ground and throw their spears toward a tall wood pole many long steps away. No spear reaches the pole, though Mo's three come closest. San, the next to last to throw, hurls his three spears past all the others and a few strides short of the pole.

Hei steps up. He grips his spear firmly, moves it backward and forward over his shoulder a few times, makes a short run to the line, and hurls the spear high in the air; it flies past San's farthest spear and past the pole by at least five steps. He turns to see Han grinning. Chief Tau grunts in admiration, and Lee breaks into a big smile.

The next contest, for accuracy, involves hitting three piles of green leaves, the first twenty long steps away, the second ten steps farther, and the third another ten. Hei's clan has the same contest, so this time he asks to go first. His three throws hit their target, the last one sticking dead center with such force that the pile of leaves flies into the air. The spectators cheer. "Amazing!" Chief Tau exclaims.

One by one, the other clansmen step up to throw. Only San and big Mo hit more than one target. None comes close to hitting the third.

Han grins at his brother again. Lee beams. Nee is glowering, but Hei's father taught him that a game won by fair means should offend no one, so he decides that Nee is simply disappointed in himself. Besides, he thinks his own turn for disappointment may come in the next competition. Though he is a strong runner, he has been told by many in the clan that Nee runs like the wind. He flexes his muscles and focuses on limbering up for the footrace.

Chief Tau holds up a hand for silence. "Take your positions, runners. You will go on my signal." He raises his spear and brings it down. "Now!"

Nee and Hei lunge forward, keeping pace with each other and putting a good distance between themselves and the other men. They expand their lead as they cross the first valley and race up a short hill into another valley. The halfway point is a cluster of trees that hides them from sight. Nee slows, comes from behind Hei, and trips him, sending him flying into the bushes. As Nee heads back across the valley, Hei hears his fading laughter and scrambles out of the bushes. He sets off in pursuit, anger spurring him on.

Halfway to the end of the race, Hei closes in on Nee, who glances back in disbelief and picks up his pace. Hei accelerates with a burst of energy, sprints up the hill to the campsite, and crosses the finish line to wild clapping. Nee follows him a minute later, his features distorted by exhaustion and rage.

Though Nee has cheated, it is the tradition in Hei's clan for the winner to praise the losers. He is walking toward Nee, trying to catch his breath, when San appears and takes his brother aside. Hei watches the two of them stride away from the crowd and thinks that their clan must not share his tradition.

Chief Tau approaches with Eva and Lee. "You're the fastest runner I've ever seen," he says.

"Yes, that was a great victory," Eva says. "Nee has never been beaten before."

Han limps up on his bad foot and claps his brother on the back. "I knew you'd win. Nobody can run as fast as you."

Lee gives him another of her beautiful smiles. "I loved watching you fly across the valley," she says.

Hei gives up on catching his breath.

At the feast of roasted lion, Hei is the guest of honor for

saving Lee and winning the contests. He and Han sit next to Chief Tau and Shaman Eva, and Lee stares at him shyly across the enormous campfire. His mind flashes back to Kee for a moment, and Han puts a hand on his shoulder, sensing his sadness.

When Hei catches Lee's gaze, the sadness vanishes as suddenly as it came. He turns to her father and applies himself to making a good impression. "Your clan is thriving, Chief," he says. "It is much larger than mine. How have you had such success? You must have at least forty members."

"Fifty," Tau says proudly, "and fifteen hunters." He and Eva go on to tell their guest much about the clan's ways and traditions.

As the feast winds down, an older couple approaches to consult their chief and their shaman about a problem with their son. Han excuses himself and limps off to his borrowed sleeping pallet. Hei excuses himself too, mustering his courage to go to the other side of the fire and talk to Lee.

"Does your arm still hurt?" he asks.

"It's stiff, but there's no pain." Lee's smile is as bright as her eyes are dark. "And if not for you, I wouldn't even have an arm, or any of the rest of me. I'm glad you beat Nee today."

Hei's eyes travel from her breasts down to her long legs, and he suddenly wishes that he could see through her leather skirt, a wish he has never had before.

A clansman materializes next to him. "Chief Tau wants to see you," he says.

Hei steps back, alarmed. Has the chief seen him looking at Lee's body and read his thoughts? Until Han's foot heals, they are both at the chief's mercy should they displease him in any way. He follows the clansman back around the fire and sees the older couple just leaving with profuse thanks.

"Sit," Tau says. "We have some questions for you."

Hei sits down nervously next to Eva. Questions? What questions?

"Are you married?" Eva asks.

"No." Hei's stomach sinks. Lee's parents must indeed by angered by his attentions to their daughter.

Tau nods. "Tell us about your family."

Hei takes a deep breath. "My father, An, was our clan's best hunter. He was killed trying to save one of his men from a leopard. My mother, Oni, became our leader and our strength until she fell prey to a lion when she took a party of women out to forage for plants." An immeasurable sadness overcomes him. "Now our clan can find no herds, and once again we have no chief." He tells them about the recent hyena and lion attacks that took Paa and the others, and the images in his mind require him to stop speaking several times.

Tau leans closer to the fire, his face somber. "I met Chief Paa and your father many summers ago, at a group hunt south of the big mountain. An was a great hunter and scout. I'm sorry to hear he was killed."

"As am I," Eva says. "You and your brother and your clan have suffered grievous losses."

Hei looks down, pleased despite his pain that Chief Tau remembers his father.

For a while, no one speaks. Tau is deep in thought, and the flickering fire draws strange pictures on his face. At last he says, "As for the deer, your clan is not alone. Clans in all the valleys have been having more and more difficulty finding herds and water. There has been little rain for many moons, and the rivers and lakes are drying up everywhere."

Tau's words trouble Hei greatly. "Has your clan found any herds nearby?"

"Only a few small ones, but our scouts saw deer in great numbers two days north of here, and tomorrow we're going after them on a long hunt. Will you join us, Hei? We could use a man as good with a spear as you are."

Hei hesitates, reluctant to be away from his clan much longer.

Eva reads his expression. "Han's foot is healing, but it will be some time before he is strong enough for your long journey home."

"Then I will be honored to join your hunt, Chief," Hei says.

At dawn the next morning, Tau and his fifteen hunters head north out of the camp. Hei walks with Tau, peppering him with questions.

"How did you become chief?" he asks.

"Eva's parents were chief and shaman of a large clan, and they chose me to marry her." Tau smiles. "They said they selected the strongest and smartest hunter in all the clans for the privilege of marrying their only daughter. When they grew to old to lead, Eva became the new shaman and I became the new chief, according to clan tradition."

The hunters jog northward and reach a big valley late on the second day. After they start campfires to ward off night predators, they eat a meal of dried meat, nuts, and plant roots dug near their campsite. During their foraging, they recall how their mothers and their clanswomen taught them which plants are safe to eat and which are poisonous. Hei listens, recalling his own mother's lessons, his sadness tempered this time by gratitude for her and by the camaraderie of the other men.

In the morning, as they douse their fires, a scout runs up to Chief Tau. "A deer herd, a big one!" he says, pointing to the other end of the valley. The hunters quickly follow him, and soon they come upon the herd grazing by a sun-dappled stream. Tau divides his men into three groups and outlines his plan of attack, speaking in a low voice so as not to spook the deer or any other animals in the area. Where there are deer, there are often predators as eager for prey as the clan is.

The hunters surround the deer, and by nightfall they have killed five, Hei felling one of them with a single throw of his spear. They return to camp with their load of meat, Chief Tau at the head of the procession, Nee skulking along at the rear, and soon the entire clan has heard the news of what happened on the hunt: Nee panicked at the sight of a lion, and instead of assembling his group in a tight line to shout and brandish their spears and scare the beast away, he ran. The lion went after him and was on top of Nee and would have killed him if Hei hadn't sprinted to his rescue and stabbed the lion in the neck.

When Tan hears about his son's act of cowardice, he confronts him, his face a thundercloud. "You were a fool to run, Nee. You have shamed our family."

That night, at a celebratory feast of roasted deer and lion, Chief Tau honors Hei again, for his courage in saving Nee and for his hunting prowess. Lee again sits directly across the campfire from him, smiling, and he sees Chief Tau observing his daughter's interest in him with what Hei decides is approval. When the feast ends, he goes to Lee and asks her to take a walk with him.

She rises swiftly, as if she has been waiting for him, and they stroll through the camp to a secluded spot on the other side of the hilltop. It is a clear night, and they lie down together and look for patterns in the stars. He leans toward her and embraces her, and without his intention, he feels his manhood rise. Lee moans softly, and their bodies melt together.

There is no need for words on their walk back to camp, but as they approach, Hei finds himself worrying about what Chief Tau and Shaman Eva will think if they learn what he and their daughter have just done. Still, he would do it again, so strong are his feelings for the only girl who has ever taken away the pain of losing his first love. At the edge of the camp, they stop and kiss, and with reluctance and longing, Lee goes to her sleeping mat and Hei to his.

In the morning, as the camp is beginning to stir, Chief Tau seeks Hei out. "Walk with me," he says.

Hei feels a stab of fear. Did Lee say anything to her father about last night? Is the chief about to inform him of his impending death? They walk along in silence until the noises of the camp fade and the chief stops and turns to him.

"Hei, you are a fine young man. Eva and I want you to join our clan and marry Lee." He clears his throat. "And we know Lee wants you."

This is the last thing Hei expected to hear. He hasn't thought much beyond his love for Lee, but now he must. If he marries her, he will become part of Chief Tau's clan, abandoning his own, which needs him desperately.

"You do me great honor, Chief," he says, "but my clan

needs every hunter it has, and I can't leave them now, especially after our chief was just killed."

Tau frowns. "I have not yet told Lee of my choice, but you are the only one she has ever wanted. We all want you, Hei. Take the night to think things over, and give me your decision tomorrow."

Back at camp, Hei finds his brother and confers with him about what Chief Tau has proposed. Han says that he will support Hei no matter what his decision and that he is sure the clan can manage without him. "My ankle has healed, and I can return to our clan alone and tell them what happened to Chief Paa," he says. "Now that we know there are herds to the north, we can track them and survive even if you don't return."

Despite Han's reassurances, Hei struggles with his decision. He knows his small clan needs him back—he is their best hunter—but he loves Lee and would be proud to be chief of her clan one day. These conflicted thoughts make it impossible to sleep. Just before dawn, he hears footsteps and sees two figures disappear behind the trees, one tall and one short, probably heading away from the campsite to make water. "Or to do what Lee and I did last night," he whispers, smiling to himself.

The light of morning brings him clarity. He goes to Chief Tau. "I must return to my clan," he says, "but I'll convince them to move north, for better hunting and to be close to your clan, which is larger and will give us more security. Han and I will leave today."

His anxiety about how Chief Tau will receive his decision vanishes when the chief claps him on the shoulder and says,

"A good choice, Hei. You are not only strong but wise. I can't say Lee will wait for you, but judging from the sunshine in her eyes these past days, I think she will."

When Tau tells his wife and daughter that Hei and Han are leaving, sadness overcomes Lee, but she understands Hei's reasons. She and Eva pack a pouch of berries and a two large bags dried deer meat for the brothers' long trek home, and then they walk with Hei and Han to the outskirts of the camp. Lee pulls Hei aside and hugs him with all her strength. "I'll be back soon," he tells her, and forces himself to take the first steps away from her.

As he and Han depart, he keeps glancing back to see Lee waving until she finally disappears. Setting his gaze resolutely ahead, he notices two silhouettes on a rocky hill, backlit by the morning sun.

"Hei!" Nee shouts, raising his spear. He and San are waving from a tall boulder halfway up the next hill Hei and Han must cross on their journey.

"What's this? What can those two want?" Hei says to Han as they climb the hill.

After greetings, San wanders off as if wishing to give his brother privacy, and Nee says, "I heard you were leaving today, and I wanted to thank you for saving my life, but it would have hurt my pride to do it in front of the clan. I'm sorry for the way I behaved."

Nee puts a hand on Hei's shoulder. His smile is too bright, his words too hollow, but Hei thinks it would be rude to rebuff him. He looks to Han, whose expression tells him that the choice is his alone. He is just about to accept Nee's apology when he sees San slinking back toward them with one hand behind him, as if holding a surprise gift.

"Please take this with you for additional protection," Nee says, extending his spear sideways in presentation, and then he flips it forward and thrusts it at Hei.

Hei jumps back and grabs the spear, but too late: the stone tip pierces his chest. He falls to his knees, and can only watch as San strikes Han's head with the rock he was hiding. Groaning, Hei pulls the spear from his chest and looks up through a fog of agony to see his attacker's eyes widen in fear.

"Run, San! Leave them to the lions!" Nee yells, sprinting away down the other side of the hill.

Hei raises his head and sees two lions loping toward him. Han comes to, groggy, and is crawling to his brother when he spots them. The bags of deer meat Lee and Eva packed are right by his hand, and he manages to grab them and throw them to the lions, who stop to devour the easy meal in front of them, giving Han just enough time to pull Hei up and support him as they make a stumbling scramble to the top of the boulder. They watch, sure the lions will follow, but then the beasts raise their massive heads, sniff the air, and bound down the hill.

Han can't believe his eyes. He cradles Hei's head in his hand. "They're gone. Here, drink," he says, holding his water pouch to Hei's mouth. "How bad is your wound? Take your hand off it, let me see." On unsteady legs, he goes down the hill a short way and comes back with some wood and some dark green leaves. "Chew these, they will ease your pain," he says, and builds a small fire. After a time he asks, "Brother, should we go back to Tau's camp."

Hei watches the sun set as a full moon comes up over the

horizon. "No, Nee and San might see us coming and try to kill us again, and besides, we need to get home."

The next morning, they trek off to the south, making steady progress as their injuries gradually heal, and after five days they arrive at their camp. The clan greets them joyfully until they hear the terrible news about the death of Paa and Joh.

"Why didn't you return right away to tell us of the loss of my brothers?" demands Poh, who has assumed the duties of chief in Paa's absence.

Hei looks at him squarely. "We were certain that our chief would have wanted us to continue with his mission of finding food for the clan, so we kept going north searching for deer herds, and we found some, and then we found another clan. We had to stay with them for a while because Han injured his foot and couldn't walk."

Poh scowls.

"There are no herds here," Hei says. "We must follow your brother's wishes and go north to the valley where Han and I found deer."

"No," Poh declares. "Moving that far north with women and children will take twice as long as it took you, and besides, we don't have enough food and water for such a long, foolish trip. After you left, I went out myself, and I saw a few wildebeest to the west."

"But there is plenty of game up north, and—"

Poh holds up a hand. "At the next full moon, we will go west to hunt wildebeest."

Hei looks down at the ground and shakes his head, thinking about his past troubles with Poh, who has always been jealous of his superior hunting skills.

"You know my wife died years ago," Poh says suddenly. "As chief, I must marry again, and I can choose any eligible female I want. I have decided who that will be."

Hei frowns. The clan now has twenty-five people, but only two females are eligible for marriage. One is a girl named Tu, the other is—

"Your sister Fei will be my wife," Poh says with a sly smile.

Hei shudders. Fei is five years younger than he is. At ten, she is tall and looks older, but she hasn't yet become a woman. Even if she is of an age to marry according to the clan's practice, she is too young, and she can't stand Poh. None of the clanswomen can. He bosses them around, and he beat his late wife, and he still beats his daughter.

Hei mulls over his sister's predicament until the sun has almost set. When he goes to her and tells her of Chief Po's decision, she buries her face in her arms and cries like the child she is.

He strokes her back. "I won't let it happen."

She looks up at him tearfully. "But how?"

Hei looks around the camp. This is his home, where he has lived all his fifteen years, but the only thing that matters now is saving his sister from Poh.

"We leave tomorrow, before the sun comes up. We'll go to the clan I met in the north. I will tell Han, but nobody else. He'll understand, but he will stay here—"

"Yes, I know why." Fei smiles a secretive smile.

Five days later, the sun is going down as Hei approaches Tau's hilltop camp. Eva, who is out gathering plants, sees him and runs to greet him.

"You've come back, Hei! I'm so glad—" She breaks off, noticing Fei.

"We have come to join your clan, Shaman Eva," he says, peering over her shoulder. Lee stands on the hilltop, but when she sees him with Fei, she drops her arm mid-wave and turns away.

Hei is confused but remembers his manners. "This is my sister, Fei, Shaman Eva. May I speak to the chief?"

"Your sister?" Eva's eyes light with understanding. She hugs them both and then glances back to look for Lee, who has disappeared. "The men are out hunting. Come, Fei, I have someone I want you to meet."

When they reach the camp, Hei sees Lee sitting on a log underneath a tree, staring at the ground. How he longs to see her beautiful face once again.

"We have company, Lee," Eva calls cheerfully, as if enjoying a great secret.

Lee sits unmoving, her face still in shadow.

"We have guests, Lee. Is that a proper way to behave?"

"I'm sorry, Mother." Lee stands up and looks at Hei and Fei, tears in her eyes.

"Lee, this is Hei's sister, Fei."

Lee's eyes widen. She gives Fei a huge hug, startling her, and throws herself into Hei's arms.

When the hunting party returns, Nee and San catch sight of Hei and stare in disbelief, then turn on their heels. Chief Tau watches them go, puzzled, and then he welcomes Hei and Fei warmly and invites them to his campfire. After they exchange news of their clans, Hei falls silent. He has debated whether to tell Tau what happened after he and Han left, and has finally decided he must, but he doesn't know where to start.

"Is something troubling you?" the chief asks.

Silently, Hei unrolls the long bundle he has been carrying since he and Fei left home. He holds up Nee's spear, points to the scar on his chest, and tells how Nee and San tried to kill him and his brother.

Lee and Eva blanch, and Tau's face goes black. He waves a passing hunter over and tells him to summon Tan.

"Where are your sons?" he demands when Tan presents himself.

"I don't know. They came back to camp with the rest of the hunters, but then they said they were going out again to scout for deer."

"They tried to kill Hei and his brother. We cannot have that," Tau says.

Tan is aghast. "There must be some mistake. My sons would never do something like that. Why—"

The chief holds up a hand for silence. "Go. Find them. Tell them they are never to return."

This punishment seems harsh, even to Hei. All the clans understand that banishment is akin to a sentence of death. Without a clan's protection, most exiles cannot survive long in the unforgiving wilderness.

"Go," Chief Tau repeats, and Tan, shoulders slumped, walks toward the forest to tell his sons the grim news.

Lee watches the fifteen other young clanswomen who are stretching and breathing deeply in preparation for the endurance race. Her wedding is tomorrow, and today is a celebration day, with many races and contests for both men and women. Her desire to win this race is greater than in the past because it is her chance to show the men of the clan—which now includes Hei—her speed and stamina. Her main competition is Sai, who has won all the women's endurance races for the last four years.

She turns to see Hei and Fei walking toward her. Her soon-to-be husband beams at her and then asks, "Can Fei run in the race? She's only ten, and she's never competed in a long race, but she's a very good runner."

Lee studies Fei. The girl is big for her age and as tall as she is. "I'm glad you want to run," she says. "May I offer you some advice? Don't start too fast. Run a steady pace from the beginning, and try to keep alongside me."

Fei nods eagerly.

Lee, Fei, and the other runners take their places at the starting line. A gentle wind is blowing, a few puffy white clouds drift across the blue sky, and Hei is watching.

The race starts. Three young girls sprint down the hillside ahead of the rest, and Lee and Sai follow. Lee glances over her shoulder and sees Fei only a few steps behind.

The pace holds until halfway through the course, when Sai, Lee, and Fei begin to close the gap with the leaders. They pass them in the second valley, Sai in first place as they cross over the last hill, Lee and Fei just behind her. Lee scans the crowd and sees Hei near the finish line. She nods to Fei, who is running stride for stride alongside her, and they sprint ahead like deer and pass Sai. Lee grabs Fei's arm and raises their clasped hands as they cross the finish line together.

Two winners. The camp roars its approval.

The next day, Hei watches the clan prepare for the grand

feast and wedding, and joins the hunters in carving new wood spears and making new stone knives. While they work, they laugh at the antics of the children, who are playing hide-and-seek and running short races. As night falls, the moon shines full and bright, and the smell of roasting deer meat teases his nose. He smiles. This is a good life, without petty jealousies or worries about an abusive chief, and it is his life now.

Chief Tau, Eva, and Lee approach Hei's fire. "It is time for the first ceremony," Tau says, leading them to a secluded spot on the other side of the hill. He points to a semicircle of low boulders, and they all sit down in a silence that lasts for several moments. Then Eva stands, radiant in the moonlight, and takes a leather pouch from behind her boulder.

"Hei, it is our tradition to give gifts at the time of a man and woman finding each other, but tonight I want to give you a special gift that will bond you and Lee and your future children to our family always." She reaches into the pouch and pulls out four lion's teeth strung on a leather thong. "Two of these are from the lion you killed when you saved Lee's life, and the other two are from the lion you killed when you saved Nee."

She holds the necklace out and shows Hei and Lee the precise cut mark in one of the teeth. Hei reaches out and rubs it with his finger.

"What's that for?" he says, turning to Lee, who appears as puzzled as he is.

Eva smiles."You'll see. Tau, give me the river rock and your arm."

Chief Tau hands her a sharp rock that sparkles in the moonlight, and she gently cuts his arm with it. She dabs her finger in his blood, smears it into the cut mark on the lion's tooth, and repeats the process on her own arm. Then she looks at Hei and Lee. "Come," she says, and performs the blood ceremony with them too.

"Our mingled blood on the tooth necklace will bond us together always," Tau says.

"Yes, and it will do much more," Eva says, tying the necklace around Lee's neck. The ivory teeth nestled between Lee's breasts seem to glow against her ebony skin. To Hei, the necklace seems like a kind of protection, a shield that will protect him and Lee and their children from harm.

Eva looks from her daughter to Hei and back again. "Will you take a solemn oath to pass the necklace on to your children and to teach them everything you know?"

"We will," Lee says, and Hei's heart swells as he echoes her answer, because it is as if Eva has heard his innermost thoughts.

"Your oldest daughter and her husband will add their blood to a new cut mark," Eva goes on, "and her oldest daughter will do the same, and each oldest daughter will always do the same, and our family's spirit and goodness will be passed on forever."

They complete the private wedding ceremony and walk back to the campsite, where Shaman Eva presides over a simple ceremony witnessed by the whole clan. Then the clan members go to their separate campfires to enjoy roasted deer meat and Chief Tau's special brew. Though the details are secret, Tau tells Hei that creating the special brew involves placing various plants and roots in water, allowing the mixture to sit in the full sun, and then shading it at just the right point for a time known only to the maker.

Eva watches proudly as Hei and Lee participate in another tradition, visiting each campfire to listen to stories about the clan and the ancestors while the children play and eat sweet berries and nuts. After a time, Lee giggles. "My mother ordered me to pass this necklace to my daughter, but I don't have one yet. Whatever shall we do about that?" she whispers to Hei, and leads him to the campfire laid especially for them in the most out-of-the-way spot in the camp.

That night, Lee dreams she is flying over hills and valleys, using her arms to glide up and down effortlessly, following a long winding river and a deer herd. When she tells Hei of the dream the next morning, he says, "Surely only good can come from such a dream, one dreamt in the midst of such a happy time."

The Hei-Lee Clan

It has been twenty seasons since Hei and Lee married, and five seasons since Chief Tau and Shaman Eva died after a long and happy life together. They have been hard seasons because of the same threat that loomed in Chief Paa's day and has been growing worse: the rains no longer come with regularity if they come at all, all the rivers and lakes in the great valley have dried up, and all the animals are nearly gone. There is nothing to do but what the clan has always done. They must move if they hope to survive.

Following two once-mighty rivers that are starting to dry up, Hei leads his clan steadily north until they finally come to an enormous body of water, larger than any of them have ever seen. They quickly discover that the water is salty and that those who drink it sicken and die despite Lee's plant medicines. Hei keeps hoping Lee will have dreams foretelling that the rains will come again, but her only dreams are of rivers, not of rain.

He shades his eyes and looks out across the salty sea. If he squints, he can see a sliver of land beyond the water. Are the rivers Lee has dreamed of over there? Other clans are camped near his along the coast, and the bravest scouts from some of these clans have attempted to cross on log rafts. Few have returned, but just yesterday two came back to report that the sea is shallow all the way across and that there are clans thriving on the other side.

As Hei stares at the eastern horizon, he hears a man yelling, "Come on! Line those logs up the way I told you." Hei turns to see the men of another clan arranging ten long logs side by side. "Now put those across them and tie them together," the man directs, pointing to five shorter logs and a pile of animal-hide strips beside him.

Behind him, Hei hears the lively chatter of his children, all grown now, and all named after their four grandparents. Oni married a few seasons ago and now has two young children, her sister Eva is about to marry, and their brothers, Tau and An, are ready to seek suitable mates. Hearing their voices makes Hei happy, as it always has, but his happiness is clouded by his worries about their survival.

The next morning, Hei consults with Han, who left Chief Poh's clan long ago. As soon as he married Yee, his childhood love, he took her north to find Tau's clan and reunite with his brother. Han and Yee now have children of their own, and Han is as worried about the future as Hei is.

"Come," Hei says, leading Han to the shore, where a

crowd has gathered to watch the men who built the raft yesterday push it into the sea. There are ten aboard, several of them using long wooden poles to guide it as the sun bores down on them.

"I asked them to light a big fire on the other shore to show that they arrived safely," Hei tells Han. "If we see that glow on the horizon, it will be the sign we need."

Han nods and leaves to return to his family. Hei lingers for a moment, watching the raft recede, then turns to go back to his own family and notices two men standing at the edge of the crowd, one tall and one short. He walks toward them, more certain with each step that they are his old adversaries, but they see him approaching and vanish. He tries to follow them, but the crowd is too thick, and there is no sign of them by the time he reaches the spot where he saw them. Disgraced and banished from their clan, Nee and San must have survived somehow and come to the coast for the same reason he did, because the big valley was drying up. If the two are living nearby, he will never sleep well again.

That evening, Hei goes back to the shore. He is pondering what to do about Nee and San when he sees a yellow glow on the horizon. No, it's not starlight, it's not moonlight, it's—

"Fire! Fire on the other side!" he calls, pointing, and the rest of the clan comes running to look out across the sea to the other shore.

With the fire bolstering him, Hei at last makes his decision and announces it to the clan. "That fire means we can make it across," he says. "We will go as soon as we build enough rafts."

There is silence until one of the clan's revered elders stands and speaks. "I have a bad feeling about this. An elder of another clan told me it is much too dangerous. If we fall into the water, we will surely drown, and if we don't drown, the salt will poison us. My wife and I have never been in the sea before. None of us has. What if this elder's words are true?"

"You all know me, and you must trust that I came to this decision after much thought," Hei says. "Listen to our shaman."

Lee steps forward. "I too have fears, but each time there has been a crossing, we have learned much. Just in the past few days we have seen four glowing fires on the other side. Animals are scarce here, and it is getting harder to find food each day. If we don't go, we will starve."

The old man's wife turns to him and touches his hand. "I don't want us to be left alone here. Hei, we will go."

It is impossible to cut down live trees with stone tools, so Hei's clan follows the example of the other clans and searches for fallen trees in a forest near a long river that feeds into the sea. Each of the fifty clan members helps drag the logs back to the shore, and before long, they have six sturdy rafts. Hei scans the coastline in both directions. They have competed with the other clans for logs, just as they do for food, and now they will have to guard the finished rafts overnight. Hei's youngest son the first to volunteer.

"All right, An, and Raa will join you." At thirteen, An is strong and smart, and Hei has great confidence in him, but with the danger posed by Nee and San, he wants a more experienced hunter to keep watch with him. "Han and I will take the second shift, and if the sea is calm tomorrow, we will cross at sunrise."

Three hours later, Hei and Han walk toward the shore under a bright moon. "Where are the rafts?" Han says. "I don't see them where we left them. Can they have drifted away?" The brothers pick up their pace and are soon standing where the rafts should be. In their place are two forms lying face down. Hei kneels and turns the smaller one over.

"No!" His howl of pain rends the night and brings the rest of the clan running. When Lee sees her son cradled in Hei's arms, his throat cut, she screams and throws herself on the limp body. Raa's brother rushes to Han, who is kneeling over the other body in shock. Raa's throat has been cut too.

Hei can't speak, not even to try to comfort Lee or his other children, who are weeping over their brother's body. He blames himself; he should never have let An stand guard. He stares out at the sea, his heart a stone in his chest.

Hei's cry has been heard all along the coast, and another clan chief approaches him. "I know who did this," he says quietly. "I saw Nee and San's clan leaving on your rafts."

Hei says nothing, just stares out across the water and nods. He knew who the murderers were the instant he saw An's body.

He will build more rafts. Now nothing on earth will keep him from crossing to the other side.

It takes the clan a month to build six new rafts, and it is a difficult month. The competition for logs is fierce as more and more new clans arrive at the coast, lingering only long enough to build their rafts and make the crossing. In addition, Hei's clan is grieving for An and Raa, and many are more fearful than before about the journey across the sea, but with each passing day, their sources of food and water dwindle. It is time to go.

Because of the renewed anxiety about the crossing, Hei

has decided to take half the clan across on three rafts, with the rest following only if they see the glow of the first group's fire. He and Lee will be on the lead raft; his son Tau, who at fifteen is strong and capable and almost as determined as Hei is to go to the other side and pursue his brother's murderers, will be in charge of the second raft; and Waa, husband of Oni, will take her and their two children, Jaa and Sar, on the third raft with the last group.

On the day of departure, Hei stands on the shore supervising the loading of the rafts and looking across the sea at his clan's future home. Soon after they land, his daughter Eva will marry Kan, the clan's best hunter, making the venture a new beginning for her, and for all of them, he hopes. Light chatter catches his attention, and he watches Oni and her family climb onto their raft. It is a warm, sunny day, and white clouds amble across the blue sky. The wind has picked up a little since dawn, but the water looks safe enough. He boards his raft with Lee and Eva, signaling the two clansmen who are steadying the raft with long poles to push off. He looks at the two other rafts slowly leaving shore with their anxious passengers and calls, "Stay next to each other and close behind me."

As the clansmen waving from the shore become specks in the distance, the wind grows stronger and the waves grow bigger. "Don't drift, stay close!" Hei calls again, but the waves get bigger still, until he sees a huge one roll over Waa's raft and sweep Oni and her children overboard.

"Help!" Oni screams, and Waa pulls her and then Sar back onto the raft, but he can't see Jaa anywhere. As he dives into the briny water, Jaa's head bobs up, then back down. Waa reaches down blindly, finds Jaa's arm, and tows him back to the raft, but the tiny body is motionless.

Helplessly, Hei and Lee watch from their raft as Oni cradles her son. His own heart breaking, Hei directs all three rafts back to shore.

Days later, Hei stands in darkness, staring across the sea. More fires are blinking across the wide expanse, proof that other clans have crossed safely. His own clan's six rafts lie at his feet, the water lapping at them, waiting. Food is even scarcer now, with hunger and thirst daily occurrences. He goes back to the camp and calls a clan meeting.

"We will starve here," he says. "Many others have made it across safely. We must try again."

Oni watches Sar playing in the moonlight, then whispers to her husband. She stands and says, "We don't want to lose another child. We will stay."

Never before has any of his children defied him, but Hei knows he must respect his daughter's decision. He listens to the clan members mumbling among themselves and watches as one after another goes to stand with Oni and Waa. Soon the camp quiets, divided into two groups.

"It is decided, then," Hei says. "For those of you coming with me, we leave first thing tomorrow."

That night, at their campfire, Lee takes Hei's hand. "So much loss," she says, her voice breaking. "I don't know how to bear it. First An, and now Oni will be gone from us too. We gave her the sacred tooth necklace years ago when she married, but what about our family bonding, and what about Eva? My parents meant the necklace to bind us all forever."

"Then we must make a second necklace for Eva," he says.

Lee's beautiful face brightens. "Yes, I'm sure Oni will

agree, but Eva must marry before we leave."

"But we go in the morning—"

"No!" Lee says with a sudden resolve that tells Hei not to argue. "I will see my daughter married, and I will preside over the bonding ceremony, as all my ancestors have done before me. Eva and Kan will marry, and we will not leave before then."

Over the next two days, while the clan prepares for the wedding, Eva lovingly fashions a second necklace out of the first, with Oni's blessing. She removes two of the four lion's teeth, strings them on a new leather thong, and replaces the worn thong on the old necklace. She brings the new necklace to Hei, and he cuts a precise groove into one of the teeth with the same sharp shiny rock her father had used so long ago.

The next night, just before the wedding, Lee presents the second necklace to Eva, to her enormous surprise, and performs the blood-bonding ceremony. Hei watches proudly as Lee puts her handiwork around Eva's neck.

Then Lee turns to Oni and Waa. "You are now leaders of a new clan that will stay here. Think of us as you continue your lives, as we will think of you." She opens her arms to her daughter, and they embrace, crying over what is being lost and hoping for what might be gained, a new life on both sides of the mysterious salty sea.

The sun shines brightly on Hei's clan in their new home. He listens to birds chirping and smells flowers blooming all around him as he watches Kan and his hunters poised in a semicircle over the water. He looks across the sea and wonders how Oni and her new clan are faring. Have they found enough food to survive the drought? He sighs, realizing that he may never know.

"Hyah!" Kan cries, thrusting his spear into the roiling water and bringing up a big fish that flaps and struggles for freedom. In a single motion, he flings the fish off the spear point, and it lands near Hei's feet. The hunters soon spear five more fish.

Hei smiles. They will have plenty of food tonight, though this wasn't so in the days following the crossing. As the clan traveled along the coast toward the morning sun, they had to learn how to catch fish. They made longer, thinner spears with sharper points. They fashioned traps from bamboo found inland and discovered that they could dig for shellfish. Hei shakes his head, thinking of their initial struggles. Fishing isn't man's work like hunting animals, but it keeps them alive. He has sent scouts inland to search for deer herds, but they find only a barren desert and report that all the clans in the area are heading east along the coast.

Hei wipes sweat from his forehead. It is hotter here than it was on the other side. The clan has had to build lean-to tents out of branches and leaves to shield the babies from the hot sun during the day. Tomorrow they will take down the tents at dawn and continue along the coast in search of game and plants.

As the sun sets and the sea breezes bring relief from the heat, Hei sees an old man limping toward the camp. A long wound runs from his thigh down his leg, which is horribly swollen. Hei calls out to him and waves him over. The man hesitates, then approaches, his head down. Hei notices him glancing at a fish roasting over a campfire and offers him a piece. The man tears into it as if he hasn't eaten for days, which perhaps he has not. Hei waits in silence until he finishes and licks his fingers.

"What happened to you?" Hei points at his wound.

"Raiders. Three suns ago, they attacked us at night. They killed most of my clan and took our women."

Hei's neck hair bristles. "How many were there?"

The man, who says his name is Sho, holds up both hands and spreads his fingers. "This many. They snuck up on us and struck before we could defend ourselves. They made me watch them raping my daughter. They—"

"Did you recognize any of them?"

Sho nods. "There was a tall man like you and a small one. I'd seen them walking by our camp several times. The tall one was called Nee."

Terrible memories flood Hei's mind. "We will find them," he says in a steely voice, gesturing toward his hunters gathered around their fires. "You will lead us back to your camp, and we will track them from there. We will find those savages and kill them all."

Sho guides them for two days, trying to help fish when they stop for the evening but mostly sitting under a tent holding his leg in pain. Shaman Lee ministers to him with her medicinal herbs and roots, and the wound begins to heal. The old man cries often.

On the morning of the third day, he stops and points. "There," he says. "It happened there."

They walk a distance farther, and Hei stops in horror. Remnants of lean-tos litter the beach, and decaying bodies lie about, partly eaten by birds. Sho goes from one body to another, pausing to name each one.

Hei sends scouts out from Sho's camp in every direction. When the sun is high, one of them returns saying that he has found the place where the killers are camped with the captured women.

"We strike tomorrow," Hei says. "Tonight we prepare." He turns to his men, their faces somber and determined. "Sharpen your spears. Tomorrow we hunt predators of our own kind."

The next day, the sky is clear blue and the sun sparkles on the sea. The scout leads them and stops within sight of smoke rising behind a low hill. "The killers are there," he tells Hei.

Retreating to a safe distance, the clan makes camp, and Hei's hunters gather around him, each carrying two spears and their knives. Lee brings him his water pouch, and her eyes tell him she loves him. He looks around the camp. Women and children of all ages sit at their fires, along with old men who can no longer hunt. Sho sits with the other old men. He asked to come, but Hei told him to stay and help protect the women.

At dusk, Hei and his men set out. When they see the smoke from the enemy campfires, they tiptoe closer and wait for Hei's signal. Hearing drunken laughter, Hei raises his spear silently, and his men rush the camp. The enemy warriors stumble to their feet, staring, as twenty spears fly through the air. Screaming, they scramble for their own weapons, and Hei's men unleash a second volley. Then they unsheath their knives.

Hei sees Kan stab San in the back. But where is Nee? Hei looks everywhere and finally spots the coward crawling toward a copse of bushes to hide. He is bleeding from several spear wounds. Hei stands over him, staring into his terrified eyes.

"Please," Nee begs, "please don't kill me. I'll do anything you want, I promise."

"Once, I believed your promise, and almost lost my life because I trusted you." Hei drives his knife deep into Nee's neck, his face tight with rage, then pulls the knife out slowly and walks away.

Hei has imagined this moment for many years, but now that it has come, he feels no solace. His beloved son is still gone. The loss hits him all over again, and he falls to his knees in grief.

Chief Kan and Shaman Eva sit gazing into a flickering campfire late at night. As Kan lovingly rubs his wife's neck, she says, "I miss my brother An and my sister Oni, but I miss my father and mother most of all." It has been one year since Hei and Lee died peacefully of old age.

"I miss them too," Kan says. "They were great leaders, loved by all the clans on the coast. They cared for everybody and did many good things."

Tears slide down Eva's cheeks as she looks up at the stars. "I hope you and I will lead the clan as well as they did."

Kan takes her in his arms. "I know a way to keep their spirit alive for generations to come. We will take Hei-Lee as our clan name, and you and I will take their names too."

Eva wipes away her tears. "Yes, what better way to honor them and preserve their memory."

"And one more thing. All our clan's future leaders will be called Chief Hei and Shaman Lee."

Eva smiles, her eyes bright with love. "I like that, Chief

Hei. They would be proud to know their names are not lost."

* * *

Iran, 78,000 Years Before Present

Chief Hei pauses on a trail along a river that streams down to the coast. He stares up at the black clouds that have slowly covered the sky, creating a gloom so complete that he can hardly see the tip of his spear. For several days now, he and his scouts have been looking for a new campsite inland where they hope to find good hunting.

Suddenly lightning streaks across the sky, thunder rumbles, and a heavy rain pours down. "To the trees!" Hei yells, and he crouches with the scouts under the scant cover of a few small pines. The wind is blowing almost sideways, soaking the men with stabs of cold water. Hei looks around for some larger trees and sees a dark patch up a nearby hill. Through the silver sheet of rain, it looks like a big opening.

"Follow me!" he shouts, and the group runs up the hill into a dark hole, away from the torment of the driving rain.

Hei stands there while his eyes adjust to the darkness. In the land his people have come from, there are no stories of holes such as this. For as long as anyone can remember, his clan lived on a grassy plain, constantly moving in search of deer. The old ones tell stories around the campfires of ancestors who once crossed a great water to escape animals that were killing their families. There are no such animals here, or at least none that Hei has found.

He touches the cave's hard walls, finds them surprisingly

cool and dry. The floor is smooth, and the space large enough for a man to take several easy strides. Outside the rain pounds down, the wind whips the trees, and the rumble from above is deafening, but in here it is drier than any tent could be. It feels safe.

He turns to his scouts, who are hunched up and shivering with cold. "Make a fire," he says. "We stay here tonight."

It is still raining hard the next morning. The group sits around a smoldering fire made from debris they found in the cave the night before. Hei waves to chase away the smoke and says to the others, "This would be a good place to live. It's better than our tents when it rains."

"But it's not big enough for our whole clan," one scout says.

Hei nods. "When it stops raining, we'll look for a bigger hole in a bigger hill."

At last a feeble sun comes out, and they search the nearby hills, climbing higher and higher through tangles of vines and sparse trees that cling to the rocky soil. Never before has Hei seen such rough land. They pass numerous caves, all too small, and then one of the scouts calls out, "Look!"

Hei's gaze follows the scout's to a wide opening in the hillside with huge boulders all around it. It looks like a giant smiling mouth. They approach, and Hei stops to scan the surrounding landscape. Below, a wide river snakes through a big green valley and meets a larger river to the north. Tall trees, green bushes, and thick grasses fill both river valleys, and he sees two deer drinking at the first river. This hill will make a good lookout for the clan's hunters.

He steps through the wide opening into a huge cavern, its domed ceiling at least three times taller than he is. It becomes lower as he goes deeper inside, alert for any beasts or holes or other dangers. He stops at the back wall, perhaps thirty paces from the mouth, with enough room to stand. The cave is twice as wide as it is deep. It's chilly, but it will do. The entire clan will fit, and some families can live in the smaller caves nearby if they wish.

Hei turns to his scouts. "This will be our new campsite. We'll stay here tonight, and tomorrow we'll go back and prepare the rest of the clan for the move." He squats at the mouth of the cave, wondering what Lee and the others will think of their new home. They are used to living in the open, sleeping under trees or tents made from animal skins and branches. Here in the mountain foothills, they will have to adapt to the cooler temperatures, but they will be safe. The cave will shelter them, and the rivers will give them fresh water, game, and edible vegetation.

All in all, it will be a new life, but a good one.

While the men build fires at the cave's opening, Lee walks around inside, inspecting every cranny. How strange to live in a hill! She didn't believe Hei when he told her about it, but now she and the other women are settling in like birds in a new nest. The ceiling overhead is smooth, but as she discovers now, the walls have cracks where she can store things. An indentation at the very back is big enough for her family of four to lie down. It will be cramped, but Oni, her oldest daughter, may soon be sleeping elsewhere. She is becoming a woman and already has her eyes on a young hunter, though she has yet to name him, even to her mother. Still, the shaman in Lee assures her that Oni will be in his bed before long.

Lee sets down the big hide bag that holds the family's

belongings, opens it, and sifts through it, removing stone knives, wooden cups, water pouches, and her bag of healing plants and leaves. Later she and the other women will go back down the trail and see what plants and nuts and berries they can find. In this new climate, there may also be medicinal plants that work as well as the ones she is familiar with, or even better.

Her eyes light on the leather pouch her mother gave her when she married Hei. According to the clan's legends, this bag and its contents have passed down through the generations since the beginning of time. Lee opens it and studies the necklace of two huge teeth, each nearly the length of her hand, said to have been taken from a fierce beast long, long ago. She goes outside and inspects the necklace more closely in the bright sunlight. Its leather thong is worn, and Lee reminds herself to replace it, as her mother told her to do. Cut marks circle both teeth in a pattern of ten groups of five cuts close together on each tooth, like five fingers on a hand. Her own father had cut the last groove the day she married Hei, and had told how their ancestors did the same and passed the necklace on to the next generation. So many ancestors! Five fingers, ten times, and just as many on the other tooth!

Then it strikes her. There are so many marks on both teeth that there is no space for another one. What will she do when Oni is ready to marry? The clan has yet to see an animal larger than a deer, let alone one as big as that ancient beast must have been. Well, she will just have to make do with deer teeth, she decides, because she can't break the tradition. The necklace is her spiritual tie to her parents and grandparents and all those who came before them. As she has been taught and as she believes, their spirits live forever in the necklace, and sometimes even talk with her as they did that very morning just before she woke up. She was sure it was her mother's voice, though now, in the light of day, she realizes that it could have been any one of her female ancestors speaking to her, warning her of an unnamed peril more deadly than her worst imaginings.

The Hei-Lee clan is always in peril. At any moment, a giant predator or a tiny venomous spider might take one of them. Sighing, Lee decides that her dream was no prophecy, merely an echo of a fear every human shares. She goes back into the cave, to the little nest she selected for her family, and finds a tiny niche in the rock wall. Reverently she slides the pouch into it for safekeeping until her daughter marries.

Many days later, when leaves have started to fall and cold winds are dancing through the valleys, Hei and his hunters return victorious with the meat from five deer. They drop it next to the fire pit on one side of the cave's mouth and spread the hides out on the boulders for drying. Hei finishes with the last hide and lingers to look for Lee, who has gone out to forage for plants. Seeing no sign of her, he turns to follow the other hunters into the cave and hears snuffling behind him.

He whirls around to see a huge brown beast standing on its hind legs, so close that he can smell its breath. The creature is easily twice his height, and it looks down into his frightened eyes for a long moment before it goes on all fours and ambles past him toward the raw deer meat. Out of the corner of his eye, Hei sees several of his hunters creeping toward him from the other side of the cave, spears at the ready.

While the beast is occupied with the deer meet, Hei

gestures to his hunters and leads them up the hillside to a ledge directly above the mouth of the cave. Rocks of all sizes lie in the surrounding scrub brush, and Hei picks up the biggest one he can carry and wrestles it to the ledge. His hunters follow suit and line up next to him. Below them, the beast is still feeding.

"Now!" Hei cries, and a volley of rocks rains down. The beast staggers up on its hind legs, roaring, and falls to the ground as the rest of the hunters run from the cave and drive their stone spears deep into its neck.

Hei climbs down from the hillside as clan members emerge from the cave tentatively, in case the beast isn't really dead. Relief washes over him when he sees Lee standing with Oni and a tall young man whose spear is dripping with the creature's blood.

"The teeth," Lee says, stepping forward.

"What?"

"I want the two biggest teeth."

Hei sits by the mouth of the hillside cave, watching his tiny granddaughter play with the other children, cautioning them from time to time about staying well back from the sharp drop-off below. When darkness falls, Oni and the other mothers shepherd their children into the cave, but Hei remains outside, gazing up at the stars.

Where has time gone? Many winters have passed. His son has become a renowned hunter, and Oni now has three children, all girls. As Lee had assured him, the tall young man Oni fell in love with and married has displayed great skills in hunting and leadership. Hei looks toward the cave and summons the image of his granddaughter toddling around at play. He will blink his eyes and she will be grown and he will be gone.

The earth beneath him rumbles. He rises. Is that thunder? Another rumble, and then a violent shaking knocks him down. He hears screaming from the cave and claws his way over fallen rocks to the entrance. He can't see through the choking dust that fills the air, but over the din of rumbling and screaming, he hears someone shout, "Hei! Help us!"

It's Lee, he knows it is, and with all his strength he fights through the debris of the collapsed cave toward the nook at the back that has been his family's home for so long. A few other men join him, heaving fallen slabs of rock away as they search for their own wives and children.

In the end, they find the lifeless bodies of ten women and five children, one of them Hei's granddaughter. Lee and Oni survive, clutching each other as they and the few left of their clan mourn their losses. Hei watches stonily, unable to comprehend his grief, and then the earth beneath him shakes again.

"Everybody outside now!" he yells.

The clan huddles at the cave's mouth, afraid to go back inside. Occasionally the earth trembles again, and after several nights have passed, one fact is obvious: the Hei-Lee clan must leave. Hei confers with Lee and the clan's elders and decides that they must go south to the coast and then east toward the rising sun, never to return to the place that has taken their loved ones and left indelible scars on their hearts.

18
Soccer

San Francisco, February 2000

Lisa missed reading to her parents from John's book, but she had other things on her mind these days. She was worried about her mother, who hadn't been looking well lately, and she was worried about today's matches. She was Terra Grande High School's star soccer player, and for the first time her team was competing in the three-day San Francisco Invitational Tournament at the Polo Grounds in Golden Gate Park. The tournament was for northern California's top twenty teams, and Terra Grande was ranked sixteenth. Most of the other schools had twice as many students as Terra Grande, and Lisa knew the cards were stacked against her smaller school.

"Come on, everyone," Andy called from the hallway, jingling his car keys. "We better get going, we don't want to be late." He shooed his family into the garage and opened the passenger door for Eva as the twins piled into the backseat with their big sister.

"You know, Coach Hearn said there are going to be college

scouts at your games today," he said glancing at Lisa in the rearview mirror.

"Yeah, Dad. I know. No pressure there, huh?"

"Are you nervous?" Hanna asked.

"Yes. Stomach butterflies. Way bigger than monarchs, that's for sure."

"Actually, honey, that's a good thing," Eva said, turning around in her seat. "Nothing like a good case of nerves to get your adrenaline pumping and sharpen your wits. Don't worry about winning or losing. Just play hard and enjoy the game."

"I'll try, Mom."

"I know you will, honey."

"And don't forget, you've been doing great so far," Andy said. Lisa had scored four goals on the first day of the tournament, and her team had won both their games against larger schools. On the second day, she'd scored three goals, including the second game's winning goal, and the four wins had put them in the semifinals with three of California's top teams.

One thing Andy knew: Lisa had his and Eva's genes—the genes of an exceptional sprinter and a great long-distance runner. She had speed and endurance, and her competitive drive made her difficult to defend against and fun to watch. Coach Hearn obviously recognized her talents. He played her at center midfield, where she could cover the entire field and be active on both offense and defense.

It was a cool morning, just right for soccer. Andy went off to the concession stand to buy a special treat for the twins, hotdogs and sodas, and a cup of coffee for Eva, who said she could use "a little pick-me-up." He returned to his seat just as Lisa's team took the field against Santa Cruz High School, last year's tournament champion. Santa Cruz had a fast and powerful offense; they'd scored more than four goals in each of their first four tournament games.

Playing tenacious defense, Terra Grande held Santa Cruz to one goal in the first half. The Santa Cruz players body-checked Lisa hard and often when she had the ball, but just before the first half ended, she broke through at midfield, dribbling past two defenders and scoring the tying goal with a powerful shot from fifteen yards out.

Both teams continued to play good defense in the second half. Santa Cruz doubled-teamed Lisa whenever she had the ball, and neither team could score. In the game's final minutes, Lisa intercepted a pass at midfield, broke through a hard tackle, and sprinted ten yards up field. Two Santa Cruz defenders closed in on her, but not before she struck an accurate pass to an open teammate who softly bounced the ball off her chest for a perfect shot past the Santa Cruz goalie. The clock ran out, and Terra Grande was in the finals, lined up to play northern California's top-ranked school, San Jose High.

As the game got underway that afternoon, it was obvious that San Jose was determined to prevent Lisa from scoring. She was heavily marked and double-teamed whenever she had the ball. It was another physical game, with both teams playing a tight defense. Just before halftime, Lisa got the ball at midfield and shook off a double-team to take a powerful shot from twenty yards out. The ball sailed toward the corner of the goal, hit the top crossbar, and flew out of play, and the first half ended with no score.

In the second half, Andy could see that San Jose was even more serious about keeping Lisa away from the ball. When she took a pass and broke through a double-team, a third player tackled her from behind, knocking her to the ground. A foul was called.

Andy turned to Eva. "They're playing dirty now."

She nodded, but what he saw in his wife's eyes was a competitor's fire, not apprehension. "They play dirty, she's got to play tough."

Minutes later, Lisa was tackled from behind again and fell hard, scraping her elbow. The fans booed, and the referee gave the San Jose player a yellow card. Lisa ran off the field to the bench and had a quick exchange with Coach Hearn while the trainer attended to her bleeding elbow.

Back on the field, Terra Grande took control of the ball, moved it down the sideline, and passed it to Lisa twenty yards in front of San Jose's goal with the clock running out. Two defenders went for the ball, swinging their elbows, and Lisa swung back, knocking one of them down. When the other San Jose player tried to kick the ball away, Lisa leaned into her hard with her shoulder, shoved her out of the way, dribbled twice, and struck a powerful shot toward the left side of the goal. The goalie dove for it, but the ball sailed into the net.

The crowd roared. Eva, Andy, and the twins leapt to their feet, clapping and cheering. Lisa turned toward them in the stands and raised both arms in triumph as the final whistle blew and her teammates rushed her, smothering her in hugs and high fives.

Lisa had just come home from school the next day when the phone rang. Eva picked up, listened for a moment, and said, "Why, yes, she's right here." She handed the receiver to

Lisa, whispering, "It's the Berkeley soccer coach."

Eva watched her daughter's expression turn from surprise to elation during the brief conversation. "Full ride, Mom!" she said after she hung up. "I can't believe it!"

Over the next several weeks, Eva fielded more scholarship offers, from Stanford, UCLA, UC Santa Barbara, Cal Poly, and several out-of-state schools, including previous national soccer champions North Carolina and Portland.

"I think I'll go to a school in California," Lisa said one evening at the dinner table. "That way I'll be near my friends. And my family," she added.

Eva laid her fork down. "Good thinking. I remember my undergrad years at Northern Mississippi State. It helped to have friends and family nearby in Mound Bayou and Cleveland."

"Which is more important to you, honey?" Andy asked. "Playing soccer on a good team, or getting the best education?"

"I want both."

Eva nodded approvingly. "That shouldn't be a problem. Most of your offers are from excellent universities with outstanding athletic programs. I guess your decision will partly depend on what you want to major in."

"But I don't know what I want to major in," Lisa said plaintively.

"Well, let's talk about it. Were there any departments at those schools we visited last fall that you liked?"

Lisa shrugged. "I don't know, Mom. I guess I was more interested in seeing the campuses."

"And the good-looking guys," Andy said.

That night Lisa dreamed she was flying along a winding river when she saw a woman picking strange plants along the riverbank. She glided down and asked, "Why are you picking those?"

"I'm a shaman," the woman said. "My plants help sick people. That's my job, to help people." She smiled at Lisa and disappeared.

Lisa woke up with the image of the woman's kind face in her mind. Over breakfast, she said to her parents, "I think I've decided on a major, microbiology or chemistry. I want to be a scientist."

"Really?" Eva said, pleased that her daughter wanted to follow her path into research.

"Yes, really."

"I'm not egotistical enough to think your mom and I influenced you in any way," Andy said with a wry smile, "but what sparked your decision?"

"I want to help people. I want to do genetics research. Not for family trees and genealogy, for diseases and cures. Just like you, Mom."

"Honey, you make me proud," Eva said.

Over the next week, Lisa narrowed her choice down to UC Berkeley and Stanford. Both had outstanding science programs and very competitive women's soccer teams. Before dinner one evening, in a quiet moment when the twins weren't bouncing around, she announced her final decision.

"I'm going to be a California Golden Bear," she said.

Andy laughed. "So we'll have a live bear in our family."

"My, what big teeth you have," Eva joked. "You can pass them on to your kids."

"I guess gold just runs in the family, Lisa," Andy said. "Golden Bears, Golden Gophers."

19
Crisis

San Francisco, May 2000

In two weeks, Lisa would graduate from Terra Grande High and prepare to head to Berkeley. Right now, she was working on her valedictorian speech, which honored her parents by explaining how her biracial background gave her the best of both worlds.

While Eva listened, her mind kept wandering to what she called her "lazy spells" and the short bouts of fatigue that she never mentioned to the nurse at her dialysis appointments because she blamed them on work stress. She felt so proud as Lisa described what her blended racial identity meant to her, but still she found her eyes closing. Well, it was just that she'd already heard the graduation speech several times, she told herself.

"Dinner's ready!" Andy called from the kitchen, where he was dishing up bowls of his homemade chili, a meal everybody loved, especially the twins.

When they were almost through eating, Eva dropped her spoon on the floor, and Lisa looked over at her with concern.

"Mom, your eyes look puffy again. Are you okay?"

"Just tired, honey." Suddenly she couldn't keep her head upright. "Well, maybe a little dizzy."

"Lisa, get a cold towel," Andy said, putting his arms around Eva and helping her to the couch.

"What's wrong with Mom?" Hanna asked, fear in her voice.

"I don't know, sweetie, but don't worry, she's going to be just fine."

Eva knew. In spite of all her denials, something wasn't going right with the dialysis.

The emergency room at UC San Francisco Medical Center was busy that Saturday night, but they took Eva quickly. Soon Andy and Lisa were sitting across from Dr. Coleman in one of the private conference rooms.

"We'll have to find a good genetic match for a kidney transplant soon," Dr. Coleman said. "I'd hoped the dialysis would hold until we found a perfect match, but it's not. I'll set up screening tests for Monday morning, say eight o'clock. We don't have much time. Bring all the close relatives you can round up."

Andy nodded. "I'll be here, and I'll make some calls when I get home—"

Lisa gripped his arm. "I'm her daughter. I'll take the test too."

"Are you eighteen?" Dr. Coleman asked. "You have to be eighteen to donate a kidney."

"Yes. I just turned eighteen."

On Monday, lab technicians drew blood from Andy, Lisa, and three cousins of Eva's who'd flown to California after Andy called them. Eva's parents had offered to be tested, but their own health issues would keep them from donating if they matched.

Andy and Lisa sat with the cousins in the waiting room. While Andy tried to make conversation, Lisa scribbled in her notebook, revising her graduation speech. Shortly after eleven o'clock, a man in green scrubs appeared, holding a clipboard.

"Hi. I'm Dr. Jensen," he said, shaking hands all around. "I'm in charge of kidney transplants. Mr. Koskinen, you're not a good match for your wife. In fact, there's only one good match."

"That's a relief," Andy said. "Who is it?"

"It's your daughter."

Lisa closed her notebook and stood. "I want to do it. How soon?"

Dr. Jensen looked at her as though taking her measure. "We can get the medical team together in a couple of days. But are you sure?"

"Absolutely."

Andy put a hand on her shoulder. "Honey—"

"I'm not scared. Mom needs me."

Dr. Jensen reviewed his notes. "Things will be different afterward, Lisa. For example, your mom told me you play soccer. But I already knew that." He allowed himself a brief smile. "I love soccer too, always been a fan, and I follow you and your team in the sports pages. If you donate a kidney, you'll have to give up all contact sports."

Lisa's body stiffened, but her expression remained resolute. Andy could hear whispered voices down the hall and the steady pulse of a machine somewhere, but otherwise there was silence. What was going on in his daughter's mind?

"Mom needs me," she said again. "That's all that matters now."

The operations took place on Friday. Eva's parents had flown in to lend their support, as had Andy's. He was glad they were here. Everyone sat quietly in the waiting room, too nervous for polite chat.

Andy looked at his watch for the hundredth time and went to the nurse's station. "Why is it taking so long? Is there a problem?"

"Try to be patient," said the receptionist, an attractive dark-haired woman about Eva's age. "Our doctors are the best in the world, and I'm sure everything will be okay."

Okay, okay. That became Andy's silent chant as he returned to his chair and the endless waiting.

An hour later, Dr. Jensen appeared. Andy held his breath.

"It went well," the doctor said. "Eva and Lisa are both in very good shape. You can see them in the ICU shortly."

Andy released his breath explosively and pumped his fist in the air. He hugged Hanna and Henry, and then his parents, and then Eva's.

"Thank the Lord," her mother said, "and don't be crushing an old lady."

Neither Eva nor Lisa was well enough to attend her high school graduation ceremony the following week, but Andy was there with the twins. The school principal read Lisa's valedictorian address, which captivated the audience and made Andy even prouder of her, though he didn't think it possible.

The crowd stood and cheered, and then the principal held

up his hand for silence. "Lisa had to give up her Berkeley soccer scholarship and the sport she loved in order to be her mother's kidney donor," he said. "I mention this because I received a phone call yesterday morning from the UC Berkeley president. He said the university would honor Lisa's scholarship, all four years. Soccer or no soccer, Berkeley will be honored to have Lisa as a student."

20
Jewel of the Delta

During her weeks of recovery at home, Eva used the time for some of the research she'd been wanting to do about the Yoruba tribe and Nigeria ever since she got her DNA results. One evening at dinner, she surprised Andy and Lisa—and chased away the twins—by saying, "You know, those *homo sapiens* in East Africa didn't just migrate north up the Great Rift Valley and cross the Red Sea and take their sweet time getting themselves up to Finland. Some of them went west to other parts of Africa, like Nigeria."

"Is that right," Andy said.

"It is. Look." Eva took a folded piece of paper from under her plate and spread it out on the table. "Going by John's theory that the early migrations followed major rivers, I found several rivers that people could have used to go from East Africa to West Africa, and I made my own map."

"Wow, Mom, you're getting to be quite the anthropologist."

"Don't sound so surprised, honey. I've got a brain cell or two left, and I also found out an unusual fact about Nigerians. The average worldwide birth rate for twins is less than one percent, but for Nigeria it's four percent, which seems to have

MAP, KENYA TO NIGERIA

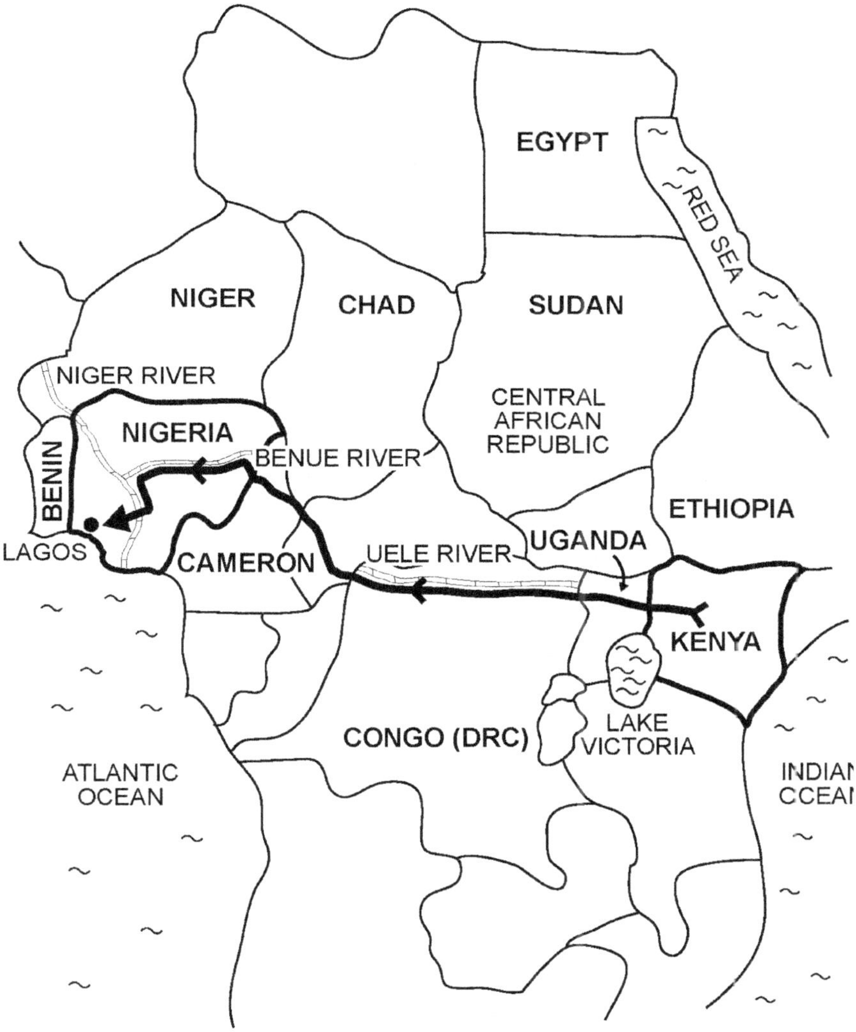

something to do with their diet of cassava, a tuber that has a high estrogen content."

"Did you eat a lot of cassava before you had Hanna and Henry, Mom?"

Eva laughed, but Andy was looking thoughtful. "Nigeria was one of the major centers of the slave trade," he said, "so that's how the descendants of some of those early folks who went west ended up in America thousands upon thousands of years later." He took Eva's hand. "Like your family, honey."

"Yes," she said, her good cheer of a moment before gone.

"You told me a little about your family history after you got your DNA test back, Mom, but I wish I knew more. I remember you said they got to Mound Bayou in 1887, but how?"

Eva sighed. "Since I've had all this time on my hands, I've been researching that too. It's hard to talk about, but it's a story worth hearing, so I'll just pretend I'm John and give you a lecture. Two of my distant uncles were friends with the men who founded Mound Bayou, Isaiah Montgomery and his cousin Benjamin Green. They were all former slaves of Joseph Davis, the older brother of Jefferson Davis, president of the Confederacy during the Civil War. In the early 1800s, Joseph left his family plantation in Virginia and established several plantations in Mississippi. After the war, his slaves were freed and left to fend for themselves, and that's how Mound Bayou came to be. It was one of several all-black communities formed in the years after the war as black farmers isolated themselves from the racial violence of the white plantations and grew their own cotton."

Eva paused. "Andy, where's that old map we did up years ago after we got married? I want to show Lisa exactly where

Mound Bayou is and what a great spot those ex-slaves picked for their town."

"Be right back," he said, and went upstairs to rummage in his office, returning with a map that was a little the worse for wear.

Eva smoothed it out and put her finger on Mound Bayou. "See, Lisa? It's right on the Mississippi, and it happens to be directly south down the river from Minnesota, where all of dad's family settled. Look, a river leaving dad's hometown, Moose Lake, joins the Mississippi River. He could have taken a canoe ride to see me."

Lisa chuckled and studied the map as Eva continued. "Mound Bayou had its own station on a new rail line connecting Memphis and Vicksburg, and Booker T. Washington helped to foster economic development by attracting capital through his National Negro Business League. The town had a cottonseed mill and a newspaper, and because the leaders emphasized education, almost everyone could read. President Theodore Roosevelt called Mound Bayou the Jewel of the Delta. The town flourished, and by 1911 its population had grown to eight thousand, but by 1920 cotton prices were falling and racial prejudice was intensifying in the Deep South. Blacks left in droves for jobs in the North, starting the Great Migration of African Americans out of the South. More than a million blacks left over the next twenty years, including many residents of Mound Bayou. Today the town's population is about two thousand."

Eva paused again. "All right, lecture's almost over, but I guess I better get myself into the picture. I was born on our farm in 1955, and I was told that my great-grandmother Nina

MAP, MISSISSIPPI AND MINNESOTA

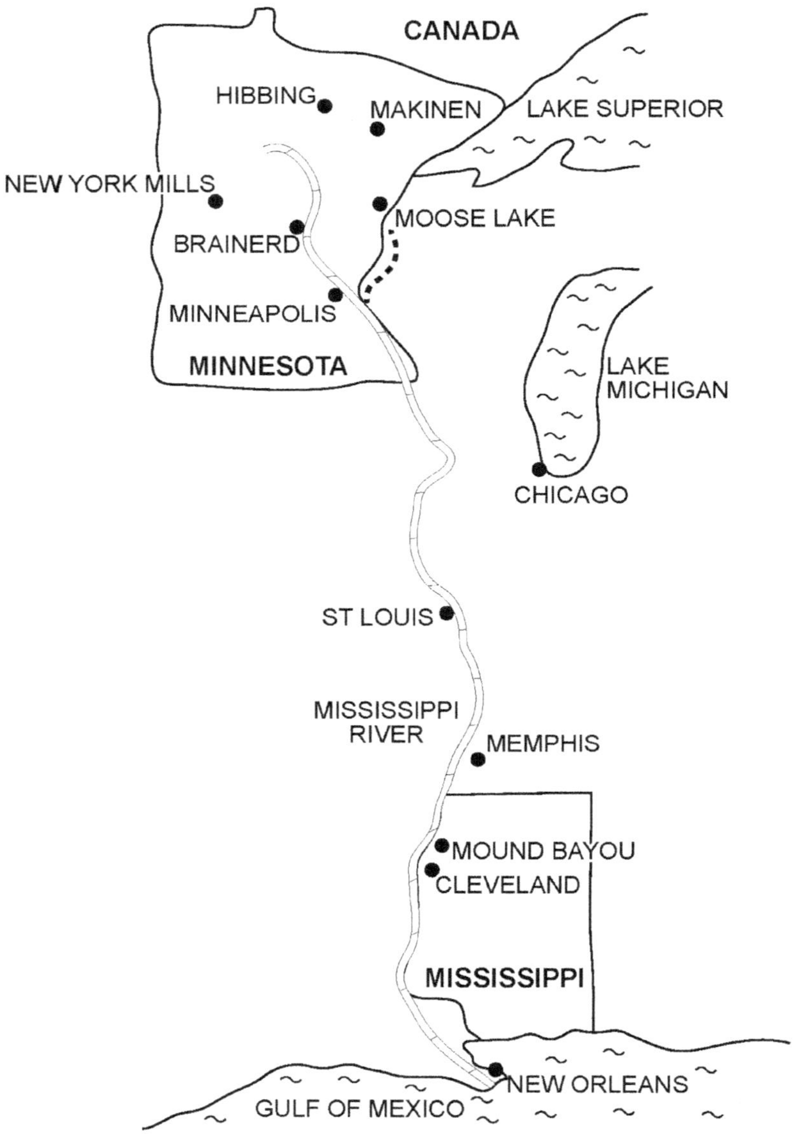

Jackson helped deliver me. As a girl, she was one of the first to live in Mound Bayou. She saw it all, the good and the bad."

***

Mound Bayou, Mississippi, 1920–1955

From the caboose of the Vicksburg-to-Memphis train, Manny watches the Mississippi cotton fields fly by, thankful once again for his porter's job. He squints as if he can see the Mound Bayou farm where he and his five siblings grew up, breaking their backs clearing land and picking cotton. His parents, Nina and Herbert Jackson, did well with it, but hey, this is much better.

The locomotive whistle shrills, and he stands and walks to the passenger cars, bracing himself against the seats to keep his footing as the train slows. The brakes squeal, the engine hisses, and the train stops at the Newton station. He opens the doors and steps down into a rainy, windswept spring day.

A thin white woman runs from the station, her arm over her eyes against the rain. She slips, and her suitcase skitters across the wet pavement. He grabs it just as it's sliding under the train and helps her up, careful to take only her elbow. A black porter, a white woman—even a hint of familiarity can cause him trouble.

"Are you all right, ma'am?" he asks.

"Yes, but it's chilly in all this rain."

"Here," he says, guiding her up the steep steps into the car. "What's your seat number? I'll bring your suitcase to you."

"It's 12A."

"Yes, ma'am, and your car's half empty, so you can sit wherever you want until Memphis."

Manny helps two other passengers aboard and walks through the cars as the train picks up speed. When he reaches the woman's seat and sets down her suitcase, he sees she is crying.

"What's wrong ma'am? Can I help you?"

She looks up and wipes her eyes. "No, I'm all right," she says, but she doesn't stop crying.

"What's wrong?" he presses.

"Well . . . my brother just died," she says, choking back her tears, "and I'm going to his funeral."

"Oh, Lord. I'm so sorry for your loss. I'm Manny, let me know if you need anything at all," he says as he leaves her.

Two days later, as Manny's train is ready to pull out of the Memphis station, he sees the same woman walking toward his car.

"Manny?" she says

He smiles. "Yes, ma'am. Here, let me give you a hand," he says, stepping down to help her aboard and leading her to her car. He sees that she's crying again and asks if there's anything he can do.

"No. I just feel so sad. My brother was too young to die."

It isn't a porter's place to ask questions, but if ever a soul was in need of comfort, it's this pretty, sad-looking white woman. "What happened to him, ma'am?" he asks, sitting down beside her.

"He was roofing a building, but he lost his footing and fell off. He was trying to earn enough money to leave home because our father started beating him after our mother died last year. Peter was such a sweet boy, not a thing like Pa and George, our older brother. He just couldn't take it anymore in Newton, and now I'm going back there," she says through a hiccupping sob.

Manny glances around. No one is in sight. "What's your name?" he asks.

"Oh, forgive me for going on like that. I'm Ellen." She glances down at her folded hands. "Will I see you again?"

"Well, I live in Mound Bayou, and that's where I usually get off, but it's only one stop from Newton. I could meet you there next Wednesday if you like," Manny says, all too aware of the risk he's taking.

"Oh yes," Ellen says, her blue eyes clearing.

They meet a week later, and then the next week and the next. After a year of these clandestine rendezvous, they make plans to head for Chicago, where Manny has been promised a job with the same railroad.

A month before they are to go, he takes Ellen to visit his parents at the Mound Bayou cotton farm. He hasn't told them about the move to Chicago, but he's done his best to prepare them for his white girlfriend. His parents are more tolerant than most in the South, but still he feels the awkwardness as they all struggle to find something to say.

Ellen breaks the silence. "Thank you for Manny. He's the most wonderful man I've ever met, and that must be because of you."

Nina smiles, and Manny knows he has to tell her now. "Mama, we're going to Chicago to get married. Ellen's four months pregnant, and we can't live together here."

Nina grips her husband's arm, her knuckles white, and

Manny knows she's thinking about Charles, his younger brother, who moved to Chicago to work in a factory and married a Choctaw Indian girl. Nina has often said that the news pretty near killed her, but now Manny sees her look at Ellen and relax just a bit.

"How 'bout I write and ask Charles to help you find a place?" she says, giving Manny and Ellen a smile that costs her some effort. "Y'all going to need a nice place for my grambaby."

Ellen studies her belly in the closet mirror and sighs. She can't wait to get to Chicago and start her new life. Charles has written back to Nina to say that's he's found a good apartment, and Ellen is sure everything will be all right once they get there.

Needing a few things for dinner, she leaves the house and walks the three blocks to the grocery store. On her way home, she hears a voice behind her. She turns to see Charlie Miller, an old boyfriend.

"Ellen!" he calls loudly. "I seen you with that nigger, and you're pregnant, ain't you? What the hell you up to?"

"I have to go," she mumbles.

Three days later, on her way to the station to meet Manny, Ellen sees her father's car drive by. George is with him, and . . . is that Manny in the back? She runs toward the car, but it speeds away.

The next day, Manny is found hanged by his neck from a tree on the outskirts of Newton.

A week after Manny's funeral, unable to bear living in her father's house for another minute, Ellen moves to Mound Bayou to live with Manny's family. She tells herself that it will just be until she has the baby, and then she'll go to Chicago like Manny wanted to do. Nina treats her like a daughter, and she has never felt so much love, but she knows that neither she nor her child will ever be accepted in Mississippi.

While she's hanging laundry on the backyard clothesline one morning, Hank Benson comes walking up. He's a big man, and he was Manny's best friend. She's seen him working at the grocery store now and then, and she's heard that he sells bootleg liquor.

He stands there in the yard, nervously rubbing his hands together. "I got something to tell you," he says. "It's about your daddy and your brother."

If it's about her father and George, it can't be anything good, but she feels obliged to hear him out. "Why, sure. Let's sit down over there in the swing."

Hank follows her, and the swing squeaks under his weight. He looks down at his hands. "Last Sunday, me and some friends drove over to Newton and followed Sam and George to their regular fishing spot on the river. Nobody lives there, just a few huts and such around. I parked way behind them, and we waited for them to go down to their boat."

He falls silent and frowns at his hands. The swing squeaks as they go back and forth, back and forth, and the scent of honeysuckle drifts in from over by the well.

Finally, he goes on. "We saw Willie, an old black man who always sold them bait, walk over to them, and when we snuck up closer, we heard him say that he had a case of whiskey he'd sell them cheap."

Where is this going? Ellen wants to shake him and tell him to get to the point, but she stays silent.

"Sam said it was probably moonshine but if it was any

good they'd buy it. Old Willie pulled out a couple of bottles for them to taste, and they agreed to buy the case after they got back from fishing. Well, the next day, somebody found their boat drifting several miles down the river with two empty whiskey bottles in it. They never did find Sam and George."

Hank stares down at the ground, and she knows the rest.

Weeks later, safely settled in Chicago, Ellen receives a letter postmarked Mound Bayou, with no return address. Enclosed is a Newton newspaper article about her father and brother disappearing while fishing on the Mississippi River. A handwritten note scrawled at the bottom reads, "RIVER GOD REVENGE."

Ellen has never in her life wished anyone harm, but she can't find a scrap of grief for her father and George. She names her baby boy Manny and never returns to Mississippi.

21
Hilda

Andy came into the family room waving a letter. "Remember how I said I always wondered what happened to Hilda Koskinen?"

"Huh?" Lisa looked up from the Berkeley course catalogue she'd been studying intently.

"You know, my grandfather Antti's sister. He and Matti and Tuomas were the ones who came over to America in 1890. Hilda and their other brother, Johan, stayed on the farm, but I never could find out what became of her. She just seemed to disappear from the family."

"Right, I remember now," Lisa said.

"Well, I just got this letter from Johan's grandson Matti Koskinen, who runs the family farm now, and he explains what happened. Here, I'll read it to you, unless you're too engrossed in Berkeley."

Lisa closed the catalogue. "I'm all ears."

Andy sat down with the letter. "Okay, here goes. 'Hilda married a man named Vakko Karila, and they lived on his farm outside Kokkola, not far from ours. During Finland's short but bitter 1918 Civil War, known as the White and Red

War, farmers from the same community and relatives within the same family took opposing sides. Vakko Karila supported the Reds, who were backed by Soviet Russia, while Hilda's brother Johan supported the Whites. The two families argued bitterly over which one held the right position in the conflict. Vakko's brother, Jaakko, left central Finland and went to southern Finland to join the Red militia. When the Whites won the war, Jaakko was imprisoned and executed. The Karilas moved away from Kokkola, and the Koskinen and Karila families never saw or spoke to each other again.'"

"That's so sad," Lisa said. "I hope nothing ever divides our family that way."

***

Finland, Portugal, Brazil, 1919–1938

Twenty-one-year-old Heikki Karila and his younger brother Tapio do not want to farm. They want to be sailors and see the world. They move to Helsinki and find jobs on a cargo ship headed to Lisbon, Portugal. There they find the Ancora Bar, where a lot of Finns like to drink, and where sailors from all over trade ship information and occasionally blows. They communicate through a patchwork of words from their various languages, and everyone seems to speak a little English.

On Heikki's third visit to the Ancora, a fight breaks out at the table next to him. One of the men falls against his table, sending his beer crashing to the floor.

Heikki stands. "Stop it! That's enough! There's no need to—"

Two sailors jump him. Heikki pushes them off and swings hard, and in seconds they're both lying on the floor, rubbing their bruised chins. Satisfied they'll be no further trouble, he sits down and calls for a fresh beer.

The bar's owner, a rugged Basque named Asier, brings it to him. "My God, you're strong," he says. "You attack like a tiger."

Heikki shrugs, sipping his brew.

"I mean it. Why don't you come work for me as a bouncer?"

"Well, I really want work on a ship," Heikki says.

"Yeah? You know Portuguese?"

"Portuguese?" Heikki sets his beer down.

"The ships only hire men who speak it. Tell you what. You work for me, I'll teach you."

Heikki is motivated and catches on fast. In just three months, he learns enough to talk with the Portuguese sailors. For a while, he and his brother share a room above a ship supply store, until Tapio gets lonely for his girlfriend and returns to Finland. A week later, Heikki signs on with a Portuguese ship sailing to Brazil.

They lay up at the Rio de Janeiro port for a week, to unload and take on new cargo. On the first evening, several shipmates take him to the Amados, where they sit at a large U-shaped bar in a rustic room filled with ladies of the evening. An attractive woman bartender greets them with a smile.

"What do you handsome sailors want to drink?"

Heikki smiles back. "I'll have a beer."

Several bar girls join them, and soon his shipmates are all laughing and having a good time, but Heikki just stares at the bartender, thinking how beautiful she is.

He nudges one of his mates. “Who is she?”

“Nina? Studying at the university to be a teacher, I think. All the working girls like her because she helps them with the unruly customers.”

When business slows down, Heikki moves over to where Nina is wiping the bar. Soon they are deep in conversation, talking and laughing. He loves her beautiful smile and her striking brown skin. Finally, he musters the courage to ask her for a date.

“Oh, I couldn’t. I can’t take customers from the girls. Look, let me introduce you to someone I think you’ll like. Sally?” she calls out, and a pretty woman with flowing brown hair saunters over.

“This is Heikki,” Nina says. “Why don’t you two take that table over there? I’ll bring you drinks.”

Heikki finds Sally attractive and enjoys talking with her about her background and interests. One by one, his sailor friends and their female companions retreat to the rooms upstairs, but Heikki just keeps talking and drinking.

Nina comes to their table with another strong beer. “Would you like to take Sally upstairs? I can give you a nice room.”

Heikki blushes. “Not tonight.” Seeing Sally’s frown, he says quickly, “I’ll be back tomorrow night. I promise.”

She kisses his cheek. He gives both women a big tip and staggers back to the ship.

He returns the next night, and Sally rushes over to join him. They sit at a table in the corner and pick up their conversation from the night before. After an hour of drinking, he takes her upstairs, and they make love. Heikki realizes he likes her, not just physically but as a person.

The next night Sally is waiting for him at the same table. They are laughing at a joke she's just told when four locals enter the bar. One of Heikki's mates has already pointed these men out to him, warning that they are part of a Rio port gang known for drug dealing, extortion, robbing drunk sailors, and abusing bar girls. The one who seems to be their leader approaches the table and says to Sally, "Join me at the bar."

"No. Not tonight, João, I'm busy."

His face clouds over. He pulls her from the chair by her arm.

"Leave me alone!"

Heikki rises to his feet. "She's not interested."

João stares at him. "Go find another girl, sailor."

Heikki turns to Sally. "Do you want to stay with me?"

"Yes, I do—"

João takes a punch at Heikki, who ducks and returns two quick punches to his stomach and head, sending him crashing to the floor. João gets up and grabs a chair, but before he can swing it, Heikki smashes him hard between the eyes, knocking him out cold.

The other gangsters look from their prostrate boss to Heikki in disbelief and back away.

Nina leans over the bar. "Get your friend out of here," she says, and they leave, lugging João with them.

"Well, he'll have a throbbing headache for a while," she says, mostly to herself. She turns to Heikki. "Free drinks for you for the rest of the night. The rest of these bozos just want to get laid, but you're a real gentleman."

Heikki spends every night in port at the Amados Bar with Sally. Nina seems worried that João will come back; she tells

Sally and Heikki to stay upstairs in the nice private room she gives them. On his last night in Rio, Heikki promises Sally he will return, and she promises to write.

Heikki's ship docks in Rio six months later, and he goes straight to the Amados to see Sally. When he enters, Nina comes to him with a serious look on her face.

"Please sit down," she says. "I have bad news."

"What is it?"

"They found Sally in the alley three nights ago with her throat cut. She told João she never wanted to see him again, and they argued. We're sure he killed her."

Heikki slumps into a chair. "Oh, my God."

Nina gently touches his shoulder. "I'm so sorry, Heikki."

He sits there numbly. "Bring me a drink, will you? Whiskey."

When she returns, he gulps the shot of whiskey and slams the glass on the table. "Another one," he says.

"No, you'd better go. João will be looking for you after what you did to him in front of his favorite bar girl. He probably knows your ship's in."

Just then, João and two of his thugs come through the door and head for Heikki's table. "Step outside, sailor," he says.

Heikki fixes him with a cold stare, rises from his seat, and follows him out into the alley. He is more than ready for a fight.

João doesn't have a fair fight in mind. He pulls a knife as the two thugs step toward Heikki, but with a swift motion Heikki kicks the knife out of his hand. Before the thugs can react, he pulls his own knife and plunges it into João's stomach. "That's for Sally, you bastard."

As their boss moans and writhes on the ground, the other two gangsters come for Heikki, knives drawn. He feints and knocks the first one out with a powerful blow that cracks his jaw. The second one slashes his arm when he raises it to protect himself, but he manages to land a right-hand punch to the attacker's cheek. The man staggers back, and Heikki finishes him off with a blow right between the eyes.

Nina, several bar girls, and the bouncer come out just as the fight is ending. They stare at Heikki and the three bodies on the ground in astonishment. Nina sees that his left arm is bleeding and takes him inside to a back room, where she pours whiskey on his wound and wraps it tightly with a bar towel.

"Heikki, you have to hide," she says. "Even someone who can fight like you won't be a match for João s whole gang when they come after you."

"Upstairs, you mean?"

"No, not here. They'll find you. I'll take you to a safe place, come on."

In the wee hours of the morning, they arrive at Nina's mother's home just outside of Beira-Mar, a village up the coast from Rio. She wakes her mother to tell her what has happened.

"You'll be safe here," Oni says, patting Heikki's shoulder and turning to Nina. "Is this Sally's sailor?"

"Yes. The young man from Finland."

They treat his arm and put him in their spare bedroom for the night. The next day, Nina comes home from work with news. "João bled to death," she says. "His brother, the gang, and the police are all looking for you."

Heikki considers. "Nobody knows where I am, right?

Except you and your mother?"

She nods. "I told everyone that your sailor friends took you away."

"All right, as long as you're sure I won't put you and your mother in danger, I guess this is the best place for me to stay until my arm heals."

Exhausted, he sleeps late the next morning, and after lunch with Oni, he walks along the beach, enjoying the warm weather and the white clouds floating over the deep blue ocean. His thoughts drift back to summer days on the farm in Finland, and to the green pines trees and blue lakes of his native land, a different type of beauty, but peaceful like this. He thinks about Sally, grieving, and wishes Nina were here walking with him. He misses her wise counsel, particularly the way she always knows just the right thing to say when he's worried. And he *is* worried. His ship is due to leave in a week's time. Will he be able to sneak back on board before then? Will they even take him back with his injured arm? He knows they can't let a sailor who can't do his job take up precious space and food.

No answers come, so he returns to the house. Oni has arranged for him to see the village doctor, who tells him his wound is healing well but he shouldn't lift anything heavy for at least a month, which confirms that he can't work on the ship.

As they leave the doctor's office, Heikki sighs. "That's a long time for me to impose on your hospitality, Oni. What if the gang comes looking for me?"

"They won't know where to find you. Nina lives near the bar, near her school, and she told me she never talks about her childhood home. No one knows it even exists."

In the third week of his stay, Heikki begins to feel restless. His arm is almost healed, and the beach walks aren't enough now, so he goes for a run. In his boyhood, he followed Paavo Nurmi's track career and cheered wildly when he heard on the radio that Paavo had won three gold medals at the 1920 Olympics in Belgium. Like many young Finnish boys, he wanted to emulate the Flying Finn, and in high school, he won prizes as a long-distance runner.

He finishes his run, breathing hard, and sits down on a walkway bench to watch the waves crashing on the beach. An old man sitting across from him nods and introduces himself.

"I am Salvador González. And you are?"

"Heikki Karila." He looks out over the turbulent sea and says, "This is one of the most beautiful places I've ever seen."

"It is that. I moved here from Basque country in northern Spain when I was a boy. I love it here. Where are you from?"

Heikki feels safe enough to answer truthfully. "Finland."

While Salvador talks about the village, Heikki watches a woman and her two young children wading knee-deep in the ocean. He sees a wave building up behind them and stands up, alarmed.

The wave crashes down on them, and the children disappear. The mother falls and scrambles to her feet, screaming. Heikki sprints to the shore and dives in as she feels about frantically in the water. He sees a leg sticking up, grabs it, and pulls out a little girl, holding her tightly when another large wave sweeps over them. He hands her to her mother.

"My boy! Where's my boy?"

Heikki sees a head bobbing a ways out. He swims to the

boy, brings him to shore, lays him down, and pushes on his little body until he coughs out the water he swallowed. He is pale and scared, but Heikki thinks he will be okay.

The mother hugs her son, weeping. She is thanking Heikki profusely for saving her children when she glances behind him and her eyes widen. He turns to see Salvador slumped over, holding his chest. They run to him and he looks up. "My nitroglycerin," he gasps through his pain. "I need my nitro tablets."

The woman turns to Heikki. "He lives in the big house on the path to the village, but it's too far, it's a kilometer away—"

Heikki is already running.

He gets to the house in just a few minutes, knocks loudly, and tells Salvador's wife what happened. She quickly retrieves the medication and shoves it into Heikki's hand. He runs back to Salvador, who chokes down a pill and eyes Heikki. "Such speed," he says. "It took you—what, five or six minutes to run two kilometers?"

"Two kilometers?" Heikki says, surprised himself that he covered that distance so fast.

Mrs. González and several villagers arrive a few minutes later and take Salvador home. Heikki returns to Oni's house, grateful that he helped a stranger in peril even as he wishes he had been there for Sally when she needed him.

When his arm has healed and Oni invites him to stay on as long as he wishes, he accepts on the condition that she let him work at her small grocery store. Nina's father is dead, and her brother moved to São Paulo years ago, so Oni is glad for the help. Heikki works at the store every day, and every evening takes a long run on the beach, stopping at the end to watch a boys' soccer team practice.

One evening, the woman whose children he saved notices him and walks over to speak to him. "My brother Juan is the soccer coach," she says, pointing. "That one. Come, I want to introduce you to him."

Juan shakes his hand vigorously. "I'm very glad to meet such a hero as you, Heikki. Our family owes you a great debt."

Heikki feels his face grow warm and changes the subject. "Good to meet you too. I enjoy watching your boys play. How old are they?"

"Fourteen to sixteen."

"They seem older. They're really good at dribbling and kicking."

"Well, you're welcome to watch anytime."

Heikki stops every evening to watch the boys practice, and after several days, Juan waves him over to the bench. "I wonder if you'd do me a favor. I'm going out of town for a week, and I was hoping you'd run the practices for me."

"Well, I've never coached a soccer team, but your players seem to know what they're doing. I'll be glad to help. It will be fun."

"Be sure to get them running," Juan says with a smile. "You seem to know what you're doing in that department."

On Heikki's second day with the team, the boys complain about the long-distance runs he has them doing.

"We're already in good shape," one of them says.

"Are you? Okay, let's see just how good. Whoever beats me in a three-kilometer run today won't have to run tomorrow."

The boys laugh. "Let's go," another one says. "We can all beat you."

None of them finish within twenty meters of him.

"Okay, now you teach me something," Heikki says. "I want to learn to play soccer. I'll join you in your practice drills."

When Juan returns at the end of the week, he asks Heikki to continue with the team, and Heikki readily agrees. Word spreads that Heikki the hero is helping coach the boys' soccer team, and the villagers begin turning up to see him, especially the young women.

After practice one evening, he takes the boys to Oni's store for soft drinks, and soon they begin stopping in every day. Girls begin stopping in at the same time, including some older girls who want a chance to talk to the blond, blue-eyed Finn. Oni's business picks up dramatically.

One afternoon as Heikki is helping her restock the shelves that are emptying fast of late, he mentions his surprise at the low prices she pays for the goods she buys from her wholesaler.

"Well, it's like everything else to do with running a business. The wholesaler gives me these prices, and I'm glad to pass the savings on to the customers."

Heikki has never run a store, so he has no idea if this is the norm. Maybe the wholesaler just feels sympathy for a widow trying to make a go of a business on her own. He shrugs and says, "Sounds like he's a really nice guy."

Nina is home on break from the university. The first morning, after breakfast, she says to Heikki, "I'm in the mood for a walk along the beach. I've missed that at school."

The weather is warm, and the tide is going out on the smooth ocean. They kick off their sandals and step into the water. As Nina wades ahead of him, he finds himself scanning her calves and thighs and backside. When she turns, his gaze moves up to her tight pink blouse. What's wrong with him? Nina is his friend, and he shouldn't be having thoughts like this about her. He chooses his words carefully as they speak of small things. "I could walk on this beach forever," she says, "but I should get back. I've got a paper due next week."

They return to her mother's house, and she pulls a notebook from her overnight bag and sits at the kitchen table. He sits across from her.

"What's your paper about? Can I see?"

"I guess so," she says, handing him the notebook, "but it's just a draft."

Heikki starts reading and frowns.

"What's wrong?" Nina asks.

He looks up at her. "Your handwriting. It's just like Sally's."

Nina meets his eyes and sits back. "Heikki, Sally couldn't read or write. None of the girls can. I write their letters for them. Sally told me what to say. She liked you so much."

"So that means you must have read my letters to her?"

Nina nods. "Yes, and they were so tender." She reaches out and squeezes his hand. "I knew from your letters what kind of a person you are, and that's why I helped you after the fight."

That afternoon, Heikki and Nina are helping out in the store when the boys come in from soccer practice, followed by three young women who like to flirt with Heikki.

"Are you going to the big celebration this weekend?" one asks.

"Celebration?"

"It's a dress-up dance in honor of the hundredth

anniversary of the village."

"Oh, I remember," he says. "Yes, I am. Coach Juan is loaning me a suit since we're the same size. I'm looking forward to it."

Nina is watching him with a slight frown that vanishes after the young women leave and he asks, "Will you do me the honor of coming to the dance with me?"

On Saturday evening, in his borrowed suit, Heikki escorts Oni and Nina to the village hall. They join a table with Juan and his wife and Salvador and his wife. Before long, the master of ceremonies introduces the band and says that the first dance is ladies' choice. Several women head toward Heikki, but Nina pulls him out onto the floor. Everybody at the table beams.

He takes her in his arms, and she puts her head on his shoulder. When the dance is over, they just stand there looking at each other. "Let's go outside," he says finally. She nods, and he leads her out into the warm night, to a wooden bench facing the sea. He puts his arms around her and kisses her, and she returns the kiss.

Heikki takes her hands. "I love you," he whispers.

She leans into him. "I love you too."

They go back inside holding hands and are inseparable for the rest of the evening.

When they return to the table after the last dance, Mrs. González isn't in her chair. Without explaining his wife's absence, Salvador stands. "Well, it's time," he says. "Let's go out into the garden where we can talk."

He takes them outside to an ornate wrought-iron table almost hidden among the vines. "Please be seated," he says to

Heikki and Nina. Oni remains standing.

"What about Mrs. González?" Nina asks.

"She knows what I'm about to say. She agrees that now is the right time."

It is quiet except for the waves lapping beyond the garden. What is this all about? Heikki wonders.

"Nina, you work at that bar because you don't want to accept school money from your mother," Salvador says. "Is that right?"

Nina gives Oni a questioning look but nods.

"What I have to say is about that, and much, much more."

Nina gives her mother another look. "I don't understand—"

"You will soon. Indulge me while I tell you a story."

He takes a breath and seems to be gathering his thoughts. "Twenty-two years ago I left Brazil. I lived in Portugal for a time, and then Spain. My grandfather Asier was originally from the Basque part of northern Spain, and I wanted to explore my roots. One day I got a letter from my father saying my brother was very sick. I didn't want to leave what I considered my new homes, but I returned to Brazil. I was so worried about my brother and so unhappy about being back in Brazil that I took to the bottle. One night I fell asleep on the beach, drunk, and woke up the next morning to find a young woman pulling on my arm. The tide was already at my feet. If she hadn't woken me up, I would have drowned. The woman was beautiful, bright, a delight to be with. I saw her almost every day for a month.

"Well, one day I brought her home to meet my parents. They were polite, but the girl wasn't acceptable to them. She was dark-skinned, you see. They forbade me to see her again, and I returned to Portugal by myself. I met a woman there and married her. When my brother died, my father asked me to come home and take over the family business. There was little choice—I was the only living son—so I did."

Salvador glances at Oni and continues his story.

"I wanted to see what had happened to my first love, so I went to the beach one morning looking for her. To my surprise, I saw her pushing a stroller that held a beautiful, brown-skinned baby girl. I went to her, and we talked, and when she said she wasn't married, it hit me."

He stops, reaches down, and grasps Nina's hand. "I'm your father, Nina."

Nina sits stunned. She looks at Oni. "Mother?"

"Your mother thought we should keep it a secret because I was married, and I agreed. I promised to help her financially so she would be able to raise you well."

"Oh, Mother. Why didn't you tell me?"

Tears stream down Oni's face. "I couldn't. I married Felipe, a local fisherman, and everybody thought you were his. Felipe died at sea when you were only four, and that was when Salvador had his company set up our family grocery store."

Ah, the really nice wholesaler, Heikki thinks.

"Try to understand, Nina," Salvador says. "My wife—Mrs. González and I had three children by then, and we lived on the other side of town. Our families saw each other only at big village events. We all agreed that was for the best. But now . . ." His gaze travels from Heikki to Nina. "Now I want you to quit your job at that bar. I'll pay for your schooling, and for anything else you need."

Nina says nothing. Oni hugs her. "My dearest daughter, I'm so glad you know everything now."

There is an awkward silence, and then Heikki finds his voice.

"Nina, may I walk you home?"

They leave the village center holding hands and walk silently down to the beach under a golden moon that seems to float on the warm breeze. Heikki stops and turns to her.

"I love you, Nina. I want to stay in Brazil. With you. Will you marry me?"

Salvador makes all the arrangements for a big wedding in Beira-Mar. On the day of the ceremony, Nina shows Heikki a leather thong with a long curved tooth attached to it. "This is an old family necklace Mother wants me to wear for our wedding. I know it's kind of ugly, but to her it represents a sacred tradition. Would you mind if I wear it?"

Without hesitating, Heikki replies, "Of course not! Anything you and Oni want for the wedding is fine with me."

She kisses him on the cheek. "I'll tell you about the old tooth on the way to the village."

Nina completes her degree and returns to teach the village children. Salvador hires Heikki to help run his company. Heikki continues to help coach the boys' soccer team, so well that by 1938 the team, which now includes his and Nina's seventeen-year-old twins, is invited to play in a nationwide youth tournament.

As Heikki is leaving the soccer field with Tiago and Tomas after a win against a regional team, a newspaper reporter from Rio steps forward and introduces himself.

"Your sons are outstanding players," he says, his pen

poised over a notepad. "Best around, I'd say. Coach, are you ready for the big national tournament in Rio?"

"Well, yes, I think so, but the whole team's good, not just my boys."

"Of course, but it makes a good headline. 'Soccer coach leads twin sons to victory.' Has a nice ring, don't you think?"

Paulo Cardosa reads the article in the sports pages as he rides the bus to the stadium to watch his own boy play in the big tournament. Heikki . . . Heikki . . . the name has a familiar ring. The article says the Beira-Mar coach moved to Brazil from Finland years ago and married a Brazilian girl.

Paulo reaches the stadium and finds his seat. He studies the opposing team as its players take the field. Yes! The coach *is* the Finnish sailor who killed his brother João at Amados Bar. It has been eighteen years, but he never forgets that day.

He watches Heikki's boys lead their team to victory over his son's team, and his rage grows. By the time he leaves the stadium, Paulo is plotting how to take his revenge against all three of them.

"There's a problem," Nina says over her shoulder to Heikki as she hangs up the phone.

"Why, what's going on?" He's just showered, and is standing by the bathroom door toweling off.

"That was Maria from Amados. Paulo Cardosa says he's found his brother's killer. He knows it's you, and he knows where you are. Maria overheard him saying that he and his Rio gangsters plan to kill you and the boys. My God, what will we do?"

"Damn!" Heikki slams his fist against the wall. "Damn it!"

In his youth, he would have taken on any number of ruffians like these, but he can't put his entire family at risk. His mind scrambles for a way out. "If they know where we are, we've got to leave Beira-Mar. We've got to go. And soon!"

Heikki pulls on his trousers, selects a shirt from the closet, and puts it on. Nina sits on their bed, blinking back tears. "I'm scared too," she says, "but this is the only home the children and I have ever known. Must we really leave?"

"They won't bother you or the girls, but the boys and I have to go. Maybe to Portugal. Or Finland."

That night, Heikki tosses and turns for hours. The idea of running is anathema to him, and he decides to confront Paulo. First he sends Oni, Nina, and their two daughters to live with Oni's cousin in São Paulo. He tells the boys they're spending the summer in Finland, and once he receives word that they're on a ship bound for Europe, he sends a message to Paulo to meet him at the Beira-Mar pier.

Two days later, the newspaper's report that Heikki Karila, the Beira-Mar soccer coach, has been found beaten and drowned near the village pier. Local police say it was a revenge killing by Rio gangsters.

After arriving in Helsinki, the Karila boys travel to their grandparents' dairy farm near Lohtaja. Tiago and Tomas miss their Brazilian family and friends, and they miss playing soccer, but they pitch in with the farm's many chores. Vakko and Hilda seem grateful for their help, and if they work hard enough, they can sometimes take their minds off the letter telling of their father's death.

One Saturday when they've been on the farm for a month, Vakko and Hilda take them into town. In a store window they see a flyer for a soccer game at the village park just across the street. Vakko takes them to watch it while Hilda shops. As they wait for the match to begin, Tiago whispers to his brother eagerly, "Since they have soccer here, maybe one day we'll be able to play again."

Tomas whispers back, "Father would have liked that."

They continue waiting. And waiting. Lohtaja, the underdog, is scheduled to play the season's first game against their big-city rival, Kokkola, but only nine players from the Lohtaja team are on the field. The start time for the game comes and goes, and the spectators begin to grumble.

After another twenty minutes, the Lohtaja coach appears and waves for silence. "There's been an accident," he says. "Five of our players were in a car crash outside town. None were hurt badly, but we need two volunteers or we have to forfeit."

Vakko turns to Tiago and Tomas and says, "Come with me." He takes them to the coach. "My grandsons can play."

The coach looks them up and down. "Twins, I see. Do they know how?"

Vakko smiles. "Oh, they've played a little soccer."

"Well . . . well, at least you have tennis shoes, and we'll give you jerseys, shorts, socks, and shin guards." He points at Tiago. "You play midfielder. And you play defensive back."

Tiago leans over to Tomas. "Let's play for our father."

The game starts within minutes. A Kokkola player takes control of the ball and moves it to the sideline and down the field. He makes a long pass, and Tomas intercepts it. He dribbles and passes to Tiago, who knocks the pass down with his chest and dribbles full speed down the field.

A Kokkola defender approaches him, and Tiago pivots toward midfield, still dribbling. Two more defenders close in, and he spins around, bolts between them, and accelerates toward the goal, leaving them stunned by his dextrous maneuver. One last defender approaches, but Tiago easily eludes him and strikes the ball toward the goal. The powerful shot sails fifteen meters, passes the flat-footed Kokkola goalie, and flies into the side of the net. A loud cheer comes from the Lohtaja crowd.

A few minutes later, Tomas steals the ball again, and seconds after that, there is another goal for Lohtaja.

Vakko, cheering in the crowd, knows this is a special game for Lohtaja, and for his grandsons. He listens to the fans screaming every time they advance the ball. With five minutes left in the half, they score two more goals.

Word spreads that Lohtaja is whipping Kokkola 4-0. Vakko runs across the street and finds Hilda. She and several other customers follow him back to the field to watch the amazing Karila grandsons from Brazil.

The twins play as remarkably in the second half, putting on an amazing display. The game ends with Lohtaja winning 8-1.

The coach invites Tiago and Tomas to join the team. The boys' sprint speed, endurance, and Brazilian-style ball-handling skills help lead Lohtaja to an undefeated season and a league championship, which gets them invited to a nationwide amateur soccer tournament in Helsinki. They easily win their first two games against larger cities, and the Helsinki newspapers rave about the young twin players. More and more fans show up to root for Lohtaja as the team goes on to win the tournament.

When school starts a month later, the handsome twins are already popular. Tiago and Tomas meet two pretty farm girls and marry them soon after they graduate from high school. They expand the Karila dairy farm, and they all live there together.

Years later, when Vakko and Hilda are ready to retire, they sit down with Tiago and Tomas. "The farm is yours," Hilda says. "We'll help you with the garden in the summer, but the rest is up to you."

"We have only one condition," Vakko adds. "Keep the farm in the family always."

Though Heikki had left the farm decades before, his sons are glad to remain. Despite the tragic circumstance that brought them here, the Karila farm has become their home.

22
More Revelations

San Francisco, August 2000

Fully recovered from her surgery, Eva flew to Cheyenne, Wyoming, to attend the National Microbiology Conference and came home two days later. Lisa greeted her at the front door.

"How was your trip, Mom? How was the conference?"

"Excellent. There are some interesting results on new drugs for bipolar disorder, and I went to some great panels, but I managed to leave some time for shopping."

"What did you buy? Did you get me something?"

Eva laughed. "That's just what you always asked when you were little. I'm sure the twins will have the same question. Where are they anyway?"

"Dad took them to a birthday party at the Village Pizzeria. They ought to be back in an hour or so."

"Well, that will give me plenty of time to unpack. Come on upstairs and help me." Eva reached for her suitcase.

"I'll get that, Mom," Lisa said. She grabbed the suitcase, carried it to her parents' bedroom, and plopped it on the king-size bed. Eva opened it and handed her a cardboard box.

"You *did* get me something! What is it?"

"Why don't you see for yourself?"

Lisa opened the box and pulled out a brown leather shirt with fringed sleeves. She held it up. "It's nice, Mom, thanks. It's different, kind of rustic, but I really like it. Where'd you get it?"

Eva sat on the end of the bed and kicked off her heels. "One afternoon, I was walking around the historic part of Cheyenne, where everything still looks like the Old West. I passed a store window and stopped to look at a mannequin of a Native American woman wearing that shirt. The minute I saw it, I knew I wanted it for you." She stopped rubbing her feet and stood. "Try it on. I'll be right back. There's something that goes with it."

When she returned to the bedroom, Lisa was standing in front of the full-length mirror in her new leather shirt, which fell almost to mid-thigh.

"It's a great fit," Lisa said, "and it's so soft. It'll be perfect with a pair of jeans."

"And with this. Turn around."

Lisa's eyes widened when she saw her mother holding out the tooth necklace. "But I thought—"

"Livermore Lab returned it right before I left for the conference. Dad and I were saving the news until I got back. Here, let me help you put it on." Eva tied the leather thongs of the necklace around her daughter's neck. "What do you think?"

Lisa turned back to the mirror. "Wow. The teeth look really good against the leather. They really pop. I can't wait to show Dad when he comes home."

"I'm sure he'll love it." Eva paused. "Honey, I want you to try something else."

"What, Mom?"

"Fourteen thousand years ago, women in Africa didn't wear shirts. It was too warm."

Lisa's brow furrowed as her mother's words sank in. "You mean—"

"Trust me on this, honey. Do it just for me. I want to see how it might have looked all those years ago."

"Well . . . okay." A minute later, Lisa stood in front of the mirror again.

"Beautiful," Eva said, "just as I thought. The ivory of the teeth almost glows against the gold of your skin."

"I guess you're right," Lisa said, still a little uncomfortable, "but I sure can't show Dad, or anybody else."

"Well, someday you can show your husband."

Lisa blushed, and then they heard Sukie barking. Eva snatched two packages from her suitcase, whispered something to Lisa, and went downstairs to intercept Andy and the twins in the hallway.

"Mom! You're back!" Hanna and Henry cried in unison, giving Eva a big hug. "Did you get us anything?"

"I sure did, pumpkins." She held out the two packages. "Come on into the kitchen and open them."

"Anything for me?" Andy said.

"Just this." Eva kissed him.

"The perfect gift for the man who has everything," he said, watching as the twins unwrapped their presents: a belt with a turquoise buckle for Henry and a turquoise bracelet for Hanna.

After they thanked her and went upstairs to watch TV, Eva said to Andy, "You must be tired, honey. I bet you hear your recliner calling you." She led him into the family room, where Lisa sat on the sofa reading the newspaper.

She peered over the top. "Hi, Dad. Have a good time?"

"The kids had a ball, and you know how I feel about pizza."

As he was about to sit down in his recliner, Lisa set the newspaper on the coffee table. He stopped dead. "What . . . wow . . . gosh," he stammered. "Where . . . where'd you get the shirt?"

"Mom bought it at a Native American store in Cheyenne."

Andy's eyes took on a faraway expression. "Seeing you, I can almost imagine how good the necklace looked thousands of years ago, on someone in our family."

That night, when they were alone, Eva told Andy how good the necklace also looked against Lisa's bare skin.

Lisa thought her life couldn't get any better, but in her freshman year at Berkeley, she volunteered to help the soccer coach with non-contact team drills, and he was amazed by her speed and ball-handling skills. At the end of the season, he consulted with doctors at the UC San Francisco Sports Medicine Center, and they all concurred: if Lisa wore protective gear for her kidney, she could play competitive soccer. It had worked for several professional basketball players, so why not a soccer player?

In the opening game of the next season, Lisa played like a tiger, stealing the ball from her opponents with ease, controlling it, and passing it accurately to her teammates. Covering the field with her usual endurance, she struck two powerful shots from fifteen yards out that flew past the goalie into the net. Berkeley won 4-0.

Lisa was back. Not just back, but the team's leading scorer and MVP, chosen for the Pacific all-conference first team.

San Francisco, Spring 2002

With soccer on her mind, Lisa was walking across the Berkeley campus on a late Friday afternoon when her cell phone rang.

"Hi, Dad."

"Honey, you're not going to believe this, but you have another package from Tapio."

"Really? What do you think's in it?"

"No clue, but it's bigger than the last one."

Lisa recalled her reaction when she opened the first package and saw the tooth necklace. It had frightened her, and there had been the dreams, but she was over all that now. She'd learned so much from the necklace, and from John—maybe this new package would hold further revelations.

"I can't come tonight, I have a date, but I'll see you in the morning, Dad."

Lisa arrived just as Andy and Eva were finishing breakfast.

"Can I fix you something, honey?" Eva asked. "How was your date?"

"Well, the guy turned out to be kind of a dork. I'm sure that package will be way more interesting than he was. Where is it?"

Andy reached over to the sideboard and handed her the package. She tore off the heavy wrapping to find an old hand-carved pine box with an envelope taped to its top. She opened the envelope and read aloud.

Dear Lisa,

Last week I found this box in the storage hut next to Aunt Tulli's farmhouse. I knew you and your father would be interested in having what was inside.

Your cousin, Tapio

P.S. Let me know what you think this is all about.

Lisa looked up at her expectant parents and removed the tape holding the box's two drawers closed. She pulled out the top drawer and found a leather pouch containing several small rocks, each embedded with a shiny crystal.

"It's just like the pouch for your necklace," Eva said, "but I wonder what the rocks are for. Go on, honey, open the other drawer."

Lisa slid the drawer out. Three more leather pouches lay on a lining of old cotton cloth. "What do you think is in these, Mom?"

"Only one way to find out," Andy said.

Carefully untying the leather strips that fastened the pouches, Lisa emptied their contents onto the table: three more tooth necklaces.

There was a long moment of silence around the table before Eva said, "Wow. I don't believe it. They're the same as yours, Lisa."

Andy picked up the necklaces one by one and studied them. "No, these all have twenty teeth each, not fourteen like Lisa's. I think they're bear teeth, and they have the same little cut marks in groups of five. Let's see"—he paused, counting—"ten sets of five cut marks, for a total of fifty cuts on each tooth, just like the first necklace, so the number of teeth is the only difference."

"Look, Dad, these are larger than the rest," Lisa said, pointing out two teeth on the third necklace.

Andy laughed. "Probably polar bear teeth."

"Dad, get serious. Do you think these necklaces can possibly be as old as mine? Shouldn't we have them tested?"

"Yes, of course. I'll call Dr. Cheng first thing Monday."

The normally taciturn Dr. Cheng could barely contain his excitement when he heard about the four new pouches. He told Andy to bring them right in, and the following Saturday he called to ask if Andy and Lisa could come to Livermore that afternoon.

"We'll be there," Andy said, "and I'm sure my wife would like to come too."

"Fine, I'll see you soon."

When the three Koskinens arrived at the lab, Dr. Cheng sat them down at his big conference table and spread the necklaces out. "Hang on to your hats," he said. "The two large teeth on the one necklace are lion's teeth, and they're eighty thousand years old."

Eva's mouth dropped open.

"What?" Lisa exclaimed.

"Are you sure?" Andy sputtered.

"I'm sure. These teeth are the oldest relics I've ever tested in my twenty-two-year career. Each of them has twenty teeth spanning about twenty thousand years, with each tooth pair separated by about two thousand years, just as on Lisa's necklace, though it only has fourteen teeth."

Eva turned to Lisa. "Wait till John hears about this. Do you know where the necklaces came from, Dr. Cheng?"

"I have my best researchers on it, and we have a hunch, but we don't have proof yet. They definitely span eighty thousand years, at two-thousand-year intervals, though there are three teeth pairs missing, at thirty-four thousand, thirty-eight thousand, and seventy-four thousand years ago. They probably got lost somewhere on the journey. And what a long journey it was. The amount of history you've got here?" Dr. Cheng cleared his throat. "Career-making potential, actually."

"As for this," he continued, picking up the fourth leather pouch and shaking it out, "those are raw diamonds embedded in the rocks." He held one up and rotated it so that the sharp edges glittered under the fluorescent lights.

"Yes!" Lisa said. "They needed something to make those cut marks with, and the diamonds would last forever, right, Dr. Cheng?"

"Exactly right."

Andy grinned. "So diamonds have been girls' best friends for eighty thousand years."

Eva was inspecting the necklaces intently, remembering John's migration lessons. "The eighty-thousand-year-old teeth must have come from Africa, from the Great Rift Valley."

Dr. Cheng nodded, impressed. "So the scientific evidence would suggest."

"Whew, I still can't believe it all," Lisa said. "What's next? Can I take the necklaces home?"

"You can, they belong to you, but they're priceless relics," Dr. Cheng said, and after he explained that they should be kept in special archival cases with temperature and humidity control, Lisa decided that they should stay at Livermore "as long as I can visit them sometimes."

The next week, the *San Francisco Chronicle* ran a feature article with a photo of Lisa, Andy, Eva, and Dr. Cheng. Lisa was wearing a huge smile over all four necklaces and a brown leather shirt.

23
Nina Rivaldo

California, 2005

After Lisa graduated from Cal Berkeley, she was selected to play on the US national team in the new America's Cup Women's Soccer Tournament. The team advanced to the finals and was slated to face Brazil in the championship game in Los Angeles. Lisa was her team's star player. Brazil's star was a player named Nina Rivaldo. Eva and the twins couldn't make it to LA that weekend, but Andy was there to cheer his daughter on.

The game took place on an extremely hot summer day. Both women played well, each scoring two goals. From the sidelines, reporters kept remarking on how alike they were in physical appearance and soccer skills. "They could be sisters," one said to another.

The game ended in a 3-3 tie. In keeping with the "golden goal rule," play would go on until one team scored. After three grueling overtimes, with the sun beating down relentlessly on the field and exhausted players succumbing to dehydration and leg cramps, the referees halted the game and declared the USA and Brazil co-champions.

That evening, during the post-championship barbecue at tournament headquarters in an LA hotel, the Brazilian coach wended his way through the crowd with Nina until he found Lisa standing by the pool.

"I thought you two should meet off the field," he said, making the introductions and complimenting them both on an outstanding game. He looked from one to the other. "You know, the newspapers are right. You really could be sisters."

The women smiled at each other, having heard the same before, but then Lisa took a closer look at Nina and blurted, "Where did you get that?"

Nina put a protective hand over her necklace. "My mother gave it to me. I wear it sometimes for luck. Why?"

"I'll leave you two to talk," the coach said, excusing himself.

Lisa stared at the big tooth hanging from Nina's necklace. "Do you know where your mother got it?"

"She found it at her grandmother's house after she died."

"What else do you know about it?" Lisa asked with an urgency that puzzled Nina.

"Well . . . my mother thought it was from the Tupi, one of Brazil's oldest indigenous tribes. She found it in a leather pouch in a jewelry box. She told me Grandma Nina said it was part of a sacred ritual. At first I thought it was weird and scary, but now I think it's kind of cool."

Lisa was about to say that she had a necklace with a similar tooth when Andy rushed up to congratulate her on the game and stopped short.

"Dad, this is Nina Rivaldo."

"Gosh, the newspapers are right. You two—"

"Could be sisters," they both said at once, laughing.

As Andy was complimenting Nina on her play, his eyes fell on her necklace, but before he could ask her about it, a handsome young man in a colorful sport shirt came up and gave her a bear hug.

"Great game, sis!" he said.

"Thanks, but where are your manners?" Nina said, introducing him to Andy and Lisa. "This is my brother Heikki."

Andy extended his hand. "Heikki? But that's not a Brazilian name, it's Finnish."

"It is," Nina said. "He's named after his great-grandfather from Finland, and I'm named for my great-grandmother. They met in Rio."

"Must be quite a history there, and maybe more behind that necklace of yours," Andy said. "Did Lisa tell you she has a tooth necklace too?"

"I was about to, Dad, but then you showed up."

"Sorry, didn't mean to crash the party, but I'd love to know more about that tooth on your necklace. A couple of the ones on Lisa's are eighty thousand years old."

Nina's eyebrows shot up. "No way."

"Yes, way," Lisa said. "Have you ever thought about having it age-tested? That's what we did with mine."

"Well, no, but now that you mention it, I've wondered myself."

"How long will you be in California?" Andy asked.

"Another week, we took a vacation to come to the tournament."

"Why don't you come to San Francisco? There are some great places to visit, and I think I can arrange to have your necklace tested while you're there."

"Great," Heikki said. "Could we go to a Giants game? I've never seen baseball."

"Sure, my son Henry is a big Giants fan. We'd love to take you. Henry is the English name for Heikki, you know," Andy said as he flipped open his cell phone and placed a call to Dr. Cheng.

Two days later, Nina and Heikki were sitting around the kitchen table talking with Eva and Andy about their families.

"I still can't get over your name," Andy said to Heikki. "How does a Brazilian guy end up with a name like that? What was your father's family name, do you know?"

Heikki shook his head. "I don't, but I wish I did. I never asked."

"I never did either, but maybe our mother knows," Nina said, getting up to go outside and make a call to Brazil.

"His last name was Karila," she said when she returned. "He grew up near Lohtaja, and—"

"Karila!" Andy exclaimed. "That must be Hilda and Vakko, and they must have had a son named Heikki." He turned to Lisa and Heikki and Nina. "Which means you're all cousins," he said, sudden tears filling his eyes, "and we're all family."

The next morning, Eva picked up the phone to hear Dr. Cheng saying, "I expedited the test on that tooth, and I'll get straight to the point. It's a lion's tooth, and it's eighty thousand years old."

Eva hung up and reported the news to general amazement, and then Andy turned to Nina. "We should tell your mother," he said.

"Definitely. She won't believe it." Nina grabbed her cell phone and punched in her mother's number. "Hi, Mom, I've got some news. . . . No, really. . . . No, I'm not kidding . . ."

Andy and Eva and Lisa listened, wishing they could hear the other end of the conversation. After a long while, Nina put her hand over the phone. "Hold on, Mom," she said, and reported as briefly as she could what her mother had told her.

"Mom's parents met in Rio and settled in a village called Beira-Mar. She was their second girl, and they named her Oni after her grandmother, and— "

"Oni?" Eva said. "Ask your mother if she knows where your grandmother came from."

After another exchange on the phone, Nina said, "She thinks from a very old Tupi tribe far up the coast."

"Maybe not," Eva said. "Ask her if she'd be willing to have a DNA test."

Six weeks later, Nina called Lisa from Brazil to say that Oni's test results had come in. "Her maternal mitochondrial DNA shows that her ancestors came from a Yoruba tribe in Nigeria," she announced.

"Listen to you, you sound like a textbook, but my mom's DNA tests showed the same thing." Lisa paused. "And her mother's name was Oni."

Nina drew in a breath. "So maybe we're both descended from slaves who came from the same Yoruba tribe and were transported like cargo both to the US and Brazil."

"Probably so," Lisa said, "but I bet we can show the world that we're not slaves anymore."

Epilogue

At the start of the school year in the fall of 2010, Lisa Koskinen has long since stopped dreaming of flying along rivers, but she still dreams of running, and that she does. As she circles the track at Kezar Stadium near the UC San Francisco Medical Center, where she is a genetics researcher and an associate professor of molecular and cell biology, a handsome blond man overtakes her and flashes her a smile.

The next day, as she passes the same young man on the way to her classroom, he steps in front of her and says, "Hi, I'm Heikki Pikkarainen. Are you taking this class too?"

Lisa smiles. "I bet you're Finnish," she says as the class is about to start.

"How can you tell?" he says with a laugh. "Sit with me, will you?" He points to the seat beside him.

"I already have an assigned place," she says, and steps to the podium. "Welcome to Advanced Microbiology. I'm Professor Lisa Koskinen."

Heikki waits for her after class and invites her to lunch, and though she should know better than to socialize with a student, she accepts.

A year later, Heikki and Lisa marry. On the first night of their safari honeymoon in Kenya, Lisa orders him out of their hotel bedroom and then summons him back, and he stands there transfixed by the sight of his beautiful wife, naked except for the tooth necklace dangling between her breasts.

END

MAP, CLAN MIGRATION PATHS, AFRICA TO FINLAND

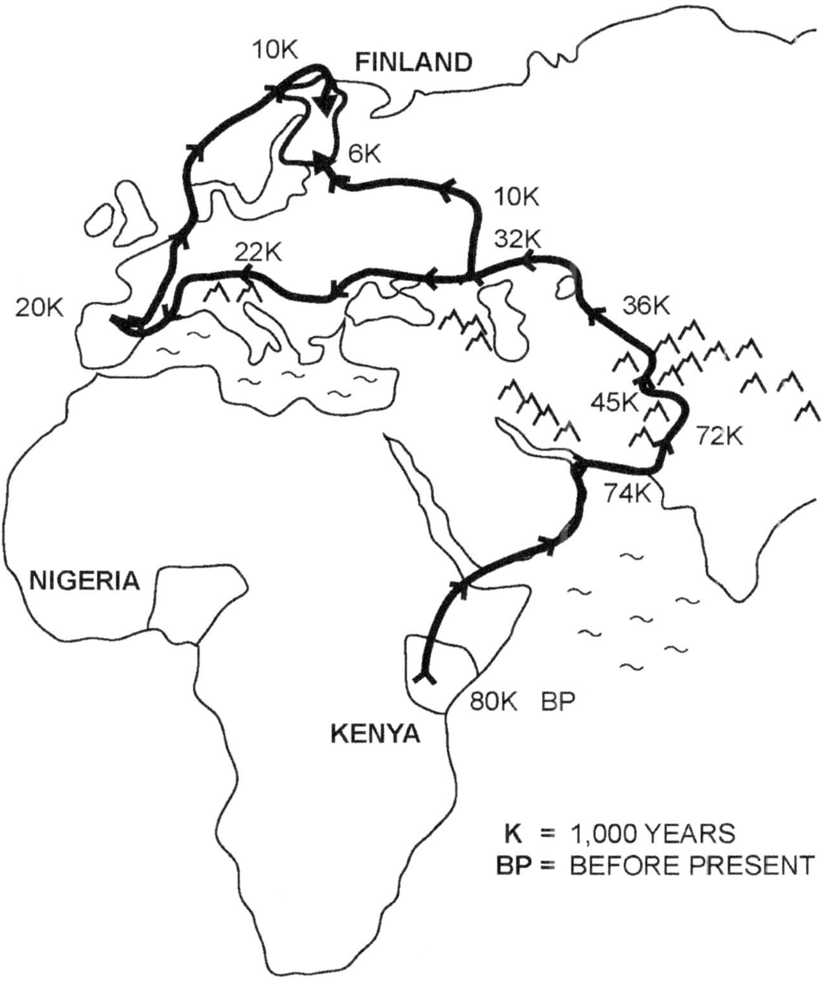

FAMILY TREE

Years Before Present	Location	Family, Clan, and Tribe Names			Location
80,000	Kenya	An-Oni /Hei and Tau-Eva/Lee Families			
			Hei-Lee		
	Red Sea	Hei-Lee Clan		Oni-Waa Clan	E. Africa
72,000	Pakistan	Hei-Lee Clan	Cee-Jaa Clan (to Asia)	Oni-Waa Clan	Kenya
45,000	Afghanistan	Hei-Lee-Clan			
36,000	Uzbekistan	Hei-Lee Clan Heikki-Lisa	Dee-Raa Clan (to No. America)		
32,000	S. Russia	Hei-Lee Clan	An-Eva Clan	Oni-Waa Clan	C. Africa
27,000	Danube R	Hei-Lee Clan	An-Eva Clan (Volga R.)	Oni-Waa Clan	Uele R.
20,000	N. Spain	Hei-Lee Clan	An-Eva Clan (N. Turkey)		
12,000	N. Germany	Hei-Lee Clan Hekki-Lisa/Saame			
10,000	N. Finland	Saami Tribe			
10,000	Russia		An-Eva Clan Antti-Eva/Heikki,Tapio		
6,000	Finland	Saami Tribe	An-Eva Clan	Oni-Waa Clan	Nigeria
1200 AD	Kemi Finland	Tauno-Sari /Lisa, Eva Lisa-Heikki	Matti-Sanna /Heikki, Antti Antti-Eva		
1750				Yoruba Tribe	Nigeria
				Oni	Brazil
				Nina	USA
1887				Nina Jackson/Manny	Mississippi
1888	Olhava Fin. Minnesota	Sari, Outti Sari Jarvinen /Amelia			
1890	Kokkola Fin. Minnesota	X	Toumas Koskinen Matti, Antti, Johan, Tuomas, Hilda	Y	
1920			Heikki Karila (Fin, Port, Brazil)	Oni/Nina. Heikki, Nina Karila	Brazil Brazil
1938				/Tiago, Tomas	Finland
1946	Minnesota	Lisa Jokinen /Amanda Jokinen	Antti Koskinen /Thomas Koskinen	Y	
1977	Minnesota	Andy Koskinen	X	Eva Jefferson	Miss/Minn
1999	SF, Calif.	Andy-Eva Koskinen /Lisa	Tapio Hakiminen (Finland)		
2005	California	Lisa Koskinen	Tiago, Tomas Karila(Fin.)	Nina Rivaldo	Brazil/Calif
2010	SF, Calif.	Lisa-Heikki Pikkarainen			

CPSIA information can be obtained at www.ICGtesting.com
Printed in the USA
BVOW08*1813131015

422276BV00001B/3/P

9 781478 763444